RUN OF THE BRUSH

RUN OF THE BRUSH

WILLIAM MacLEOD RAINE

First published in Great Britain by Hodder and Stoughton
First published in the United States by Houghton Mifflin

Published in Large Print 2008 by ISIS Publishing Ltd.,
7 Centremead, Osney Mead, Oxford OX2 0ES
United Kingdom
by arrangement with
Golden West Literary Agency

British Library Cataloguing in Publication Data
Raine, William MacLeod, 1871–1954
Run of the brush. – Large print ed. –
(Sagebrush western series)
1. Western stories
2. Large type books
I. Title
813.5'2 [F]

ISBN 978–0–7531–8017–4 (hb)

Printed and bound in Great Britain by
T. J. International Ltd., Padstow, Cornwall

CONTENTS

CHAPTER ONE

To See The Elephant

Night had sifted down upon San Antonio long before Jim Delaney rode up on his claybank from the horse market to Military Plaza. The sky was a basin of stars, the air mellow with the soft languor of the South. From Dolorosa there drifted the sound of a guitar. The rider drew up a moment, to listen to the liquid lilt of a Spanish love-song. Some young Mexican was serenading his sweetheart.

Jim murmured sympathetic approval. "Hop to it, Manuel. If I knew a black-eyed *señorita* handy, I sure would sing to her myself."

For months he had been tailing longhorns in the brush country and he was hungry for entertainment. He had come to town to see the elephant. Youth clamorous for expression was bubbling in his veins.

As he came within sight of the mesquite fires on the plaza and of the flares above the stands, the light in his eyes quickened. This was the life.

In the daytime Military Plaza was a market. At Hord's Hotel cattlemen sold their cows to shippers, sheepmen trafficked in wool, and horse-traders bargained. In the old Governor's Palace business firms bought hides and furnished supplies to ranchmen. A row of wagons loaded with hay stood in front of it. The Bat Cave was in the northwest corner of the plaza, a combined city hall, morgue, and jail, with a woodpile beside it for the exercise of the less important prisoners.

But after sundown — all night long and every night in the year — the plaza was a carnival attended largely by the Spanish element in the city. Ice-cream stands adjoined side-shows with barkers, merry-go-rounds, and three shell experts. There were *chile con carne* tables, where *tamales, enchilades, frijoles*, and *tortillas* also were served. Across the plaza a Spanish dancing-girl was doing undulant steps to the accompaniment of a tambourine.

The sight of *chile* steaming from a trivet set the mouth of the brush popper watering. Less than an hour ago he had reached town, and he had not yet had a chance to satisfy an appetite that had been growing more ravenous with the passage of time. He had last seen food at the tail of a cowcamp chuck wagon long before sunup.

Swinging from the saddle, Jim dropped the bridle rein.

"*Chile, señora,*" he ordered. "And *enchilades, frijoles, tortillas*. If I've forgotten anything, drift it this way *muy pronto*."

The fat little Mexican woman in charge smiled at the long-legged, handsome youth. "*Si, si por cierto, señor,*" she told him, and began to wait upon his needs.

The longer young Delaney ate, the more certain he became that San Antonio was the best town on earth.

Where else could one find a place still so full of the charm of the old days of the *caballeros* and yet so quick with the energy born of business? Here was the greatest wool and horse market in the world, the Mecca of the cowman. Here gamblers and bagnios throve. Yet over the placid, winding river was the same romantic moon that had looked down on Travis and Crockett and Bowie.

Delaney paid for his supper, swung lightly to the saddle, and rode past the old cathedral to Main Plaza. In front of The White Elephant Bar and Café he stopped, tied to a hitchrack, and jingled into the place.

In spite of his native audacity, Jim stopped a moment in the vestibule, a little daunted at the magnificent appointments. Back in the mesquite brush he had listened to tales of this new house of entertainment. Leaning against the circular mahogany cigar stand, he looked down the deepest room he had ever seen. The floor was laid with tessellated blocks of white and black marble. Heavy crystal chandeliers hung from the ceiling, each with hundreds of glittering pendants. The massive bar was said to be the largest ever made. Back of it were huge mirrors of French plate glass reflecting pyramids of goblets, hundreds of bottles of choice wine and liquors. A broad stairway swept up to the second floor where were the clubrooms devoted to gaming.

The money in Jim's pocket began to burn. Should he go up now and take a whirl at roulette or chuckaluck? Or should he wait until he had rambled over the town a bit?

A man at the bar gave a whoop and called him by the cognomen used by most of his friends in and around Uvalde and the Pendencia Creek country.

"Oh, you Slim! Where in Mexico did you drap from?"

Jim turned, to look at a squat homely little cowhand with a freckled face and washed-out blue eyes.

"'Lo, Sundown. Blew in with a bunch of horses belonging to King Cooper. How's the old mosshead?"

"Fine as silk. I druv a wool wagon down from Bandera. Come an' wash yore gullet."

Delaney joined his friend. They chatted. The names of common friends were mentioned. News was interchanged.

Sundown toyed with the drink he had ordered, looked up and down the bar to make sure nobody was listening, and murmured information.

"Young fellow, this town ain't healthy for you right now," he said out of the corner of his mouth. "Better get back to chousing mosshorns in the brush. Yore name is on the Rangers' list. I got it from Jim Pendleton."

"Not news," Jim answered lightly, his foot on the rail. "I've been told the State of Texas claims it wants me. But the Rangers have got four-five thousand names in that book. I'm just trailin' along in the drag."

What Jim said was not strictly true, though it had been a few years earlier. From all over the country desperadoes, many of them hunted men, had poured into the Lone Star State. Its wilds had been infested by gangs of bad men who lived outside the law. But the Texas Rangers, as efficient a police force as ever existed, having finished with the Comanches and other raiding tribes, had turned their attention to the gentry in the brush. Hundreds of the outlaws lay buried in unmarked graves in the chaparral, shot down while resisting arrest. Almost as many were in the penitentiary. Numbers had fled to safer pastures. But it was still a fact that scores of hard characters were hidden in the mesquite on both sides of the Rio Grande ready for any devilry that came to hand.

"Don't bank on that, son," Sundown advised. "The Rangers have got their eye on King's crowd. Don't you believe they haven't."

"King's all right," Jim said promptly. "He's deputy sheriff at Uvalde, and a doggoned good one. Anyone will tell you that."

"I ain't claimin' otherwise. But he has friends who trade in wet horses. You know it, and the Rangers know it. I'm telling you that yore name is on their list. If I was you I'd rock along."

"How many people in town know me?" Delaney argued. "Not a dozen, and among them probably not a Ranger. I've got money in my pocket just shouting to be spent. Oldtimer, I aim to spill a pot of paint over this town before I hightail it back to the brush."

Sundown grinned. "All right. All right. Do we go upstairs and take a whirl at the wheel? Or do we go over to Buck Scheer's Vaudeville House?"

"Let's go over to Buck's place," Jim decided. "We can gamble later."

The two men passed out of The White Elephant and down the street. Jim walked lightly, with the ease of perfect health. His reckless feet had carried him along dubious trails of adventure. He had run wet horses and had swung a wide loop. Each day had been sufficient to itself. For the future he had not a care.

No bell rang a warning in him that he was traveling now to the maddest adventure of his life, one during which a dozen times death would hang on the turn of a card. He could not know that he was to be dragged from his careless youth, as a dolly welter sends a flying longhorn crashing from its feet.

He walked gaily, arm linked in that of Sundown, a song on his lips.

They stopped at Sim Hart's cigar store to buy some Bull Durham.

"What's the matter with taking a whirl at The Green Curtain — or The Hundred and Ten?" Sundown suggested. "There's some right pretty girls at Mamie's — kinda refined — two-three of 'em play the piano fine."

Jim considered. He wanted to do the whole show, but he could not do it all at once.

"Let's drift over to The Green Curtain," he said. "It's near. If it's no fun, why, we're not hogtied. We'll mosey somewhere else."

They passed through the swing doors of The Green Curtain and had a drink at the bar. The man in the white apron caught the eye of a hard-faced citizen in a stiff shirt and a Prince Albert coat.

"Boys, meet Mr. Wilson," he said.

Wilson offered them the soft, long-fingered hand of a professional gambler. He ranged up at the bar alongside them. “Next one on me,” he announced.

It was about five minutes after this that he suggested a little game to pass the time away.

“Not yet,” Jim vetoed. “Want to breeze around a while first. See you later, Mr. Wilson.”

The friends walked upstairs. At a landing the stair-way divided. The branch to the left was evidently private. A sign on the wall said so. The other was for the public.

The two turned to the right. Jim was halfway up when he stopped abruptly. From somewhere back of the private door opposite him a cry of terror had leaped out.

CHAPTER TWO

Rose Walks Into A Room

Rose was frightened. This was a dreadful thing she was doing, to steal out at night from the convent school and to venture down alone into this sink of iniquity where all the vice of the city gathered. If the Mother Superior should find out! She would be expelled, of course, probably sent back to the ranch. Her father would think she was on the road to ruin — the same road her sister Marie had taken three years earlier. He would not understand that this was something she had to do, that she could not sit and wait any longer without knowing what had become of Marie. Pike Corcoran had his harsh and obstinate side. He could not know how impossible it was for Rose to refuse this offer of information about her sister, even though it had come from the man who was her father's deadliest enemy.

The girl was a shy and timid young thing. It was easy for her to become persuaded she was doing wrong. Yet what else could she do? After the letter from David Meldrum had come, in answer to her own, she had written again and asked him to meet her outside the school grounds. He had replied curtly that she could meet him at The Green Curtain or nowhere, if she wanted from him any news of her sister. He had set an hour — any night between nine and ten. From that her appeal could not budge him.

She had talked with the Mother Superior about Marie and had been told that all she could do was to pray to the Blessed Virgin. But the unhappiness of the girl was too keen for patience. The swift impulses of youth governed her. All her life she had been devoted to Marie, had admired her tremendously, known the fascination of her gay good looks, the radiant charm of her personality. It was not possible for her to tear her sister from the tender heart, or even to fold her hands and trust that in God's good time all would be well. It was in the Bible — or in some book she had read — that God helps those who help themselves.

There was nobody else in San Antonio she could send on this errand. Dave Meldrum would tell what he knew to no one else. He had said so in his letters. If she was going to find out what had become of Marie, she had to keep this appointment. It was a dreadful thing to do, but it was for her sister she was doing it. After all, this man was her brother-in-law. He might be as evil as common report made him out, but surely it was not quite the same as if she had been going to meet some other stranger.

Reluctantly she crossed the wooden bridge over the winding little river. Reluctantly she turned into Soledad Street and moved into that part of the town where its night life centered. A poster caught her eye. At Turner's

Opera Hall *Hazel Kirke* was being played by a stock company. It came to her with a stab of pain that Marie, so lovely and so wild, had started her career as an actress with a part in this very play.

As Rose came into Main Plaza, she drew the mantilla closer around her face. Perhaps people would take her for a Mexican girl of the lower class and pay no attention to her.

The streets were filled with men. They poured in and out of saloons, gambling-houses, and questionable resorts. Fear fluttered in the heart of Rose. Never in her sheltered lifetime had she been in such a place at such a time. She felt as if sin were pressing close to her. When a cowboy accosted her, it was all she could do to keep from crying out as she slipped past him.

By the light of one of the three new electric bulbs on the plaza, the first ever seen in the city, she caught the sign of The Green Curtain. The newspapers had been full of these lights. They were symbols of a new era into which San Antonio was about to emerge. Dixie Smith the evangelist had another description of them. He had bluntly said they had been hung in front of these houses of vice to light the way to hell.

Rose heard snatches of music, shuffling feet, raucous laughter. From back of the swing doors of the main entrance to The Green Curtain came a blend of voices. She drew back, suddenly faint from a gone feeling in the pit of her stomach. It had not occurred to her that she would have to face the staring eyes of dozens of men. That was one thing she could not do, walk into a place like The Green Curtain and ask for Dave

Meldrum. She would die of shame. They would think she was a — a common woman.

In the letters Meldrum had spoken of a side entrance. A crowd of roisterers were approaching. The desperate eyes of the girl found the little door to the left. She opened it hurriedly, walked into a small hall, and closed the door behind her. She stood there, panic in her throat.

A narrow stairway led to the second story. Slowly her feet took the treads. Dread went with her every step of the way. Where was she going? Even in her chaperoned young life she had heard of the depravity of The Green Curtain. The place was notorious. Ministers thundered at it from the pulpit. Indignant Ladies' Aid Societies demanded its suppression. And Rose Corcoran, who went to church with sedate eyes, shepherded by the sisters of the school, was walking up a stairway no good woman ever trod.

From the landing above a passage led. By the aid of a swinging coal-oil lamp she saw three doors, all closed. One of them had the word office printed on it. After a breathless pause to summon courage, the girl knocked timidly.

"Who's there?"

The abrupt, harsh response startled her. She murmured her name inaudibly.

"Come in," a voice ordered.

Rose walked into the room.

A man sat back of a table, his heels resting on it, an unlighted cigar in the corner of his mouth. In his hands were a pencil and some bills he had apparently been checking. He was broad-shouldered and of fine proportions, black-haired, hawk-nosed, intensely masculine. The face was strong and handsome, the eyes hard and cold. Rose guessed him about thirty-five.

"Who are you? What do you want?"

He asked the questions without removing his feet from the table or the cigar from his mouth. In the timbre of his voice was a steeliness almost cruel.

"I'm — looking for Mr. Meldrum," she faltered.

"What do you want with him?" he asked curtly.

His gaze did not lift from her. He was wondering what under heaven this girl, so young and immature and unsoiled by life, was doing in a house where only women of a certain kind came.

"I have had letters from him — I came —"

The sentence died away on her tremulous lips.

But now the man knew. His feet came from the table, the cigar from his mouth. He rose and bowed from the hips, an ironic smile on the hard, reckless face. More than six feet tall, he stood straight as an arrow.

"Charmed to meet you, my dear," he said. "I have heard your sister speak of you. What she said did not do you justice. She did not tell me you were a beauty. Perhaps you may have been a little gawky then. Time takes from us and gives to us. I seem to remember a child who came into Eagle Pass from the Cross Bar B, all thin legs and flying hair. But now — I give you my word you will be the toast of the town when you are discovered. I use a brother's privilege in telling you so."

A wave of color beat into the cheeks of the girl. She drew the mantilla closer around her slender bosom. He called himself her brother, but his possessive eyes stripped the clothes from her. She hated and feared him. Always she had done so since he had shot down and left for dead her father, long before his revenge had swept Marie to destruction. Yet for the time she crowded back the emotion. She had come to get information from him.

"Please, where is Marie?" she asked.

"So you decided to come, at last." In his dark eyes she could see an unholy excitement burning. "Does your father know you were coming?"

"No." She hurried on. "I ought not to be here. You ought not to have made me come. But since I did come, please tell me at once where my sister is."

He knew his question had been a foolish one. Pike Corcoran would never have let her enter The Green Curtain. If he had wanted to find out anything, he would have come himself, with a smoking gun if necessary. She had come secretly. He tasted his triumph, and it was sweet to him. Once more he would score off Corcoran, the man who had ruined his business at Eagle Pass and driven him out of town. First one daughter, now the other.

"So you're playing a lone hand," he said. "I reckon Pike is not interested in Marie since she married a low character."

Rose brushed that aside. "Is Marie here — in San Antonio with you?"

"Not here," he answered, with a curious smile.

"Then where? More than two years ago she wrote us she was married to you. Since then we have heard nothing."

"Not surprising. I think Pike mentioned in a note to her that she was no daughter of his and he would return unopened any future letters she wrote."

"Yes, but —Where is she? You must know. You said you would tell me if I came."

"And so I shall, my dear. But why hurry? We must get acquainted — take time to become friends. If you will sit down —"

"No — no! I must go — at once — as soon as you have told me."

"At once — or as soon as I have told you?" he murmured, and his smile was hateful.

"I have been unhappy all these years," she cried. "It is dreadful to know nothing about my own sister. You wouldn't refuse to give me what comfort you can, would you?"

"Not at all. But don't rush me. I'm not a wolf. I don't bite. If I have information you want, there is no reason why you shouldn't pay for it."

"Pay?"

"With a few minutes of your society. I'm not too old to appreciate my charming sister-in-law."

She shied from that like a startled filly from a flapping paper.

"Is Marie well, please?"

"Oh, yes. Far as I know. Our matrimonial ship ran on the rocks. Marie is a little —Shall we say, high-strung?"

"Is she acting?"

"Yes, with a traveling theatrical troupe."

"What is the name of the company? To what place must I write a letter?"

"How valuable to you is that information?" He drawled his words, opaque eyes fixed on her, with a look in them that set drums of fear beating in her breast. "Worth a kiss or two, for instance?"

The girl gazed at him, fascinated by fear. She ought never to have come here. The man was predaceous. He had compared himself to a wolf. The comparison was just. It had been madness for her to trust herself in this notorious haunt of evil. She drew back, a tumult of terror beginning to stir in her.

"I'll go now," she breathed.

"No hurry. We're relatives, and ought to get more acquainted, my dear." He walked past her, locked the door, and dropped the key in his coat pocket. The man was in no haste. He stood there, gloating over her, while fear choked up in her throat. "Sit down. I want to know more about you. How old are you?"

"No. I'm going on eighteen. Let me go. I'll be missed."

His grin was wicked. "You can explain you were with one of the family. Tell your father that. He will enjoy it."

It flashed to the girl's mind that this man's hatred of her father had been one of the prime motives for his marriage with Marie, and that if he could score again by ruining the reputation or character of Pike Corcoran's other daughter, it would fill him with glee. But in Meldrum's face just now there was stamped something more startling than revenge. He moved slowly forward, not lifting his gleaming eyes from her. Panic filled the pulses of Rose.

The room had three doors. Rose backed toward one of them. She was in frantic haste to be gone.

He jeered at her. “Keep right on going. You’re heading for my bedroom, if that’s what you’re looking for.”

Meldrum was almost close enough to touch her before the cry of terror broke from her throat.

CHAPTER THREE

Behind A Locked Door

Delaney looked at the blank door opposite him and spoke to Sundown, drawling out the words:

"One of the girls been hittin' it up, looks like."

The freckled-faced cowhand grinned. "Seeing snakes, don't you reckon?"

Jim waited. He was not quite satisfied with this explanation, reasonable though it was. A man could not waste time on the troubles of dance-hall girls, most of which were self-made and of the moment. Still, there had been something so full of naked fear in that cry . . .

It came again, a scream of panic terror. "Help! Help!"

The shout died away in a gasp. Jim guessed that a hand had closed on the throat uttering it.

He went down the stairs three at a time to the landing and up those leading to the closed door. His fingers turned the knob. The door was locked. His weight crashed against a panel. The wood splintered. He flung himself at it a second and a third time. Through the shattered panel he plunged into a room.

A man glared at him. The fellow was holding a struggling girl, one hand pressed against her mouth to stifle screams. He flung her against a wall and turned his attention to Jim.

"What the blue blazes do you mean by breaking into this room?" he demanded harshly.

The girl's hands moved in a piteous little gesture toward young Delaney. "Save me!" she begged.

Jim let his gaze sweep over her for a fraction of a second, then he brought them back to the man, whom he recognized as Dave Meldrum, the big mogul among the city gamblers.

"What's the row?" asked Jim.

"I'm asking you," Meldrum said, menace in every dripping word. "Has some yokel got to burst the door into my private room every time a dance-girl loads up on tanglefoot?"

"I'm not a dance-girl," Rose cried. "I don't belong here. I came —"

"What would a straight girl be doing here?" Meldrum interrupted sardonically. "She'll be saying presently she's from Saint Mary's Convent School."

"I am from there," Rose broke in quickly. "I came to see him — about something. He locked the door and wouldn't let me go."

"She came to see me about a job in the house," Meldrum sneered. Then anger pushed explanations from his mind. "Get out of here, you dolt," he ordered Jim, "unless you want to go on a shutter."

A second time Delaney's eyes strayed to the girl. Her story was unlikely, hardly credible, yet he knew it was true. She did not belong in this cesspool of humanity. She was a good girl. What under heaven had brought her here?

"I reckon I'll take her with me," he said quietly.

Jim knew his words were a declaration of war, that very likely he would never leave this house alive, but he did not know that with one swift decision he had turned his back forever on the path leading to shame and dishonor.

In two strides Meldrum was at the table. As his hand slipped into a drawer for a revolver, he raised his voice in a shout.

"Wilson — Dutch — Fat, come a-runnin'."

"Look out, Slim!" Sundown yelled.

Delaney spoke to his squat friend. "Hold the stairway, Sundown, till I get the girl out."

"Y'betcha!"

Meldrum let out one scorching, scabrous epithet before his .45 smoked.

Feet pounded along the treads of the stairway. Guns roared. Scarfs of smoke drifted in front of the lamp hanging from the ceiling. Jim's forty-four was out, pumping lead at Meldrum. He knew that Sundown was holding the shattered door and that the cowboy was wounded. An agonized voice on the stairs cried, "Oh, God!" One for the freckled cowpoke.

Jim knew all this, though he never lifted his eyes from the figure flinging bullets across the room at him. Something shoved against Delaney's shoulder. He knew he had been wounded, but felt no pain. His next shot struck the weapon from Meldrum's hand. A sheer fluke.

Sundown was on the floor. Two men ran over him into the room. Soon there would be others, gamblers, thugs, allies of Meldrum. Jim sent his last shot crashing into the lamp and flung his gun after the bullet.

The light went out, and the room was in darkness. Swiftly Jim moved toward the girl crouching against the third door.

"Come!" he murmured in her ear.

The door opened to his touch. They passed through it. He shut and locked the door, a fraction of a second before someone flung himself against it.

By the light of the electric bulb outside Delaney saw that they were in a bedroom. The first thing he did was to push a wardrobe against the door.

"That'll hold 'em, for a minute," he said.

The big eyes of the girl were fastened on his. She said nothing. Panic terror was still riding her soul.

Jim walked to the big French window. Outside of it was a small railed porch. The young man went to the bed and tore the covers back. He dragged out the sheets.

Men were hammering heavily on the door. Their oaths and threats came through to them. Jim knotted the ends of the sheets together.

He helped Rose over the railing. She clung to one end of a sheet and he paid out the linen rope. She dropped to the ground.

A man smashed through the door into the room, another at his heels. Jim went over the railing, clung to the porch floor an instant, and dropped. He fell on a pedestrian and took the man to the ground with him. Instantly Jim jumped to his feet. He caught Rose by the arm.

"This way!"

"Hold on, young fellow. What's all this shooting and funny stuff?"

A burly, red-faced policeman barred the way. Delaney's brain reflex was swift as light. If this girl was arrested now, her reputation would be gone forever.

The smooth rippling muscles of Jim's left arm contracted. A hard fist shot forward. The officer went down inert as a bale of hay.

"Stop 'em!" someone cried.

But nobody did. Delaney dodged across the road to the hackstands, still clinging to the girl. He bundled her into the first one he saw.

To the hackman he shouted an order. "Get going! A straight girl trapped in The Green Curtain."

The hackman wasted no words. There had been sinister stories of young girls brought down from St. Louis and Memphis for profligate purposes. He was an honest Jehu with girls of his own at home.

"Where?" he demanded from the box, after he had got started down Soledad.

"Anywhere from here!" Jim cried. "Move fast, fellow."

The sidewalk in front of The Green Curtain was a scene of confusion. A man stood on the little balcony above and shouted down commands. Another policeman ran across the street in pursuit of the cab.

But the fugitives had too big a start. Their cab swung out of Soledad into Houston, crossed the river, rattled up to Alamo Plaza. The lights of the Menger Hotel attracted Jim.

"Drop us here," he said.

The driver stopped. "If you're lying to me, young fellow —"

"He's not!" Rose cried. "I'll thank you all my life."

Jim paid the hackman and led Rose into the Menger by the servants' entrance in the rear.

"Where are we going?" the girl asked.

He led her into the deep shadows of the palms in the patio before he answered.

"Is it true, what Meldrum said — that you live at Saint Mary's Academy?" he countered.

"Yes."

"I daren't let the hackman take us there. He might have talked. It would have got out who you are." Questions thronged to his mind. He asked only the one necessary for him to know. "Did you tell anyone at Saint Mary's where you were going?"

"Only Polly Stuart, my roommate. She won't tell, if that's what you mean."

"Can you get back into the building without being caught?"

"Yes. There's a place I can climb the wall. And a thick vine leads to our window."

"Then we'd better start. Wait here till I find out if the way is clear."

He vanished into the gloom. Rose leaned against the trunk of a palm. Her nerves were still keyed to high excitement. It was not ten minutes since she had heard the crash of guns, since she had seen a man slump to the floor with limbs and body gone suddenly slack. Probably she and her rescuer were at this moment being hunted. They might be caught, flung into the Bat Cave. She would be disgraced forever. What would happen to this young *vaquero* she did not know.

It had all been her fault. She should never have undertaken so foolish a thing. If she had not been so headstrong at least one man — perhaps two — would be alive and well who now were dead. Her slender body began to shake with a nervous chill. She had done wrong. God would punish her.

Time dragged while the young man was away. It seemed to her hours before his tall slim body crossed a moonlit patch of the patio.

CHAPTER FOUR

Jim Borrows A Horse

"We'll take a whirl at it now," Jim said.

She followed him from the patio to a back door. By way of Crockett Street they reached the plaza. He turned to the night, moving with long, light strides. She had to run to keep up with him. In front of the moonlit Alamo, where Travis and Bowie and Crockett died in the most heroic defense of American history, a hack was standing. No driver was in sight.

Rose looked at her rescuer, a question in her eyes.

He nodded. "You guessed it. I'm a horse thief now. Teach the owner not to leave his hack while he goes into a saloon and gets him a drink."

Rose stepped into the cab. Jim climbed to the driver's seat, gathered the reins, and started.

He drove swiftly. Fifteen minutes later he pulled up at the adobe wall which surrounded the grounds of Saint Mary's School.

Rose walked to a corner which had rough edges offering hand and foot holds. She turned to her companion. In a low voice tremulous with feeling she thanked him.

"I'll never forget — never," she said.

"I'll see you safe in," he told her.

From the top of the wall he gave her a hand. In spite of her slender immaturity her body was, he noticed, compact of supple strength. She swarmed up like a sailor. Modestly she gathered her skirts close and lifted her slim ankles over the top. Presently they stood on the ground together. Through an orchard she led the way to the dormitory.

The girl looked up at him, her face suffused with color. "You must go now — please."

He knew she was thinking of the climb up the thick vine. If he was standing below, skirts would not conceal from him long stretches of stocking-clad leg.

"I'll be drifting," he agreed, and lifted his hat.

"My name is Rose Corcoran," she told him.

"Mine is Jim Delaney."

She gave him her small hand fearfully. The sisters had never told her the proper behavior for such a situation. It was one they could not have imagined.

Her fingers rested in his brown palm for an instant. He looked into her deep, innocent eyes and reflected that she was after all only a child. But a child had no business at The Green Curtain.

Swiftly she drew her hand from his, turned away, and buried her face in the foliage of the vine. She was sobbing violently, into fingers that covered her eyes.

"What's the matter?" Jim asked, aghast. "I ain't going to hurt you, girl."

"I know," she wailed. "It's not that."

He frowned. The ways of girls were outside his ken.

"Nothing to cry about. You haven't been caught. Meldrum won't give you away. That would make trouble for him."

She explained, her body still shaken by spasmodic sobs. "I did wrong. If I hadn't gone there, nobody would have been hurt. I'm — a — a murderer."

"Don't talk crazy," he said sharply. "Not yore fault Dave Meldrum is a skunk, is it?"

"It's my fault a man, maybe two men, have been killed tonight." She broke down again, with another wail of grief.

"Don't you! Don't you!" he begged. "That's not the way to look at it. I don't know why you went, but it wasn't to make trouble. Meldrum did that. You're not to blame. I'm not. If a rattler strikes, it has to be stomped out."

"But the man who . . . helped you. I saw him fall. I'll never forget how he looked as he went down."

A muscular spasm contracted the face of Delaney. He spoke, after a moment, very gently.

"Sundown wouldn't have had it any other way. He was only a stumpy li'l' brush-popper, but he was a man to ride the river with. We've been friends, him and me, ever since I was a tad, and I've always known he would be there when the call came. If anyone is to blame, I'm the man. I gave him the stairway to hold and took the easy job myself. Consequence is, I got out whole and left him riddled."

Jim spoke with sardonic bitterness. That was not how he had expected the fight to turn out, but when guns are blazing, results cannot be predicated with certainty.

Rose turned on him, tears still on her cheeks. "You did not choose the easy job. That's not true. I never saw anything as — as brave. How dare you say that?"

Her flare of feminine ferocity took Jim completely by surprise. He felt a little bit of a fool and not a little elated. It was in his defense that her starry eyes were alight with indignation.

"Shucks!" he said lamely. "All I did was lock a door and run away. Poor Sundown now, he —"

"All you did was fight that terrible man and his friends, for me whom you had never seen before, and for all you knew I was a — a bad woman."

He moved uneasily, embarrassed at her frankness. Nice girls ought not to mention women of the other world. They were not supposed to know about them.

"What's the sense in talking foolishness?" he protested. "I used my eyes and my brains."

"I don't know how I can ever repay you," she burst out. "You're only a boy and —"

"Wouldn't wonder if I was 'most grown stuff," Jim interrupted. "And I didn't do anything anyhow to make a song about. There are 'steen hundred guys in this man's town would've done just the same."

"I didn't mean you acted like a boy," she explained, afraid that she had offended him. "I only meant, you look so young. And you can't fool me. I know very well many men wouldn't have done what you did, stand up to a notorious gunman like Dave Meldrum when all he had to do was to call half a dozen of his men to help kill you."

"Have it yore own way, Miss Corcoran," he shrugged, with a grin. "I'll be lightin' out now if you don't mind. You shin up to yore room. Don't worry about spilt milk. What's done is done. Forget all about what happened tonight."

"Never. Not if I live to be a hundred."

In her voice was a tumult of feeling. Irradiated by the moonlight, the warm, breathing life in her so quick with animal grace, she was the sweetest and most glamorous young creature he had ever seen.

"Well, keep it under yore hat anyhow," he warned. "We don't know how this is going to jump. You're not in it, whatever happens. If they arrest me, I'll wiggle out somehow."

"Where are you going now? What are you going to do?" she asked.

"I have friends. I'll be saying 'Adios,' Miss Corcoran. Glad to have met you."

He turned and walked back into the orchard. From a safe distance he watched her climb to the window of her room.

Five minutes later he was driving the hack back toward town. Better get a doctor right quick, he decided. His shoulder was beginning to hurt like sixty. He would drift into Jack Corcoran's and hole up there; that is, if Jack's bride hung out a welcome sign for him. You never could tell about old friends' wives until you had met them.

His mind pulled up, struck by an odd coincidence. Her name was Corcoran, the same as his old bunkie Jack. Could she by any chance be his cousin, the daughter of Pike Corcoran, one of the leading cattlemen and bankers of Texas. Not likely, and yet possible.

CHAPTER FIVE

I've Got My Tail In A Crack

Corcoran let out a whoop at sight of his friend. He would have fallen upon him with violent affection if Jim had not warned him back in time.

"I got a busted shoulder, boy. Look out."

"Come here, Milly," Jack called. "This here usta be my side-kick before I was a brand snatched from the burning."

Milly came forward smiling, hand outstretched. She was a very pretty brunette, with long eyelashes curving over dark, mischievous eyes. Jim knew at once he was going to like her.

"Awf'ly glad to meet you," she said. "Jack is always speaking about you."

"Don't you believe a word he says about me, Mrs. Corcoran," Jim answered, grinning. "He was a burning brand, like he says. But I'll bet two bits he did the snatching and not you."

"I'll never tell you about that," Milly replied, white ivory teeth flashing in a smile. "But anyhow come in. You'll be staying with us while you are in town. I'll want to worm out of you all about his wild oats before he was snatched."

Jim sat down gingerly on the edge of a chair. "I won't hold you to that offer, ma'am, though I'll say 'Much obliged.' Fact is, I've got my tail in a crack."

The eyes of the girl bubbled. "If Jack's stories are true, that isn't anything new."

Delaney turned a reproachful gaze on his friend. "That the way you talk about me when I ain't around?"

"There was the time you hid the old bridegroom's false teeth," Milly suggested.

"He was in that his own self, Jack was, up to the hocks."

"A case of the pot calling the kettle black?"

"Yes, ma'am." Jim took a breath and plunged at his story. He might as well wear away his welcome at once, since it had to be done. "First off, and least important, I'm a horse thief. The horse is hitched to yore fence right this minute."

Imps of mischief danced in Milly's black eyes. "Good gracious! Will they hang me and Jack too?" she asked cheerfully.

Delaney shook his head. "I'm not loadin' you. Wish I was. I took the horse and the hack hitched to it because a girl was in a jam, and I had to get her out of it."

"How romantic!" the young woman said, sparkling with animation. "Is the heroine a horse thief too?"

"Wish I could laugh with you," Jim said. "I can't. This is serious business. I've just come out of a shooting difficulty. Two men, or more, were killed, I reckon." He gulped out tragic news. "One of 'em was Sundown."

Jack Corcoran jumped to his feet. "Sundown! Where? When?"

"Less than an hour ago. At The Green Curtain."

The gaiety died out of Milly's face. Why did wild young cowboys go to such plague spots as Dave Meldrum's place? They invited trouble when they did so.

"Tell us," Jack told his friend.

Jim began at the beginning. He wasted no words. In twenty short sentences he had finished. The Corcorans listened breathlessly. Their comments were characteristic.

"But — how can she be a good girl and at The Green Curtain?" Milly asked.

Her husband said, in a low voice, "Good old Sundown!"

Jim answered the wife first. "She is," he replied simply. "If you had seen her, you'd know."

"What could she have been doing there?"

"I don't know." Jim looked at Milly, then at her husband. "I know you, Jack, but not a blamed thing about this girl you married. Can she keep a secret?"

Corcoran grinned. "She knew just when we were going to get married three weeks before we slipped off to the preacher, and she never told a soul. This girl tells nothing she hadn't ought to tell."

The next question Jim asked seemed irrelevant. "How did yore Uncle Pike take to the bride?"

"Like a duck to water. Says he didn't think I had so much sense in my coconut as to grab off a girl like Milly."

"And yore missus likes her in-laws?"

"Have to ask her about that," Jack said.

"I don't know what this is all about, but I'm not keeping it a secret that I think Pike Corcoran is a fine man," Milly admitted.

"Got a daughter, hasn't he?"

Milly looked at him sharply. She had heard the story of Marie Corcoran's tragic marriage to Dave Meldrum, but she did not intend to discuss it with a stranger.

"What are you getting at?" she snapped.

"A daughter at the convent academy here?" Delaney went on.

"Oh!" Milly could answer that question. "You mean Rose. Yes. She is a dear sweet girl. I don't see what that has to do with tonight's trouble."

"Only that the girl I got out of The Green Curtain told me later that her name was Rose Corcoran."

"But — but —"

Milly's quick mind jumped a gap. "She must have gone there about Marie."

"My God! To The Green Curtain!" exclaimed Jack. "Has she gone crazy? Pike Corcoran will give her hell for this. He'll sure punish her plenty. She deserves it too."

"That's the point," Jim explained. "Pike mustn't ever know. I don't reckon Dave Meldrum can afford to tell any names."

"We can't tell that yet," Milly said thoughtfully. "We can only hope not."

Jim referred to another angle of the trouble. "Hadn't been for me Sundown wouldn't've been in The Green Curtain. I'm to blame for what happened."

"Hadn't been for you Rose would still be there," Milly added. Her gaze fastened to his shoulder. "Were you wounded in the fight?"

"Meldrum plugged me in the shoulder. I don't reckon it's bad."

"Help him off with his coat, Jack," Milly ordered sharply.

After looking at the blood-stained shirt she made a swift decision. "Go get a doctor, Jack."

"Wait a minute, lady," Jim drawled. "What doctor? I've got to have one who will live under his hat. No gossip, or I'll be bogged down."

"Doc Russell," Jack proposed. "He'll keep his mouth shut."

"Take the hack and drive close to his place, Jack," Milly directed. "Leave it there and come back in the doctor's buggy."

"I could go to the doctor's," Jim offered.

"So we won't get into trouble," Milly guessed. "Well, you won't. You're going to stay here with us."

"I wouldn't fight you about that," Jim answered with a grin.

"But you think I'm pretty bossy. Well, I am. Walk into the next room and lie down on that bed. I'll 'tend to you till the doctor gets here."

The young man rose obediently. "Since you're asking for my thoughts, ma'am, I'll give them to you free gratis. I was wondering if there is any more like you at home, not yet snatched."

Beneath the dusky tan of Milly's cheeks a flush ran. "Go along with you," she said. "I know all about you Irishmen and your blarney. Jack is one himself."

Jim lay down on the bed. In spite of his protests, Milly pulled off his boots.

"A young lady like you hadn't ought to wait on me thataway," he demurred.

"Do you think Jack married a useless little fool? Besides, I don't want your dusty boots on my nice quilt . . . Is your shoulder hurting you much?"

It was, a good deal. The ivory teeth in his brown face flashed a reassuring smile. "It kinda telegraphs me word that there's a pill there, compliments of Mr. Dave Meldrum, but I can make out to stand it."

"It isn't bleeding much. I think I'll let it alone till Doctor Russell gets here. He won't be long."

The doctor was a bearded man of middle age, undemonstrative and efficient. He asked only one question, "How long since you were shot?" The where and why of it appeared to be none of his business. He examined and dressed the wound, gave Milly a few directions, and left a sleeping draught.

"You got off lucky, young fellow," he said. "If you are going into the business of stopping bullets, you couldn't have picked a better spot in your anatomy."

Jim did not ask him to say nothing about his call. He knew Doctor Russell would do as he thought best about that. Moreover, he was of opinion that Milly would put his case more effectively than he could do.

As to that he was right. Milly and Jack followed the doctor into the outer room, closing the door behind them.

"He was shot in The Green Curtain trying to help a good girl," Milly said at once.

The eyebrows of the physician lifted in a whimsical, satiric quirk. "So that's the story. The usual one is that he did it himself by accident. I think I like the accident story better."

"But it's true, Doc — what my wife says," Jack confirmed.

"You were there, Corcoran, were you?"

"No. But Jim wouldn't lie to me. I've known him always."

"Did he mention what the good girl was doing at The Green Curtain?"

Russell had put his finger on the weak spot of the story.

"He doesn't know, but I think I can guess," Milly answered. "I wish I could tell you the name of the girl, but I can't. Jim heard her scream. He and his friend broke a door into Dave Meldrum's room. Meldrum was holding her mouth so the girl couldn't scream. He began to shoot and called for his men. They came running. Jim's friend was killed, and probably one of The Green Curtain crowd. We don't know what story Meldrum will give out, but we know this is the true one. Jim and the girl escaped through a window and jumped into a hack. Fifty people must have seen that part of it."

"Sure this wasn't just a fight about a dance-hall girl?"

"Yes." Milly confided one bit of information. "She was a school girl. I can't tell any more."

"You want me to keep this visit quiet, of course. That's why you are telling me this."

"It's not the law we are afraid of, but Dave Meldrum's gang," she explained. "If they know he is here, they won't rest until they have killed him."

Russell reflected a moment. "I'll not say anything about him without giving you warning. On the other hand, I'll make no more definite promise until I have investigated the facts."

With this the Corcorans had to be content. They carried the news to Jim that he was safe for the present.

The wounded man nodded. "Got to trouble you some more, Jack. My horse is hitched to a rack front of the White Elephant. A claybank with white stockings."

"I'll look after it," Jack promised.

CHAPTER SIX

Jim Reads A Newspaper Story

Jack Corcoran owned and ran the Travis Corral. He had bought it on a shoestring, and since he could not afford to hire much help, he did all the work he could himself. But he was still recently enough married to go home to dinner every day at noon. He had to break the day by at least one half-hour with his bride.

Into the room where Jim was lying, he came and tossed a copy of the *San Antonio Express* upon the bed.

"Boy, you're sure some wolf, and last evening was yore night to howl," he said. "Read what good citizens think of yore didoes."

Jim read.

BOLD ROBBERY FRUSTRATED

A Bloody Tragedy at The Green Curtain

Two desperadoes attempted last evening to rob The Green Curtain, one of the most notorious amusement houses in the city. With much audacity they broke down the door to Dave Meldrum's private office. The proprietor of the place resisted their demands and reached for a gun, at the same time calling for help.

Meldrum fought a gun battle with the two bandits until the arrival of William Clark, "Dutch" Nagle, and Frank Wilson, all employees of The Green Curtain. The firing then became general. In all between thirty and forty shots must have been fired.

William Clark, commonly known as "Fat," was shot and died almost instantly. A bullet from a Colt's forty-four passed through the left ventricle. The older of the outlaws was badly wounded and is not expected to live. He was taken by the police, who were on the scene almost before the gun echoes had died, to the Sacred Heart Hospital.

Meldrum says he believes one of his dance-hall girls was in league with the robbers, since she left with the younger one immediately after the fracas.

Their departure was dramatic. The bandit retreated with her into Meldrum's bedroom, locked the door, and lowered the young woman by means of a sheet-rope to the street, after which he jumped to the ground. Officer Simmons attempted to arrest the man and was knocked cold. The fugitives jumped into a cab and escaped.

The girl had just come to The Green Curtain to work, and was known to Meldrum only by the name of Rosie. He does not know from where she came.

The police have an accurate description of the escaped outlaw and confidently expect to arrest him within twenty-four hours. Apparently he is wounded, since spots of blood were discovered on the floor of the bedroom.

There was more of the story. It included the offer of a reward of five hundred dollars by Dave Meldrum for the capture of the younger desperado, alive or dead.

Jim did not read it all at once. At the end of the third paragraph, he looked at his friend.

"Sundown is still alive!" he cried, his voice trembling.

"I stopped in at the hospital on my way home," Corcoran said. "I acted like I was just one of these curiosity hounds. He's still hanging on, but he's mighty low. The docs don't figure he'll make the grade, but I heard a nurse tell a sister he might at that."

The eyes of the wounded man were shining. "He's a tough old fellow. Jack, wouldn't it be great if he fooled the docs?"

Thirty-four, it may be mentioned, was old to Jim, who had not long turned the corner into his twenties.

"Yes," agreed Corcoran, but with a troubled frown.

"You don't think he will," Jim said.

"That ain't it," Jack replied. "Maybe he will — and what will Meldrum do about that?"

Jim's jaw dropped. He stared at his friend, aghast. "You mean —?"

"What do *you* think?" Jack asked. "Meldrum has his story all fixed pretty. You boys were outlaws and the girl was helping you. He has gone to right smart trouble to make everything dovetail in nice. It would hurt his business — maybe put a permanent crimp in it — for folks to think he had been holding a good Texas girl against her will. You know. White slavery. Santone wouldn't hardly stand for that."

"Your idea is that Meldrum will —"

Young Delaney stopped. To put the sinister thought into words was to make it more real.

"Dave is a killer. We know that. Is he going to give Sundown a chance to get well enough to tell his story? Not on yore life. Soon as Sundown gets even a little better, if he does, he will be bumped off. Meldrum made one mistake. He thought Sundown was dead. Before he found out different, the police had broken into the room. He won't make a mistake like that twice."

The man in bed sat up, his looks wild. "I must go to him. God! he may be killing Sundown now."

"Hold yore horses, Slim. Meldrum isn't a fool. He expects Sundown to die any minute, and he knows the doctors won't let him talk even if he could. He won't try to fix Sundown's clock unless he has to do it. That would make a lot of talk, and he doesn't want that."

"What you expect me to do?" Jim asked. "Sit and wait till the sidewinder strikes? No, sir."

"My motion is to have him guarded."

"I could send for some of King Cooper's boys, but with the Rangers so busy right now, this isn't a healthy spot for them. Still —"

"If they came, the police wouldn't let them stick around Sundown's room close enough to protect him."

"So where do we get off, if I don't go myself?"

"Finish reading what the *Express* says," Corcoran suggested.

He picked up the newspaper, found a paragraph, marked it with a thumb nail, and passed the *Express* back to Delaney.

> The escaped bandit was called Slim by his confederate. He is over six feet tall, has broad shoulders and slender hips, and weighs about 175 pounds. Hair reddish-gold, face tanned brown. Eyes deep blue. Dressed like a cowboy. Wears trousers in boot tops. Under twenty-five years of age. Has boyish appearance. Very good-looking. The description fits that of one James Delaney, who is wanted by the Rangers to explain his activities in running wet horses.

"Do you reckon if you showed up at the hospital there would be no questions asked?" Jack wanted to know.

"I'll have to take my chance of that."

"It won't be any chance at all. Inside of half an hour of your arrival, you'd find yoreself in the Bat Cave. No, I've got a better idea than that. Pike Corcoran is my uncle. You know that. Politically his say-so pretty nearly goes in this town. He made the mayor, and the mayor appointed the chief of police. Uncle Pike doesn't like Dave Meldrum a little bit. Point of fact, he hates every bone in the skunk's body. Never mind why. If he asks for it, Chief Harper will appoint a police guard to look after Sundown. He can give it out that it is to protect him from his own friends who might kill him for fear he will give them away. Or they can say it is to keep him from escaping."

"Will Pike Corcoran do it for you?"

"I reckon he will. My father and Uncle Pike are mighty close to each other. The old boy has always been good to me."

"Still, I don't see why he should go out of his way to help an outlaw shot down while holding up a place. That's how he'll get the story."

"Not how he'll get it from me," Jack differed. "You got to remember, too, that Uncle Pike knows Sundown. Knew him when the old coot rode for my father. He may grumble, but I'll betcha Uncle Pike buys chips and sits into this game."

Jim was not at all satisfied. "Looks like some of Sundown's friends ought to guard him personally. Say a cop is planted at the hospital. Maybe he'll go wandering off down the corridor after some pretty nurse. Or maybe Meldrum will have his scalp collected, too, if he's in the way. That's the kind of a Comanche Meldrum is supposed to be. 'Course he'd fix it, like you say, to make it look like his outlaw friends bumped Sundown off so he wouldn't squeal."

Corcoran nodded. His forehead wrinkled in thought. "I wouldn't put it past the wolf . . . Unless orders were give him to lay off Sundown if he wanted official protection in this town any more. That would hold him."

Milly came into the room and announced dinner.

"I'll get busy right away," Jack promised his anxious friend.

He came in just before leaving the house to make an addendum. "I may have to tell Uncle Pike how come this fracas. O' course I won't tell him the girl was Rose."

"All right," consented Jim fretfully. "Pretty soon the whole town will know who she is if we go around whispering secrets."

Jack grinned. "The doc said we'd know when you were getting better because you'd be sore as a bear with a busted paw."

With which parting shot he left.

CHAPTER SEVEN

Chief Harper Gives An Ultimatum

In Meldrum's office at The Green Curtain three men sat in heavy consultation.

One of them was a heavy-set man, age about forty, with prognathic jaw and faded blue eyes cold and dead as those of a cod. His manner was usually unfriendly, often sullen. He was called "Dutch" Nagle.

"Up to you to say when, Dave," he said.

"Maybe I won't have to say it," Meldrum replied. "He's barely hanging on. Doctor Neely expects him to wink out any hour. I don't want to take any steps not necessary. Too bad we didn't put a slug through his head before the police butted in. Your fault, Wilson. You told me he was dead."

"He was out cold," the faro dealer answered resentfully. "How was I to know he'd come to life again?" He added, by way of defense: "The cops were hammering on the door even then. It would have been smart to start shooting again after everything was quiet. How would I have explained it? Easy to say now I ought to have done this or that."

"Frank is right," Nagle said. "Anyhow, what's the use of beefing? Question is, what do we do now? Me, I'd make sure if I was you, Dave. No can tell when this bird Smith will make one of those dying depositions that won't read so good in the *Express*."

"I've fixed that with Neely," Meldrum said curtly. "I'll get word in time if any talking is going to be done."

"Suits me if it does you," Nagle said. "His squawking can't hurt me any. I wasn't keeping a straight girl here against her will."

"I've already told you she got excited unnecessarily," Meldrum explained impatiently. "She went crazy, like a little fool."

"Don't tell us," Nagle jeered. "Tell the police — tell the good pious folks of Santone. Maybe they'll believe you, seeing you have such a good rep."

Meldrum looked at the man with cold disfavor. "Some day you'll let your tongue run you into trouble, Nagle."

"When I do I'll ask my sixgun to get me out of it like it always has done," the heavy-set man replied sulkily, his codfish eyes on the owner of The Green Curtain.

There came a knock on the door which was at the top of the stairway leading from the street.

"Who's there?" demanded Meldrum.

"Harper. Want to see you, Dave."

Meldrum unlocked the door and let in Wesley Harper, chief of police of San Antonio. The chief was a red-headed, red-faced man. He limped a little, from a wound received at the battle of Shiloh. His frame was strongly built. Once his muscles had been like iron, but with increasing years he was growing soft, flabby, and fat.

"Howdy, boys," he said, with an inclusive nod. "How are cases?"

Meldrum pushed a chair toward the chief. Harper eased himself into it, his fleshy body overflowing. From his vest pocket he took a black cigar, bit off the end, and lighted it.

"Any line yet on the holdup who got away, Wes?" asked Meldrum.

"No, sir. He seems to have done crawled into a hole and pulled it in after him. I reckon he beat it outa town back to the brush."

"Your men are certainly efficient, Chief," Meldrum complimented, with an edge of sarcasm.

Harper blew out a fat smoke ring and watched it drift ceilingward.

"What you expect, Dave?" he asked. "If you four boys couldn't get him when you had him right in this room, how would you figure on us to do it when we don't know where he's at?"

"Did I say I expected it, Wes?" Meldrum retorted, his black eyebrows lifted in satiric insult. "I've been here long enough to know better. When he's got, we'll get him ourselves."

"No need to get sore, Dave," the chief protested. "If this bird is in town and stays here, we'll arrest him. But our jurisdiction doesn't run all over Texas. You better go roast the Rangers. They been lookin' for him quite a while, I hear."

"I always did think they were overrated," Wilson cut in. "One thing they know is how to blow their own horn. You can't pick up a newspaper without seeing what wonders they are."

Harper differed, amiably. "You didn't live west of the Brazos in the days when the Comanches were raiding. I've seen the burning houses of our neighbors, and the scalped bodies of women and children as well as men. The Rangers stopped that. I've a notion, Frank, you wouldn't think they were overrated if you were on the dodge. They get the men they go after, finally; if they don't bring 'em in, they leave 'em buried nice in the shinnery."

"Shoot 'em down without asking any questions," Nagle snarled.

"As to that, Dutch, honest brush-poppers don't show fight when Rangers drop into their camp. I never heard of the Rangers killing anybody who wasn't asking for it." The chief knocked the ash from his cigar into a spittoon. What had been said so far was just casual conversation. He had to put into words an ultimatum, and he found it a little difficult. "This fellow you shot up, Sundown Smith. He's a mighty sick man. I don't reckon he'll pull through."

"I don't reckon he will . . . permanently," Meldrum said grimly.

The eyes of the chief met his. "Don't make any mistake, Dave. He is going to get his chance."

"What you mean?"

Harper continued to look steadily at the cold, hard, handsome face of the gambler. “I mean that no accident is to happen to this cowpoke.”

“Why are you telling me?”

“Thought you’d like to know. I have a man on guard in his room at the hospital.”

“Afraid his pal may bump him off so he won’t squeal. That it?”

“His pal — or someone else. That’s the idea.”

“Who else?” asked Meldrum. He added a sneer: “If one of your trusty flatfeet is on the job, he’ll certainly be safe, won’t he?”

“I’m mentioning to you that we expect him to be safe. If an accident happened to him, it would be unfortunate.”

“For him?”

Harper said what he had to say, straight from the shoulder. “For you, too, Dave.”

“That so? I don’t get it.” The eyes of Meldrum were hard as steel.

“You would be asked to leave town before night . . . and to stay away.”

“Who would do the asking?” Meldrum cut back, his face white and rigid, his voice harsh.

“Yeah, I’d like to know that too,” Nagle murmured.

The chief turned his gaze on the heavy-set man. “This order would include several of Dave’s friends,” he said.

“It would be an order, would it?” Wilson interposed.

“You could call it an order, Frank,” the officer told him.

"Whose messenger boy are you, Wes?" Meldrum demanded insolently.

The chief flushed. "No need to go back of me. I'm telling you."

"You're running on an errand," The Green Curtain owner told him, an insult in his voice. "Who for, I say? This doesn't come from Bryant. He makes the motions of being mayor, but we all know who pulls the strings to make him jump."

"If you know so much, why ask me, Dave?"

"I don't have to ask you who is boss of this town, Wes. So Colonel Pike Corcoran is serving notice on me, is he? I'm to do as he says or get out of town?"

"I don't recollect mentioning Pike."

"I'm mentioning him. Since you're toting messages, take one to him from me. Tell Corcoran he never saw the day he could run me out of town. Tell him he may be a big man in Santone, with his ranch and his bank and his gang of politicans, but he's no bigger to me than he was when I pumped a bullet into him at Eagle Pass some years ago." The black eyes of the gambler smoked with vindictive hatred. "Tell him if he wants war, he can have it, right from the chunk."

"If you have anything to tell Pike, go unload it yourself, Meldrum," the chief said, his beefy face dark with anger. "I'm giving this order, not Pike. And get it right. I'm not threatening you. I'm warning you what will happen if this Sundown Smith is hurt. The Green Curtain will be closed down and won't ever run another day."

"You mentioned running me out of town," Meldrum said bleakly. "Talk like that isn't supposed to be safe."

"Public opinion would do that," Harper answered, ignoring the threat. "I would merely be the official representative of it."

"What would I be run out for? Because two hold-ups tried to rob me and we resisted them? Because a two-bit bandit gets what is coming to him?"

The chief looked hard at him. "There's a rumor they weren't trying to hold you up."

The gaze of the gambler did not yield a fraction of an eye-blink. "Just a pair of playful cowboys who wanted to find out how hard the wood in that door is."

Harper was on thin ice. He had been told none of the facts behind the story.

"Folks who saw the girl after she had come down from the window to the street say she didn't look like a dance-hall girl," he fenced.

"Did you ever see a straight girl in The Green Curtain? Thought you had more sense than to believe in fairy tales." Meldrum asked a question boldly. He had to know how much information was back of the chief's remark. "If she wasn't one of my girls, who was she?"

"I'm repeating to you a rumor," Harper said cautiously. "I don't have to guarantee it. Use your horse-sense, Meldrum. Ever since Dixie Smith held his revival meetings here, the good folks of this town have been for closing your place. Dixie Smith said The Green Curtain was the worst —"

"I heard what he said," interrupted Meldrum. "I sat on a front seat and he said it right at me. That's not important. Churches always knock places of amusement. They get so much kick out of doing it they would hate to see them closed. Talk turkey, Harper, and quit dodging. You didn't bring me a message from the preachers, but from Pike Corcoran."

"I haven't seen Pike for a week."

"Not necessary," Meldrum sneered. "You've seen Bryant, and Bryant has seen Pike."

"Have it your own way." Harper rose, walked to the door, and turned. "But don't make any mistake about this Sundown. If anything happens to him — why, you'd better have all your arrangements made to start business in some other city."

"I've never had any notion of bumping off this scalawag, not till he gets out of the hospital, anyhow. But you've put it in my head. Maybe I'll do it. Run back and kick in with your report to your dummy boss Bryant and let him relay it to *his* boss Corcoran. Carry my compliments with you and tell them both to go to the devil. That will be all, except — shut the door behind you, if you really must go."

Meldrum's splenetic laughter followed Harper as the chief clumped down the stairs leaving the door open behind him. But his affected mirth died away as soon as the officer was out of hearing. He walked swiftly to the door, with his catlike tread, and closed and locked it.

"We'll have to let this Sundown alone, boys," he announced. "After all, his story won't blow us up, unless the girl comes out and backs it. I'll have to see her and fix that."

"You're going to lie down and take it," Nagle jeered.

Meldrum's face was venomous. His lips were a straight, cruel line.

"Don't be a fool, Dutch. Did you ever know me lie down? I'm going after Corcoran, but not half-cocked. I don't figure on playing into his hands by any crazy gunplay. This Sundown is only a white chip in the game now. I'll get Corcoran, and I'll get him right. My idea won't be to sit in with a hand dealt from his deck. Not none. I advise you not to push on the reins, my friend. When I need your help, I'll let you know, and it will be *muy pronto*."

"I'll bet it will," Nagle grumbled. "Soon as there is any work to do that takes nerve."

"I didn't ask for it that day at Eagle Pass when I dropped him on the street, did I?"

"No," retorted Nagle. "Better if you had. He would have stayed down."

Meldrum swept a hand impatiently toward the door. "*Vamos*, boys. I have a letter to write."

After the others had left the room he sat frowning at the paper in front of him. Presently he began to write.

> *Dear Sim*, Johnny will have already told you all about how Fat was killed the other night. [So the letter ran.] There has come a new development. Pike Corcoran has horned into the business. It came about this way. One of the two birds who raised the rumpus in my office is at the hospital,

still alive, but liable to kick off any hour. Pike guessed we might be figuring on a settlement with the fellow and has served notice through Wes Harper that it is to be hands off. Otherwise, The Green Curtain will be closed.

For the present I will do nothing. Would it not be a good idea for you and one or two of the boys to drift to town? Anyhow, I would like you to come yourself, so that we can have a little talk. I would ride down to the ranch, but I do not like to leave town right now, as some might say I was hunting cover. Looks like this feud has busted wide open again. Suits me down to the ground.

Hoping to see you soon

DAVE

The address on the envelope was "Sim Glidden, Circle G Ranch, Eagle Pass."

CHAPTER EIGHT

Pike Corcoran Asks Questions

Jim was on a sofa in the parlor reading a Nick Carter story when Milly opened the door to let in a visitor whose advent lit the welcome sign in her face.

She lifted her lips to be kissed, after which words tumbled over one another in her pleased excitement.

"I'm so glad to see you, Uncle Pike. You'll stay for dinner, of course. Jack isn't home yet, but he'll be here soon. This is Jim Delaney. He's staying with us just now. We've wanted you to meet him."

Pike Corcoran liked the wife his nephew had picked. There was something forthright and honest about her. Moreover, she did not make a picture hard upon the eyes. Her mobile face was charming. So, too, was the young rounded figure; plump as a quail's breast, was the way he put it. Her gaity and audacity pleased him. He did not like sycophants. This girl acted as if she did not give two hoots about his financial rating. No doubt Pike was wrong about this. Milly had too much sense not to appreciate his position in the community as a potential asset to Jack. None the less she was fond of him for himself.

The older man looked down at the young cowboy. "Do you shoot the town up every time you come here?" he asked gruffly.

All over Pike Corcoran's ample width, depth, and height the word cattleman was branded. It was stamped on the tanned, leathery face, in the wrinkles radiating from the steady gray eyes, upon the strong, slightly bowed legs. From the white Stetson just lifted from the iron-gray hair to the expensive high-heeled boots into which corduroy trousers had been folded, there was complete corroboration. However much of a politician he might be, he was a Texas cowman first, last, and all the time. So Jim judged.

"Not always, sir," Delaney answered innocently. "This was a special occasion."

"Hmp!" Pike grunted. "Nice business. Did you get much of a haul at The Green Curtain?"

"The only thing my partner and I brought away was about a half a pint of lead divided between us."

"That all? Didn't I hear something about one of Dave Meldrum's dance-hall girls?"

"Incorrect information, sir. We helped a girl get away — a good girl he was insulting."

"A good girl at The Green Curtain? Sounds fishy." Pike snorted incredulously.

"Sure does," Jim agreed. "True, just the same. No use asking me what she was doing there. I don't know. But when I busted the door down, Meldrum had his hand over her mouth to keep her from yelling. She was scared clear through."

"Who is this good girl you found in Dave's private room at the worst vice spot in Santone?"

Jim's face grew wooden, his eyes blank. "I haven't any information on that point, sir."

"Where is she at now?"

"I wouldn't know about that."

"You know where you left her, I reckon."

"No, sir. My memory has plumb gone back on me."

Corcoran shifted the attack. He realized that the young man's memory would not improve.

"Don't you know this town is too big to be stood on its head by brush-poppers on a tear? It isn't any honkytonk wide spot in the road any more."

"That's right, sir," Jim assented amiably.

"What were you doing at The Green Curtain — that is, if you didn't go to hold it up? Pigeons fly there to be plucked. Don't you know that?"

"Yes, sir." Jim was respectfully responsive again. "Thought I'd like to see the elephant while I was here. I don't drift this way often."

"Well, you saw it plenty. I don't recollect any waddy in some time making a bigger rookus than you did." Corcoran spoke dryly. One could have guessed condemnation in his manner, but would have missed the mark. This smiling youth, so blandly innocent, interested the ranchman a good deal. Pike was used to judging men. Unless there was strength back of this artless exterior he was much mistaken. What he meant to find out was whether it would likely be used for good or evil. "I hand it to you, young fellow. Not many men could have come out of that room alive and taken the girl with him."

Jim declined the invitation to brag on himself. "I had luck," he said simply.

Pike Corcoran scored another mark to his credit. The first had been when Delaney had served notice the girl was to be kept out of the story. The lad was not only a fighting fool. He had his code to be observed, and he had a wisdom beyond his years. But the question in the cattleman's mind was not yet answered. Most of the bad men he had known would have fought for a good woman. In the evil warp and woof of their lives that golden thread ran.

"How did you ever get Sundown to go into so crazy a thing with you?" Corcoran asked. "When I knew him he was a good honest run-of-the-herd cowhand."

"Still is," Jim confirmed.

"If you boys were holding up The Green Curtain —"

Delaney cut short that hypothesis. "You're following a blind trail, Mr. Corcoran. What other story could Dave Meldrum tell except that one? If you want to know why Sundown followed me, I'll tell you. Because he's a square-shooter and there every way from the ace. When the girl screamed I said, '*Vamonos*.' He sashayed up those stairs with me. I gave him the tough end of the job, to hold the door while I was lighting a shuck with the young lady. He made good, like I knew he would, 'long as he could stand and pull a trigger-finger. Me, I beat it and left him there."

Jim finished, bitter self-reproach in his voice.

"Jack says that is silly," Milly cut in sharply. "Don't you think so, too, Uncle Pike? It was Jim's business to save the girl, and Sundown was already through fighting. Nobody was paying any attention to him any longer."

"I wasn't," Jim admitted ruefully. "That's a cinch."

"I mean that they weren't firing at him any more," Milly explained. "There wasn't anything you could do for him."

"All I'm saying is that I dragged him into it, and he gets all shot up while I come through with a scratch. Maybe I couldn't help it, but it oughtn't to have been that way."

The cattleman glanced at the paper-backed story Jim had been reading at the time of his entrance.

"You studying to be a dime-novel hero?" he asked, with a flicker of a sarcastic grin. "Some would say you had done graduated already."

Jim flushed. He was acutely aware that the melodramatic angle of this exploit lent itself to ridicule. If the boys decided to take it that way, they would run on him the rest of his life.

"Looky here, Mr. Corcoran," he said, in a voice apologetic. "I ain't to blame because of all the fireworks. Doggone it, here I come to town after chousing mossheads for months. All I ask is peace and quiet while I enjoy myself, and before I've been in the burg an hour I'm hightailin' it for cover. What in the Sam Hill was I to do? Tell me that. How was I to blame? What would you have done? O' course you can say I hadn't any right to be at The Green Curtain.

Maybe not. I usta write in my copybook that 'evil communications corrupt good manners,' and a heap of other nice Sunday-School maxims. But I came here to have some fun. And first off, I'm acting like one of these dadgummed dime-novel guys, as you said. It has all been wished on me. I walk in, and she starts popping."

"Hmp!" Corcoran gave another snort. "Funny. All you want is peace and quiet, so you shove for Santone, knowing Lieutenant Brisbane of the Rangers is on your tail and has his headquarters right here. Nothing could be more reasonable."

"Shucks, a fellow can't live in the mesquite all his life," Jim explained. "Maybe my name is in that little book the Rangers keep, along with 'steen hundred other names. I'm only a kid. Mighty few of the force know me by sight. I didn't figure I was in any danger."

"But you admit the Rangers are looking for you."

"I don't admit a thing. And if they are — why, even the Rangers get off wrong foot first sometimes."

The cattleman rolled and lit a cigarette. "Know King Cooper pretty well, don't you?" he asked.

"Pretty well."

"I've heard malicious folks claim he and his friends run wet horses and cows."

Delaney's blue eyes grew wide with innocence. "Why, King is a deputy sheriff — and a mighty good one. Anyone will tell you that. After next election he will be sheriff."

"So I've heard," Corcoran assented dryly. "My mistake. A deputy sheriff couldn't deal in stock run over from Mexico."

"I reckon he usta be a wild young hellion once," Jim admitted.

"But he is a reformed character now?"

"He's no Dixie Smith. I reckon if someone brought a fuss and laid it on his doorstep, he'd pick it up. But he doesn't go hunting for trouble. And he is no rustler, far as I know."

"There is a lawyer in this town has defended him on seven murder charges."

"Found innocent, wasn't he?"

"Found not guilty. That's right. The story is that he has killed so many Mexicans he doesn't count them. Lieutenant Brisbane will tell you, when you have the pleasure of meeting him, that King's home is a headquarters for desperadoes and renegades and stock thieves."

"King is loyal to his friends," Jim said. "Some of them impose on him. O' course I know his reputation as a gunman. Everyone in Texas knows it. But he has done no killing since I first met him. We have to take a man as we find him, don't we? King is right kind and hospitable. You wouldn't want to see a finer-looking man."

"I've seen him and know him. It is easy to like a man with his personality. He doesn't come into this, except as far as you are concerned. According to Brisbane, you are one of his friends who have stretched the law considerable." Corcoran lifted a big brown hand, to forestall for the moment any comment by the other. "I know it's none of my damn business, if you want to look at it that way. I'm not asking any confession from you."

"And I'm not making any," Jim returned coolly. "Maybe I slipped up on the law some. Maybe I didn't. But I'll say that Lieutenant Brisbane would have some difficulty proving anything on me. He's doing right smart bluffing, don't you reckon?"

"Then you wouldn't mind meeting him and talking it over?"

Jim declined the suggestion with a grin. "I don't see any profit in that. Wouldn't buy me a thing. He's the law. I'm just a run-of-the-brush cowhand. If he decided to throw me in the calaboose, he could do it. With yore permission, sir I'll postpone the honor of meeting him. But in regards to another word you used — about all this being none of your business. I'll say that when you reached out to save Sundown's life, you made it your business. I'll take all the plain talk you want to hand me."

The cattleman was pleased. This youngster did not go off half-cocked. He could look at both sides of a question. The kid used his brains.

Corcoran moved forward cautiously. "For the sake of argument, we'll say you've been too free with cows and horses across the border. Have you ever had the back luck to kill any of the owners or *vaqueros* riding for them?"

"No."

"Or any Rangers pressing you?"

"Never even took a shot at one. Fact is, I never have killed a man."

"It was Sundown, then, who killed the fellow at The Green Curtain?"

Jim hesitated. "I'm taking the blame, if any, for that."

"But actually Sundown did it."

"Well, yes. I'm telling you that, not the public. Officially I did it. Poor Sundown only came in to back my play."

"If anyone gets into trouble about it with the authorities, it ought to be you and not Sundown. That what you mean?"

"With the police or with Meldrum's crowd. Yes."

"If Dave knew where you were, your notion is that he wouldn't wait for the police to arrest you."

"What would you think, Mr. Corcoran? He doesn't want the true story of the difficulty at The Green Curtain to come out. Better to bump me off."

"So you figure he'll rub you out, given a chance."

"That would be my guess."

"Mine, too." Corcoran leaned back in his tiptilted chair, both hands in his trouser pockets. "Safest thing for you to do is to go on the dodge into the brush country soon as you're fit to travel."

"I aim to do that when I know Sundown is all right."

"Then everybody will be fixed up nice except Pike Corcoran," the old-timer said casually.

"I don't reckon I get that, sir," Jim said after a moment.

Pike looked hard at the youth, appraising him thoughtfully, then decided to make him an offer.

CHAPTER NINE

No Crazy One-Gallus Brush-Popper

The cattleman smiled sardonically. "You two boys will be out in the brush where Meldrum can't reach you, but I'll be sitting right here in town. And I'm the fellow served notice on him to lay off Sundown."

"He wouldn't dare touch you, would he?" Jim asked, and then answered his own question. "You're not small fry like me and Sundown."

"Dave shot me down on the main street of Eagle Pass some years ago," Corcoran mentioned.

Jim's eyes asked questions. "I've heard you had trouble with him."

The cattleman's face grew grim. "I never liked him any better than a tarantula. He is and was a bad citizen. Even before we had personal trouble, he had worn out his welcome at Eagle Pass. I had to serve notice on him to get out. Before he went he took a crack at me."

"You think he would do it again?"

"I'm poison to him. Hatred of me is in his blood. We won't go into the reason why. I have opened up this feud again by butting in to save Sundown. From now on I won't be sitting easy a minute."

"Would San Antonio stand for it if he injured you?" Jim demurred. "I don't think it. You are the leading citizen, and he is a gambler with a bad reputation."

"Meldrum would have one of his plug-uglies do it. I wouldn't be killed in the open. Nobody would know for sure who did the job. Of course Dave would have a cast-iron alibi. With me out of the way, nobody in town would be strong enough to ride herd on his devilry." The cattleman smiled wearily. "Even in a fair fight I probably couldn't hold up my end with him or one of his bunch of killers. Meldrum himself is a dead shot. That's what they say of Dutch Nagle, too. I never had time to fool much with a gun. But it wouldn't be a fair fight. They would bushwhack me as I was coming home at night, or they would pump lead into me through a window of my house. I don't own a mess of killers as he does."

"What about the Rangers? Couldn't you appeal to them?"

"You know better than that, boy," Pike said ruefully. "The Rangers run down killers after their dirty work is done. Until then the Rangers don't take chips in the game. They don't claim to be mind readers."

"Could you drive him out of town — say, by organized public opinion?"

"Not until he does something to justify it. There is politics in this, son. The whole gambling element would band together in support of Meldrum. The others would figure it would be their turn next."

"You could go to your ranch, the Cross Bar B, and stay there for a while."

Corcoran flushed angrily. "I could, but I won't. I'm not going to be run out of town by a scalawag like him."

"Then what do you aim to do?" Jim plumped at him.

The owner of the Cross Bar B studied deliberately the tanned young face of the cowboy. He saw recklessness written there, but no trace of evil. He saw, too, a close-gripped jaw and unflinching eyes.

"You're no crazy one-gallus brush-popper," the older man said. "I expect you'd do to ride the river with. From what Jack tells me your education has been all around, up, down, over, and under."

"Jack and I slept in the same blanket," Jim replied. "He might be called a prejudiced party."

"How would you like to hire out to be shot at some more, young fellow?" Corcoran demanded abruptly.

"I expect that proposition would stand some more explaining," Delaney said quietly.

"Unless I get busy I'm going to cash in my checks right soon. I'm a law-abiding citizen, but not that easy. I'm going to get a personal guard of my own. When Meldrum hears of it, he may lay off me. I'll broadcast the news that I am expecting an attack from him. If he starts anything, it will be at his own risk."

"Are you aiming to start the war or wait for him to do it?"

For a moment passion distorted the strong face of the cowman. He clenched a big fist and brought it down on the palm of the other hand.

"Nothing I'd like better than to stomp him out like a rattler. I owe him that much twice over. But I want the good people of this town with me. I'll let him get in wrong."

"How could I throw in with you?" Jim asked. "The Rangers would pick me up first thing."

"That could be fixed if you went with me and surrendered. You say they can't prove anything against you."

"I said I didn't think they could," Jim corrected.

"Anyhow, I would go bail for you until your trial, so you would be free that long. I could have it pushed off probably. It wouldn't be my fault if you skipped out later."

"What about this business of The Green Curtain? Won't the police want me?"

"I can take care of that, even if Meldrum presses it, which I don't reckon he will."

"You would want good men for yore little army," Jim suggested.

"Good bad men," Corcoran corrected with his grim smile.

"You think there would certainly be trouble?"

"Sure as God made little apples. Three men is all I want. Jack wants to come in as one. Maybe I won't let him, on account of him being married. Buck Burris will be one of the three."

"I'll be another, Colonel," Jim decided. "You've done hired a hand."

Corcoran looked hard at him. "One that will go all the way with me?"

"I've never thrown down on my boss yet," Jim said simply.

"I'm not hiring just a guard," Pike said. "You'll find there's more to it than that. This thing goes back a long way. Trouble from early days. It involves some big men."

The cowman's manner suggested reservations.

Jim looked at him, then said, "I reckon that would call for an explanation."

"Meaning you wouldn't go in blindfold, on my say-so?"

"Meaning that if I was going into this up to my neck, with a chance of not coming out alive, I would have to be trusted with the facts."

"Fair enough. When the time comes, I'll tell you all you need to know."

"All there is to know," Jim corrected.

Pike shrugged. "You ask a good deal, young fellow. When I hire a hand, he obeys the orders that I give."

"May be so," Jim drawled. "To fix line fences on the Cross Bar B. I kinda gathered this was a more responsible job. Let's get this right, Colonel. I'm no warrior with a lot of notches on my gun willing to hire out as a killer. If I work with you, I'll know all about the why of it. And if the game doesn't suit me, I won't buy chips in it."

"You're independent, for a waddy who has been on the dodge."

"We can go different ways with no hard feelings."

"No, sir, you're going my way," Corcoran said heartily. "I like you, boy. When the right time comes, I'll tell you the story."

From the kitchen appeared Milly, smiling.

"Jack's here. Five minutes till dinner. If either of you wants to wash his hands you had better get busy."

Inside of the prescribed time they sat down to fried chicken, hot flaky biscuits, and mashed potatoes with gravy.

CHAPTER TEN

A Law-Abiding Citizen Votes For Temporary Peace

Pike Corcoran leaned back comfortably in a tip-tilted chair, his high-heeled boots resting on the desk. He was enjoying the verbal passage of arms between Lieutenant Brisbane and young Delaney. The Ranger officer had laid a few traps and Jim had side-stepped them with a manner so innocent he almost deceived the old cowman.

Brisbane was a long brown man who had combed the chaparral for outlaws for several years. He was no babe in the woods. Just now his sardonic face wore an expression of complete skepticism.

"You seem to know all the bad boys of West Texas, Delaney," he said, in a slow drawl. "Likely you hang around them just to be a good influence."

Jim grinned audaciously. "Betcha I don't know any more of 'em than you do, Lieutenant, and I don't hang around after them any more than you have."

"Know Charley Pitman?"

"Yes."

"Were you with him on the nineteenth of last January?"

"I'd have to figure that up," Jim replied. "Out in the brush one day is just like another."

"I'll jog your memory. Pitman was tailing some Mexicans who had run off a bunch of stock from his pasture."

"Oh, that day. Yes, I met up with Pitman and his boys when they were chasing the rustlers."

"Did Charley mention to you that the Mexicans were recovering their own cows, wet stuff Pitman had bought from thieves for a song?"

"No, he didn't say anything about that."

"You rode with him."

"We were traveling in the same direction."

"What happened?"

"Why, nothing happened while I was there except that we chinned for a spell and then I said 'Adios.' "

"You weren't with Pitman when he caught up with the Mexicans and shot two of them?"

"No, sir."

"Any alibi?"

"Yes, sir, this time I've got one. I left the boys near Horse Creek and rode across country to Uvalde. When the trouble took place, I was in town."

"I dare say you can prove that by King Cooper and some of his friends," the Ranger jeered.

"That's right. And by Jim Johnson, postmaster at Uvalde. I stopped for my mail when I hit town."

"Which was at what time?"

"Lemme see. I was just in time for dinner at Hop Lee's restaurant. Must have been about half-past twelve, I'd say."

"Johnson and Hop Lee can swear to the time, can they?"

"If they haven't forgot. There was a young lady in Johnson's store, a daughter of the preacher, Brother Temple. She was buying goods for a dress from the clerk. How come I to notice her she was so pretty. Maybe she would remember me being there."

The officer made a note of the names. "You don't seem to have forgotten a thing, Delaney," he said dryly. "Funny you've got all your witnesses so pat."

"You wouldn't think it strange if you spent as much time in the shinnery as I do, Lieutenant. It's a red-letter day when I get to town."

This was reasonable enough. Brisbane himself had spent too many months looking up gentry on the dodge in the mesquite not to know that visits to civilization stuck in the memory.

"This boy's story sounds right likely to me, Brisbane," the old cattleman suggested amiably. "I wouldn't wonder but what he has scattered a wild oat or two. Who hasn't? Kids all wobble some if there is much pepper in them. They have to kick over the traces while they are colts. Question is, Where does this young man go from here?"

"I would say to the penitentiary, if I had a little more evidence," the Ranger replied curtly.

Corcoran waved that aside. "Heck! You know that's not what I mean. Is he through with his foolishness and ready to be a good citizen? I'd say, yes."

"When did he get through with it? Was he all finished when he went up to The Green Curtain and raised hell the other night?" Brisbane asked.

"You're so doggoned suspicious," Corcoran reproved. "I will say this. If I had a boy of my own, I'd want him to act just like Jim here did then."

"I'm accepting his story," the lieutenant said grudgingly. "I've talked with Sundown Smith. And I don't mind admitting that no matter how bad Delaney is, Meldrum is worse. If you'll put up a bond for him I'll let him go free for the present. Later we can try him if the evidence justifies it."

"Fair enough. I need this boy right now. With that scoundrel Meldrum on the warpath against me, I'm not sitting high and handsome."

"Meldrum is a smooth proposition," the Ranger replied. "He has done enough evil to condemn a dozen men, but we've never been able to get evidence to prove it. There's not a man in Texas I'd rather crowd than Dave if I was sure of my ground. I mean legally sure."

The face of the cattleman set rigidly. "His chickens will come home to roost one of these days."

Corcoran and Delaney walked up Commerce Street. They stepped from the sidewalk to pass a pile of coffins which an undertaker had put in front of his establishment by way of advertisement. As they did so, the two men came face to face with Dave Meldrum and his henchman Dutch Nagle. Both parties came to a halt, since neither would step aside to let the other pass.

The cold gaze of Meldrum passed from Corcoran to the young man beside him. Recognition was instant.

"Got you this time!" the gambler cried. "Right where there's a coffin ready for you."

Jim watched both of The Green Curtain men. Not the slightest movement of either could have escaped his eyes. Meldrum had not yet reached for his gun. Nor had Nagle. Yet the young man knew that in a space of time that could be counted in seconds, their weapons would begin to roar.

Delaney stood poised on the balls of his feet, wary and lithe as a tiger. He was ready for what might come.

The old cowman spoke, hatred smoldering in every word. "Take care what you do, you damned villain. This boy has cleared himself before the law."

Meldrum's mouth was a thin, cruel slit. A cold, fierce eagerness shone in his eyes. "He has cleared himself, has he, for holding up my place and killing one of my men? By God, if there's no honest law in this town, I'll make it for myself."

Dutch waited for the signal, a still, hard steadiness in the fishy gaze that made all the difference between indifference and deadliness. Soon now, he thought, and chose the button on Delaney's vest at which he would fling his bullets.

"Don't you!" Pike Corcoran advised. "Safer for a double-crossing coyote like you to kill from ambush."

That was true. A bell of warning rang in Meldrum. He could not pick a fight with Corcoran in San

Antonio and kill him. Already he had injured him too much, and people would not forget that. Nor would they forget that Pike had given an amusement park to the city, that he was a deacon in the church, and supported all good causes.

"You taking up this outlaw's cause?" Meldrum demanded with a leer. "You throwing in with rustlers and bandits?"

The man was playing for time to make up his mind. A moment ago he had been all for battle, but now the lights in his shallow black eyes were not so confident. Why put all his chips on a bet that was not sure? This cowboy was a fighter. Corcoran would pump a gun as long as he could lift a wrist. Even if, by skill or chance, he and Dutch escaped alive, the town would be closed to them forever. No, there was a better way than this to score off these two enemies.

"I don't discuss my plans with riffraff like you," the cowman cried. "Get out of our way. Or come a-smoking."

"That last suits me fine," Nagle snarled thickly. His hand twitched toward the gun butt at his thigh.

Meldrum caught the man's hairy wrist. "Not now, Dutch," he ordered.

For the owner of The Green Curtain, without lifting his gaze an instant from the enemy, saw watching eyes at windows and at doors. He saw passers-by scurrying for cover. There would be a score of witnesses to tell their stories later. Their tales would be garbled, but the sum of them might stir up that strange lust for vengeance in the mob that is savage and cruel as the pounce of a tiger. He had seen lynchers at their work, had listened to the cry for blood lifted from a thousand hoarse throats. Towns had those curious uncontrollable spasms of rage. It might not be as bad as that if he and Dutch killed these men in a street duel, but at the very best there could be nothing but loss in it.

"What's eating you, Dave?" demanded the harsh, guttural voice of Nagle. "They're inviting it, ain't they?"

Meldrum spoke louder, for the benefit of all within hearing, unctuous virtue in his tone. "They're doing just that, Dutch, but we are honest, law-abiding citizens and not killers. If Pike Corcoran wants to tie up with bandits and use them as personal gunmen, we can't help it. I'm not looking for trouble, least of all with this man Corcoran. Far as this scalawag Slim Delaney goes, I'd arrest him dead or alive right here if it wasn't for his friend. But when the prominent bosses of the city support criminals, we'll have to let them outrage public sentiment until we can get them out of the saddle."

Meldrum had made his choice, and it was not for immediate battle. That was clear to Jim. His motives the young man could guess. The gambler wanted to play safe, and he wanted to placate general opinion by getting across the idea that he was being wronged. Delaney had a word to say, for those who might be listening. He said it now.

"Anybody who wants to find out why the fight at The Green Curtain started can do it by reading the *Express* tomorrow. You're not a good enough liar to get away with that fairy tale you told, Meldrum."

"It's not safe to talk that way to me," the gambler said, a threat in the words. "Be careful, young man."

Jim met him eye to eye. "I will, especially at night. I'd hate to be shot in the back. Yore big words don't scare me any. To me you are only another crooked gambler. Not necessary to tell me I'll be dry-gulched if you can do it without risk. Don't I know it?"

Dutch Nagle's dead eyes rested venomously on Delaney. "I'd say now, Dave," he murmured.

"No!" Meldrum said sharply.

Now that the chances of blazing guns were less imminent, men were sifting back into the street. A policeman was approaching. Two half-grown boys had pushed to the front and were taking in the scene with all their eyes and ears.

"That's Dutch Nagle," one whispered audibly to the other. "Parky Jones says he's got five notches on his gun."

The officer asked a question. "What's the trouble?"

Meldrum got in his answer first. "No trouble at all, Simmons. We bumped into the guy that knocked you cold the other night. All you got to do now is to arrest him."

The big red-faced policeman looked at Jim. "By golly, it is," he said, staring at him.

The ivory-toothed grin on Delaney's brown face was friendly. "Sorry I had to be rough, Officer," he said genially. "O' course I took you by surprise or you would have nailed me. I had to get away from those killers in The Green Curtain and I had no time to explain. No hard feelings, I hope."

"I'm going to arrest you," Simmons said bluntly.

"Sure," Jim agreed. "I gave myself up to Chief Harper soon as I could walk, and we talked this all over to his satisfaction. But take me back to him. He'll be pleased to know you're right on the job."

"Hand me that gun."

Delaney lifted his eyebrows toward Corcoran. There was both a question and a suggestion in that look.

"Not so fast, Simmons," the cattleman demurred. "He'll go along with you all right. I'll guarantee that, for I'm going too. But right now, with wolves running loose on the streets, he'll keep his gun."

The officer knew where his bread was buttered. "All right, Mr. Corcoran, if you say so." He tucked an arm under that of Jim and said, "We'll be going."

Jim smiled cheerfully. "You're certainly friendly, Mr. Simmons."

The gunmen watched the trio depart, escorted by the two youngsters and a fringe of idle bystanders still hoping for some excitement.

"He was my meat, that waddy Delaney," Nagle said sourly. "I could of got him cold before ever he had his gun out — if you hadn't quit on me."

"You'll always be a fool, Dutch," his employer told him with chill contempt. "We couldn't kill him without killing Corcoran, too. This town wouldn't stand for that. Use your brains, if any."

He resumed his interrupted way to The Green Curtain. Nagle went with him.

CHAPTER ELEVEN

Polly Meets A Villain And A Hero

Every Saturday, at noon, Rose Corcoran walked from the academy to her father's house to spend the weekend with him. On this occasion her roommate, Polly Stuart, went with her as a guest. Polly lived on a ranch near Laredo and went home only during the longer holidays. She was always pleased to break the week by joining Rose.

The girls chattered about the details of school life, with little gusts of laughter, with giggles, with absorbed seriousness. A pair of singing meadow larks had about as much experience of life as they.

They followed a footpath through a grove of mesquite bushes. Out of a thicket came a man with swift catlike tread. He was tall, straight, handsome, and immaculately dressed. His hat was lifted from a black head in a sweeping bow.

The gaiety went out of Rose's face as the light goes from a blown candle. She stopped, drew back. "What do you want?" she asked, her face colorless.

"Don't be alarmed," Meldrum said suavely. "I won't hurt you." He looked at Polly, then at Rose. "Can I see you alone — for a few moments?"

"No!" Rose cried sharply. "Don't leave me, Polly."

Polly had not the remotest thought of leaving. Life at the academy was dull, and she did not intend to pass up any excitement that came her way. Vicariously she had thrilled at her roommate's experience the other night. She had sighed at the romance and danger of it. But she preferred to get her stimulus at first hand.

Meldrum lowered his voice. "I wanted to talk with you — about Marie."

"I don't want to talk with you about anything at all," Rose told him. "I don't want ever to see you again. Go away and leave me, or I'll scream."

"Don't be foolish," the man snapped out. "I told you I wasn't going to hurt you. I wouldn't have done you any harm the other night, but you lost your head. What I want to tell you now is that I have set inquiries afoot about Marie. As soon as I know where she is, I'll let you know."

"I suppose you're Mr. Meldrum," Polly cut in.

The gambler looked at her. "Yes."

"Well, if you want to know, I think you are a horrid man," Polly told him impetuously. "But if you mean what you say — about Rose's sister — you can send any news you get, care of me. My name is Polly Stuart."

Meldrum bowed again. His smile was sarcastic. "It is a pleasure and an honor to meet you, Miss Stuart, but it happens my business is with Miss Corcoran."

"Since you've finished it, don't let us keep you from going," Polly said acidly.

"Did I say I had finished it?" he asked smoothly. "I want also to suggest to you both — since you seem to have stepped into this, too, Miss Stuart — that it won't do Miss Corcoran any good if it gets out that she visited The Green Curtain. Undeservedly, of course, the place has a bad reputation. I came to assure my recent visitor that I shall keep the secret."

Polly was quick-witted. "Very kind of you. And I suppose you would like to know that we'll keep it too?"

"I wouldn't want a young girl's reputation ruined unjustly," he replied virtuously. "If you have read the papers, you will have noticed I protected you, Miss Corcoran."

"Yes, we noticed that," Polly said, in what she hoped was a crushing retort. "Wholly on Rose's account, no doubt."

"Yes," admitted the gambler. "Well, I'll continue to keep your secret, Miss Corcoran. And as soon as I hear any news of Marie, I'll send it to you, care of Miss Stuart."

He gave Polly another bow and smile. That blonde young lady's pug nose went into the air. She was indicating hauteur.

"Once more let me assure you, Miss Corcoran, that I had no wish to frighten you," Meldrum went on evenly. "You were a little highstrung and misunderstood what was in my mind. I regret the incident very much."

He turned and walked rapidly away.

"Darling, he's perfectly fascinating!" Polly exclaimed. "No wonder he breaks women's hearts."

"I think he's the most hateful and the most dangerous man I ever saw," Rose said, with a flare of anger.

"Dangerous, yes. That's partly why he is so fascinating. Did you see his eyes? Marvelous. Of course he's wicked. But perhaps —"

Polly did not finish the sentence. She was looking dreamily into space. Her roommate looked shrewdly at her.

"Perhaps a good woman's love might save him yet," she snapped. "Don't be a little fool, Polly."

Polly's laughter rippled out, gaily. She had a sense of humor, and she could turn it on herself. "You caught me that time, Rose. But he *is* handsome. Even you can't deny that."

"Handsome is as handsome does," Rose said primly, quoting a maxim of one of the sisters at the convent school.

Pike Corcoran was not in evidence when the girls reached the house. Rose led the way into the parlor, where a young man was sitting in a rocking-chair reading a newspaper, his big white dusty sombrero on the table. Polly had never seen him before, but he had something that struck a lively spark of interest in her brown eyes. That something was a combination of youth, good looks, and easy nonchalance.

At sight of him Rose cried out in astonishment. "You!"

He rose, in one lithe, swift movement of rippling harmony. His glance flashed warning. His words repudiated acquaintance.

"I reckon you are Miss Corcoran," he said. "Yore father said he was expecting you. He's upstairs, in the room he uses for an office. I'm employed by him to look after some business. My name is Delaney — James Delaney."

It was Polly Stuart's turn to exclaim. "Rose's hero!" she cried.

Jim looked at her. She was a roly-poly ashen blonde, very pretty. Her eyes fairly bubbled with excitement.

"Don't josh me, Miss," he said reproachfully. "I reckon you are Miss Corcoran's roommate, and somebody has been talking."

"I know everything," Polly told him. "All about how you saved her —"

"My, my!" interrupted Jim. "So little, and you know everything. I reckon you're at the head of yore class."

"You didn't tell me you were wounded," Rose said. "Are you all right now?"

"Watch me at dinner," he suggested.

"Father doesn't know?"

"He knows I helped get a girl out of The Green Curtain. Everyone knows that. It is in the paper again today. But he doesn't know who she is. Nobody need ever know that, unless one of you talk — or Meldrum."

"I don't understand what you are doing here. Did you know my father before — before the other night?"

"No. Your cousin Jack's house was where I holed up. We are old pals. Jack brought your father into it to protect Sundown. That's how come I to meet him. We've gone into business together, in a kind of way. I'm sort of a minor partner, you might say."

"How romantic!" Polly murmured.

Again Jim took in with a steady gaze her petite charm. He smiled. "You must be right, since you know everything. I don't get that angle on it myself."

Rose promptly repudiated her friend. "Polly is always reading silly books," she said sweetly. "That's how she comes to be the way she is. Outside of that, she's really a nice girl."

"Not permanent, you think?"

Jim was looking at Polly. He turned to Rose and touched his head.

"No, she'll get over it, the doctors say," Rose told him smilingly. "Just as she did over the mumps."

Polly broke through their persiflage with an "Oh, you!" and a wave of the hand that brushed it aside. "We met that villain not ten minutes ago, Mr. Delaney. On our way here. He stepped out of the mesquite and stopped us."

"Meaning just who?" Jim asked.

"Dave Meldrum. That's who."

The young man's drawl concealed his interest. "Thought gamblers weren't supposed to be acquainted with young ladies."

"Goodness! That wouldn't bother him. He's cheeky enough for anything."

Rose explained quietly. "He wanted me not to speak of — of what happened the other night."

"He's trying to duck trouble," Jim surmised aloud.

"Just what we thought," Polly agreed. "I told him so too."

"The less you tell him the better," Delaney counseled. "I wouldn't have anything to do with him."

"That would be good advice for you, too, wouldn't it, Mr. Delaney?" Polly said sweetly, her nose tilted a trifle in the air.

"Y'betcha!" Jim assented promptly. "I'll sure leave him alone if he does me. But that's different. Young ladies ought not even to speak to riffraff like him. It isn't proper."

"You should get a position at the academy to teach etiquette," Polly said.

"What's more, the man is dangerous. You ought to know that."

"I do," Polly replied, with a giggle. "I told you so, didn't I, Rose? A man as handsome as he is, with such polished manners —"

"Behave yourself, Polly," her friend ordered.

"He is an enemy of Mr. Corcoran," Jim called to Polly's attention. "A bad man, a killer, a criminal at heart. Not a man to joke about."

Imps of mischief danced in the brown eyes of Miss Stuart. "There seem to be so many of that kind," she sighed demurely. "I was reading in the *Express* the other day about one who held up The Green Curtain, and all these things and more were said about him. Of course, I know they can't be true. I have met him, Mr. Delaney. He doesn't look like a — a bandit. Outlaws all wear beards and a lot of guns, don't they?"

"Polly," her friend reproved, scandalized.

Jim met the wide-eyed, innocent audacity of Polly blandly. "I wouldn't know about that. I'm just a cowboy out of the brush. But don't you think maybe the *Express* got a wrong steer from Meldrum about the lad who busted in on him?"

"May be so." Polly was enjoying her own impudence hugely. She fell into the drawl of the cowboy. "You wouldn't saw off a whopper on us, would you? We'd hate to think you're just a poor dogie cowhand who would buy wooden nutmegs instead of a regular Sam Bass."

"If I haven't bought any wooden nutmegs, it is because nobody has offered me any," Jim said, grinning.

"Why do you wear such a big hat, Mr. Dogie?"

"I'll tell you about that," the young man confided. "I wear this big hat because I couldn't find a bigger one."

"I suppose you have the brush cleared out some before you ride through it."

"This is my town hat."

"What does 'on the dodge' mean, Mr. Delaney?" Polly asked. "The article said he was on the dodge, whatever that is."

"Maybe it means he is shy of young ladies. I expect that's it. Likely they scare him something terrible. But we'll leave that young scalawag out of it right now. What I'm telling you is that you can't be playful with this fellow Meldrum any more than you can pet a rattlesnake."

"Don't waste time on Polly," Rose told him. "She likes to talk."

Jim's approving gaze lingered on Miss Polly. "I don't know as I would call it a total waste of time," he drawled.

"That's nice of you," Polly dimpled. "Rose means that Mr. Meldrum doesn't really fool me, even if he has a good bow."

Rose flamed to momentary passion. "I hope I never see him again. He's the — the — vilest man."

"I hope you never do," Jim nodded. "You've got him sized right."

"We'll run along now and get ready for dinner, Polly," her friend said.

"Talking about the *Express*, have you seen it today?" Jim asked. "If not, maybe you'd like to look it over. I'm through with it." He handed the paper to Rose.

In his manner was something a little more significant than politeness. Rose guessed there was news in the paper he wanted her to see.

The two girls went upstairs to their bedroom. Before the door was closed, Polly began to pour out exclamatory approval.

"Oh, darling, he's perfectly fascinating! As handsome as Byron was and —"

"Don't be a goose, Polly. He's as much like Byron as I am like old fat Aunt Becky." Rose was running down the columns of the *Express*.

"I didn't say in the same way, did I? Goodness! You're so literal. Like Lochinvar then. 'No laggard in love and no dastard in war.' I don't care what you say, it's the most romantic thing I ever knew."

Rose had found what she was looking for on the second page. It was a statement signed by James Delaney and Sundown Smith giving their account of the affair at The Green Curtain. In it very little was said about the unknown young woman except that she had begged them to rescue her from Meldrum and was manifestly in great terror.

Presently her friend's voice brought her back to the present. "— so strong and kinda heroic. If you didn't have miners on him —"

Rose interrupted, blushing. The directness of her friend's approach to forbidden themes would not have been recommended by the sisters at the academy. The thoughts of Polly hovered around love and she was quite frank about it. She did not follow the fashion of the period, which was for young women to sigh in secret and feign a modest disinterest in the subject.

"Have a little sense, Pol," Rose said impatiently. "Just because he dropped me from a window, he doesn't have to play Lochinvar to me. I don't even know him. We haven't been really introduced yet."

"What luck you have!" Polly retorted enviously. "You meet him in a thrilling adventure. I'll probably be properly introduced to my fate at a church social, and he'll be about as exciting as a sick calf."

"Oh, all right. Keep right on being romantic, you goose."

"A splendid villain. A gallant hero. A lovely heroine. I don't see —"

Rose threw a pillow at her. After the scrimmage was over, she handed Polly the article in the *Express* to read.

"He protects your good name," Polly said, after she had finished the article. "See what he says. 'She was a very young girl and we helped her get out of town.' It's going to be all right."

"I hope so." Rose was still far from sure. "I do hope Father never hears of it. What he'd do to me would be something awful. I can't see now why I ever did so crazy a thing, except that I wanted so much to hear about Marie."

A voice came up the back stairway to them. "You-all ready for dinner yet, Miss Rose?"

"In half a minute, Aunt Becky."

The girls fell to primping.

CHAPTER TWELVE

Pike Corcoran Digs Into The Past

Filled to repletion with a good dinner, Pike Corcoran lit a cigar, leaned back in his chair, and began to talk.

"I was brought up on the Brazos, son, in the days when the Comanches were still raiding. Many a time I have helped bury a neighbor man or woman who had been scalped by the red devils. Life was rough and simple in those days. We lived in houses of unhewn logs snaked out of the woods by a bull team. The floor was puncheon. A stick-and-dirt chimney with a rock back was used for both cooking and heating. All our furniture was home-made. About all the cooking implements we had were a skillet, a Dutch oven, an iron pot, and a teakettle. I never saw a match until I was pretty well grown. At nights we banked the fire with ashes. If it ever did go out, we carried a chunk of fire from the nearest neighbor, maybe a mile or so away. Out of a green cowhide we made rope hobbles, clotheslines, doors, bed springs, seats of chairs, overcoats, trousers, brogans, and shirts."

"You were a sort of Jack of all trades," Jim nodded. "In the brush country we're still some that way."

"But not so much since we've got so doggoned civilized. Well, I did my four years in the Civil War and came out like the rest of the boys clean busted. It was all free grass in those days and pretty nearly free cattle. During the war there hadn't been anybody left at home to tend the cattle and they had gone wild. Like a lot of other lads, I hired out to brand mavericks. My boss was a man named Glidden. I reckon it would be more accurate to say my bosses were a family named Glidden. There were six brothers of them, big, wild, hard-drinking fellows, mighty quick on the shoot. All they did was ride around on horseback and raise hell. Likely you have met some of them. There is still a mess of 'em around."

"Yes," Jim said. "And heard a lot more."

"You would. They were, and those of them still left are, a bunch of tough *hombres*. After a while I figured I could do better working on my own. I picked me a brand, the PC, and got busy. At the end of three months I had a nice bunch of about three hundred longhorns branded and earmarked. I knew I had better get my claims down on the books of the county clerk. Finally, I took a day off and rode to the county seat to record the brand. The clerk sure enough handed me a jolt. Sim Glidden had already entered my brand and mark in his own name. I had been working real hard for him instead of for Pike Corcoran. If I had stayed on his payroll, I would have been thirty dollars a month better off."

Jim lit the cigarette he had been rolling. "Then what?"

"I went to see him and kicked like a bay steer. He and two of his hell-roaring brothers, Bill and Mart, were in the Rawhide Saloon. They laughed at me. So did everybody else, except the decent citizens. What could I do? There were six of them, and they had plenty of friends. And they had the law on their side. I recorded another brand and began again."

"You prospered more than they did, I reckon," Jim volunteered.

"I did well. Pretty soon I began to see the day of free grass wouldn't last forever. I bought scrip and acquired land. Mavericking became a thing of the past except for outlaws. My herds increased by means of brands I would take in from fellows moving on to the big stretch of country opening to the north. There came a time when I had twenty thousand head in my name. Then came the years of the big steal. You have heard of that?"

"Yes," Jim said.

"I've been told that more than one hundred thousand head of cattle were stolen from Texas in three years," Corcoran went on, after a puff at his cigar. "The thieves took our cows by wholesale. The way of it was that there had been a drouth in West Texas and a great number of cattle had drifted down into our section or been driven there. The scalawags who claimed to own them took back home all the cows they could find, regardless of the brands. Of course, we organized to protect ourselves. Whenever we heard of one of these forced night drives, we would pass the word around and gather our neighbors.

"One night Buck Lander busted into my place with the news of a big drive slipping north through Box Cañon. Inside of three hours seventeen of us were in the saddle. We rode all night. The sun was just rising when we topped a hill and looked down into a valley dotted with a big herd of cows standing on their heads. The rustlers were letting them graze after an all-night drive. I reckon Bull Glidden, who was in charge of the thief outfit, figured they were out of the danger zone. They saw us coming, and believe me those waddies lit out like a bunch of wild Nueces steers. All but Bull and two others. We cut them off and drove them into the rocks. Bull wouldn't surrender. We rubbed him out with his gun still roaring. The other two threw up their hands. One of the captured men was a known outlaw named Rocky Parks, a bad man sure enough. He was a cousin of the Glidden boys. We hanged him right there. The other was a young lad none of us knew. There was quite a powwow. I voted to let him go, since he was only a kid. Four or five of the others were with me. Finally we talked the balance of our outfit into our way of thinking. That's where I made the biggest mistake of my life. The kid was Dave Meldrum, and I reckon he never forgave me for saving his life."

"I had heard he was in with the Gliddens' outfit, but I didn't know he was a rustler," Jim said.

"He wasn't one for long," Corcoran replied. "Not his line. Sim Glidden used him for more important business. Dave became his right bower and still is. Sim has brains, and he used them to get rich. He didn't care how. If anyone got in his way, he rubbed the man out, providing it was safe. But he is no fool. When his brothers wanted to go on the warpath against me and the other cowmen who had settled the hash of Bull Glidden and Rocky Parks, Sim held them back. He knew law was coming into Texas and he wasn't big enough to buck it. Not openly, anyhow. He had to work under cover. But don't think for a moment that he forgets. If and when he finds it not too risky, he will certainly wipe me out."

"Meldrum ran a gambling-house at Eagle Pass, didn't he?"

"Yes. Sim financed it. He was a silent partner, like he is now at The Green Curtain. Meldrum's place at Eagle Pass became a notoriously evil den. The strong-arm men stopped at nothing. When one of them killed a nice young Easterner who had come out to buy into a cattle ranch, I organized the citizens and served notice on the whole outfit to get out. We brought pressure on the district attorney to close the joint. That afternoon Meldrum shot me down in the street, then forked a bronc and rode out to Sim Glidden's Circle G Ranch. He lay out in the brush until I began to get well. There wasn't a chance for the sheriff to get him, with the whole Glidden tribe looking after him. Later he was tried before a Glidden judge and got off with a twenty-five-dollar fine for assault with intent to kill."

"So Sim Glidden, not Meldrum, is the real power," Jim said thoughtfully.

"Meldrum is dangerous as a wolf," Pike explained, voice harsh as a file and bitter with the memory of wrongs. "But he would be easy enough to handle if he did not have back of him the Glidden brothers, their sons, and all the riffraff that tie up with them. Most of that bunch are not in town, fortunately for me, but they are thick as fleas all around the Cross Bar B. I'm expecting every day to hear of trouble down there."

"There and here too," Jim suggested with a grin.

"Yes." Colonel Corcoran dropped the butt of his cigar into a spittoon and rose. "Well, boy, now you know the whole story. This thing you have started again may quiet down or it may not. My guess would be that it won't. This Fat Clark you and Sundown bumped off at The Green Curtain is another one of the Glidden forty-eleven cousins. You haven't got into this game so deep yet but what you can cash your chips and light a shuck into Colorado or New Mexico. If you are wise, that is what you will do."

Jim, too, was on his feet, a long, lean brown man who even in repose suggested force that might lash out with disastrous effect. Corcoran felt the strength of the man, in spite of the gay, boyish insouciance. Touch that drawling ease with the proper match, and he was likely to be as violently explosive as a dynamite stick with a fuse attached.

"I reckon since I've bought a stack I'll rock along for a while," he said lightly.

"What I'd look for you to do," the cattleman answered, with deep satisfaction. "Son, you'll do to take along. I'll promise you one thing; if this works out right, you won't be sorry you threw in with me."

"We'll talk about that when I've made good," Jim replied.

Corcoran noticed that he used the word *when* and not *if*. This young fellow had confidence enough in himself to carry him a long way, yet was at the other end of the pole from a braggart.

Later, Jim reviewed the conversation and found one hiatus in the tale Corcoran had told. Up to a certain point he had covered the ground frankly, then had slid away from facts he could not bring himself to mention. The part of the story which had to do with his daughter Marie still hurt Pike too much for discussion.

Jim wondered what magic Meldrum had used to seduce into marriage with him the daughter of the man whom he had tried to kill.

CHAPTER THIRTEEN

Time To Rub Him Out

Sim Glidden sat slumped in a chair, his stony, heavy-lidded eyes fixed on Meldrum. The flesh of advancing years had grown on him, but he was still strong and muscular. For reasons of business and politics he often put on an air of geniality. His laugh was loud and frequent. He did a good deal of back-slapping. But his lips were like a steel trap, and in the hinterland back of his masked, smiling face lay much malignity and evil.

Just now he was not taking the trouble to be a good fellow. No need of that with Meldrum. The two understood each other.

"It *would* be over a woman, Dave," he jeered. "Can't let 'em alone, can you?"

"I didn't ask her to come here," Meldrum retorted coldly. "She knocked on the door of this room and walked in big as cuffy."

"A lot of them walk in here from what I've been told."

"Not making that your business, are you, Sim?" the gambler asked evenly, eyebrows raised.

"Not in general. But in this particular case there seems to be some mystery about it. I don't get it."

"What don't you get? Is it my fault a couple of lunkhead cowboys busted through the door and started trouble?"

"I don't know. Tell me about it. This fellow — what's his name, Slim Delaney — claims she is a straight girl. If so, that's important. You don't ever learn that in this country a good woman has to be treated with respect — unless she is your wife."

The last proviso slipped out, apparently as a casual addendum. But Meldrum understood there was a sting in it. The gambler let his cold eyes take in the other. Glidden leaned back, as motionless as a lizard in the sun. Yet Dave knew the inert heaviness was deceptive. All the man's movements were slow, unless there was a call to action. Then Sim was the fastest-moving slow man in the world. Instantly he could come to explosive attack.

"Do straight girls come to The Green Curtain, Sim?" Meldrum asked curtly.

"They wouldn't if I was running it. Who was this girl, anyhow?"

Ever since the shooting difficulty, Meldrum had been weighing in his mind the pros and cons of coming clean to Glidden on this point. The cattleman hated Corcoran as much as he did. Would Sim keep the secret? Or would he make public the truth, knowing how it would tear the heart of his enemy? The owner of the Circle G was a wily old bird. He was not in business for his health, and he must know that to give out the name of this girl might make trouble that would wipe out The Green Curtain. Incidentally it might ruin Dave Meldrum. That last would be a minor consideration to Sim. It might even give him pleasure. But he would not be likely to destroy a large investment to gratify even his hatred of Colonel Corcoran.

"She was the daughter of Pike Corcoran," Meldrum said slowly, watching the other man.

"Your wife."

"No. His other daughter."

Glidden's bulky immobility did not betray his startled surprise.

"You're taking her on now, are you? Why, she's only a kid. Better fold up and slide for parts unknown before this is made public. I can't protect you, and I won't try."

"Wrong on both counts, Sim," his partner retorted coolly. "I'd never seen the girl to talk with before. She came to me for information. And the story won't be made public. She can't afford to have it known any more than I can."

"What information?" asked Glidden.

"Wanted to know where her sister is."

"You told her?"

"No, I didn't."

"Where is Marie?"

Meldrum smiled as he gave Glidden a second surprise. "Right here in town. Playing in stock under the name Grace Dunlap. The company blew in last week. It is to be here two months."

"You have seen your wife?"

"No. We're not on speaking terms."

"Does her father know she is here?"

"I'd say not, but he may find it out any day if she is recognized by any old friend on the street. That's not very likely, though, since she didn't live in this town more than a month or two."

Sim came back to the more important subject of the younger daughter. "You're not lying to me, Dave?" he demanded harshly. "There is nothing between you and the younger girl?"

"Not a thing. I've told you just how it was."

"Except that you couldn't resist pulling yore usual stuff with women," Glidden jeered.

"I'm not to blame because the little fool misunderstood me."

"Is it yore idea that this fellow Delaney knows who she is?"

"Not likely. If he knew, he'd likely tell her father, to curry favor with him. Pike didn't act like he knew, the day we met on the street."

"What about this Slim Delaney? Does he amount to anything?"

Meldrum considered before he replied. "He's a fighting fool. Whether he's anything more than that, I couldn't say. I've been told he is one of King Cooper's men. The Rangers think he was with Charley Pitman when he bumped off two Mexicans who were stealing back their own rustled stock from him. Delaney has fixed up some kind of an alibi. I don't know how good. But he knows too much. I've been wondering if it wouldn't be a good idea to get a couple of greasers to frame him."

"Once my boys get hold of him, he won't need any framing — after what he did to Fat Clark," the cattleman said grimly.

"I would be there with you on that both ways from the ace," the gambler nodded.

"But there may be something in yore notion at that," Glidden said thoughtfully. "Might see if you can fix it up."

"Dutch is crazy to bump him off."

"Why not let him? Save trouble all around."

"If it wouldn't get us in bad," Meldrum said doubtfully.

"We'll repudiate Dutch if it does. Tell him so. It's the dark of the moon now. He doesn't have to do it on Main Street at noon."

"Corcoran will raise a roar. He'll claim we're back of it."

"Do we care how much he roars? I'll be at the ranch. You can be there hunting with me. Whatever happens we won't know anything about it."

"All right. I'll fix it with Dutch . . . Then what about Corcoran? He won't sit still and take it, especially if he hears about his daughter coming to see me."

The stony eyes of Glidden were expressionless. "I've had enough of Pike. Time to rub him out."

"Here?"

"Not here. Down at the ranch."

"You'll invite him down to be killed?" Meldrum suggested sarcastically.

"He'll invite himself down." Sim added an explanation. "Hadn't been for me keeping the boys from him, he would have been dead long ago. I'll step aside now."

"And give the boys a hint?" Meldrum said.

"If it's necessary." The owner of the Circle G dismissed the subject and turned to affairs financial. "Now I'll take a look at the books, Dave. The Green Curtain ought to make more money than it does."

"That so?" sneered Meldrum, tossing a ledger upon the table before his partner. "How much money you want to make out of a shoestring investment, Sim?"

Glidden did not answer. He was turning over the pages of the ledger.

CHAPTER FOURTEEN

Marie Declines

Polly and Rose waylaid Jim in the hall upstairs just after supper.

"Where is Father?" Rose asked in a low voice.

"He is having a little snooze downstairs in the parlor," Delaney answered.

"Are the blinds drawn, so nobody can see into the room?"

"Yes, Miss Rose. We wouldn't forget a little thing like that."

"He'll sleep about half an hour. I want to talk with you."

Rose hesitated. Except her father's office, which was locked, there were none but bedrooms on the second floor.

The slight embarrassment of her friend Polly understood. She brushed it aside as of no importance. "It doesn't matter whether it's proper, Rose. We want to be alone. Come into our room a minute, Mr. Delaney."

Delaney followed the girls into the bedroom. He closed the door behind him and stood with his back to it.

"It's about my sister Marie," Rose said shyly. "You've heard about her, I suppose."

"Some," Jim replied.

"She went on the stage. Father wouldn't forgive her for it. He thinks the theater is sinful and that no good woman becomes an actress. When he heard of it, he was wild with anger and wrote Marie a letter casting her off. Soon after that she married Dave Meldrum."

She looked up at the brown, lean-flanked man, her blue eyes begging for a merciful judgment.

"I would call that last right rash," he said.

"What she did was wrong," Rose cried impulsively. "But if you knew Marie, so lovely and gay and generous, you would understand how I feel. It doesn't matter what she has done. She is my sister — and I love her."

The color in the dusky cheeks was high. The red lips above the beautiful pearly teeth were parted. The pupils of the dark eyes were very bright with excitement.

"That's the way to talk," Jim said quietly.

"Father doesn't think so. I am forbidden ever to speak of her. Mr. Delaney, I heard some news today. Our black cook, Aunt Becky, met her on the street. I've got to get word to her how I feel, and that I must see her."

"Of course she must," Polly agreed. "It's awf'ly thrilling."

"What is yore sister doing here, Miss Rose?" Jim asked.

"She is with the play-acting company that has come to town for two months. That's what she told Aunt

Becky, and she made her promise not to tell me. But Aunt Becky did."

"Does Dave Meldrum know she is in town?"

"Marie said not. She doesn't ever want to see him again, she told Becky."

"You want me to take a message to her," Jim guessed.

"If you will, please. I haven't anybody else to send that I can trust. Marie is playing tonight at Turner Hall under the name Grace Dunlap."

Jim looked into the pleading eyes, almost as dark as purple plums, and he knew that he would do as she wished. He did not like it, from one angle. He was in partnership with her father, and it was not exactly loyal to act as a go-between without his knowledge. The thing would not be easy to explain to Colonel Corcoran if he found out. But he was not going to desert Rose when she needed a friend.

"I'll take yore message," Jim told her.

From underneath the pillow of her bed Rose drew an envelope. She gave it to the young man.

"You'll be sure she gets it herself," the girl said shyly.

"Don't worry about that."

Rose was worrying about something else. "Do you think I'm a bad girl? I'm disobedient. Father ordered me never to write — or anything. I'm doing just what he told me not to do. But Marie is my sister. Is it wrong for me to — to —"

The question died on her lips, but it was still urgent in her troubled eyes.

"I wouldn't know about that," Jim said gently. "If you think it is right, why, then it is for you." He added, with a warm smile of approval: "All I can say is if I had a sister doing what you are doing, I'd tell her to hop to it."

"Of course," Polly said, with decisive scorn of doubt.

"I would be proud of her for not quitting on someone she loved," Jim concluded.

"I'm glad," Rose murmured, another wave of pink beneath the tan of her cheeks.

"My goodness, but Rose is silly," Polly declared bluntly. "I would obey my father whenever he was reasonable, but if he told me to never see my sister again, I would certainly quit honoring his pigheadedness first chance I got."

"I reckon if you got married, you would expect to obey yore husband," Jim said, with a skeptical grin.

Polly giggled. "I'd explain that to him after we were married."

After long and careful observation Jim slid out of the back door of the house. He had no intention of being shot from ambush if he could help it. By unfrequented streets he made his way toward Turner Hall. Having arrived there, he bought a ticket for the play *East Lynne*.

The seat he chose was one close to the wall. Before the curtain went up, his eyes ranged over the audience to make sure that no enemy was sitting near him. During the intermissions he scanned once more the faces of those in the rows behind him.

He had not seen many plays in his life, and this one greatly interested him. It was sheer melodrama, but he did not know that. The acting was overstressed. Villain was plainly labeled villain in lines and manner. The hero was one of God's noblemen, as one of the characters said. But out of the meretricious performance stood the acting of Grace Dunlap.

She had the quality of glamour, so rare among actresses. Nobody could have denied her loveliness, its wistfulness, but more arresting was the enchantment of her voice and the mobility of her charming face. When she crossed the stage, it was as though her motions were set to music. Romance walked with her. Her smile was adorable and provocative.

Jim Delaney watched her with fascinated attention. He had expected to see a woman hard, handsome, worldly-wise. Not one like this, who seemed to quiver and palpitate with emotion.

When the melodrama was finished, Jim wrote a line on a bit of paper and asked an attendant to take it to Grace Dunlap. The man grinned. Jim had wrapped the paper around a silver dollar.

The young man waited in the aisle until his messenger returned.

"This way," the man said, and led him back-stage to a dressing-room.

Jim knocked on the closed door.

"Please wait a few minutes," a musical voice called back to him.

After a time the door opened. The young woman facing Jim was a blonde, and the well-cut dress, tight about the hips and body, sheathed a torso supple and graceful as that of a panther. When she stepped aside to let him enter, there was a flow and rhythm to her movements he had never seen in any other person. Her eyes were amber, her hair a sunburnt tokay. Rose held in her youth the promise of beauty, her sister its fulfillment. Marie was an arresting, an exciting personality.

"You have a message from someone to me?" she said.

"From your sister Rose." He handed her the envelope.

"I have no sister," she said, but she did not return the letter. In her voice was a note compounded of sadness and bitterness.

"She thinks you have."

"Tell me about Rose Corcoran," the actress commanded suddenly. "Is she well? And happy? What is she like? And you — Are you her friend?"

"I have seen her only twice, but — yes, I am her friend."

The actress studied him with a faint mocking humor in her long eyes. This straight brown youth was one to like at first sight.

"And would be more?" she asked, a whimsical tilt to her eyebrows.

"God forbid," he said swiftly.

"And why?"

"No need to go into that. I'm a *vaquero* from the brush country, and I've ridden a lot of forbidden trails."

On swift impulse she offered him a small warm hand. "I've ridden a lot of them myself," she said. "My name was Marie Corcoran. It is Grace Dunlap now."

"Mine is Jim Delaney. I've had others, but that's the right one."

"Sit down and tell me all you know about Rose," ordered Marie.

"She goes to the sisters' school here. If I gave you a hundred guesses you'd never choose the place where I first met her."

"Then we'll skip the first hundred," she said, "and begin with a hundred and one."

"I'm telling you because I want you to know how much she loves you and what she risked to find out where you were."

"Now you've paved the way, I'll make my guess. In church?"

"In Dave Meldrum's private room at The Green Curtain."

The mockery went out of her face instantly. He could see panic fear take her by the throat.

"God! You can't mean —"

"No." He cut through her wail sharply. "She went there to find out from him where you were living."

"And you say you found her there?"

"We heard a woman's scream, my friend and I. We broke a door down and found her in Meldrum's arms, fighting like a wildcat and scared to death."

The blood rushed stormily to her heart. "I read about it. Was that girl Rose? You killed one of the scoundrels and helped her escape through the window. The paper said you were holding up the place. It said that the girl —"

"It said what Dave Meldrum gave out. All lies. What I want you to get is that Rose was there because she loves you."

"Does my — does Colonel Corcoran know the girl was Rose?"

"No. He mustn't find out. Nobody must know it." He smiled. "Can a secret be kept that seven people know?"

"Rose must have been mad to go there. Why didn't she send you — or someone else? Even I have never been inside The Green Curtain in my life."

"She didn't know me then. We met in Meldrum's room."

Her tawny eyes were bright with approval of him. "And you took her out of there, in spite of Dave Meldrum and all his ruffians. I could love you for that."

Jim grinned, slightly embarrassed at her gush of enthusiasm. "You will have to love old Sundown too. He stayed and had all the lead poured in him while I was jumping out of the window."

He waited while she read the letter from her sister. There were tears in her eyes before she finished.

"She told me that she has to see you," Jim said.

"The dear girl!" she cried, in a low voice full of impassioned tenderness. "Of course she mustn't. I've made my bed, and I must lie in it. There is a lot of backwoods silliness about this Puritanism which thinks an actress must be bad. But Rose can't afford to fight it — not for me, who have been wild and reckless. I am the wife of a gambler, and I'm beyond the pale."

She spoke with surprising intensity of bitterness. Jim had no convincing answer. What she said was true. The wife of a man like Dave Meldrum, an enemy to society, automatically became an outcast when she married him. But resentment moved in young Delaney. He responded to the allure of this woman's warm charm. There was a disturbing quality about her. In her blood was something winelike that had set her feet to dancing along strange paths. Life had enchanted and betrayed her. But no matter what she had done, the conviction was firm in him that she was fine and true.

"I don't know what's right about this thing," he replied evenly. "All I can say is that she has been unhappy about you and will be till she has met you."

"And won't she still be unhappy after she has met me?" she asked, with a hard, enigmatic smile.

"*Quien sabe?* What I'm trying to tell you, ma'am, is that yore sister craves to see you again. Don't you reckon you might meet her — once?"

"No!" the actress said vehemently. "I'm out of her life. I'll stay out. It's best for her. If you will, you can take a message to her. Say I love her more than anything on earth, but that her path goes one way and mine another."

"It will bring her a lot of grief, that message."

"To meet me would bring her more."

Marie took from her neck a fine gold chain with a cameo pendant. "I bought this with my own money," she said, and her voice wasn't quite steady. "Ask her to wear it sometimes — when she is alone in her room. Now go, young man."

He offered his big brown hand and buried in it her small one. “Good-bye. If I can ever help you . . . any way . . . any time . . .”

“You can’t.” Impulsively she flung at him a question. “Are you in love with Rose?”

The color flamed in his cheeks. This was no way to talk.

“No, ma’am. I good as told you that already.”

The lines on her face broke to swift mirth. “I didn’t believe you then, and I don’t now,” she told him with gay impudence. “Get along with you out of here.”

He turned and walked from the room.

CHAPTER FIFTEEN

In A Lumber Yard

As Jim went out of the theater after the performance, he was alertly aware of those about him. The crowd had vanished during his ten-minute talk with Marie Corcoran. A drunk was weaving down the opposite side of the street. A boy and a girl, absorbed in each other to the exclusion of all else, sauntered toward Commerce Street in front of him. A hack loaded with cowboys on a tear raced past. Pedestrians came within the orbit of his vision and vanished. His roving eyes picked up faces, made swift decisions that eliminated them, moved instantly to others. Jim did not expect to be molested, since he had no reason to suppose he had been observed by the enemy, but he did not want to be taken at advantage. Therefore his senses were keyed to wariness.

It was as he crossed Houston that the first bell of warning rang. The intoxicated man was still moving parallel to him on the other side of the road. Into the night a shrill whistle was lifted. It had come from the weaving figure opposite. Delaney knew there was no drunkenness in that sharp signal.

The mind of the cowboy functioned with lightning precision. Like seeds squirted from a lemon three men plunged precipitately out of a saloon just ahead of him. Two others had come from nowhere to block the road in his rear. A high wall cut off his retreat to the left. Back of the drunk on the other side of the street was an open lumber yard. It might prove a poor port in the storm about to burst upon him, but it was the only one available.

Jim scudded across the road, straight for the man who had shadowed him. As he ran, guns were already roaring. He could hear the angry bark of their crossfire.

The man on the opposite sidewalk shot once, then with a yelp of fear turned and legged it. He had no mind to meet the enemy alone at close quarters.

Delaney plunged through the wide-open gate. Piles of stacked lumber were on each side of him, and between these were shadowed recesses. Into one of these he dived, cut back of one of the piles, clambered over some waste sticks, and found a moonless spot to lurk beside a stack of two-by-fours.

As he waited for the attack, his mind pieced together the probabilities. He had been recognized at Turner Hall and a reception prepared for him. When he did not show up outside, Meldrum's men had taken it for granted he had escaped them. They had left one man on guard, in case by any chance he showed up later. Then, by a sheer fluke, he had walked straight toward the very saloon where they were solacing themselves with refreshment.

The sounds of moving men and of voices came to Jim. His attackers were searching the lumber yard, but with a discretion that recognized possible danger. They had their prey trapped. It would be bad business to get too close unexpectedly.

"Hold the gate, Cole," a heavy voice ordered. "Gun him if he makes a break to get out that way."

Dutch Nagle in command, Jim decided. The young man stood poised, tense as a panther crouched for the spring. His forty-four was out, close to his side. Soon someone would discover him. Then the guns would roar again. There must be at least five of them. Long odds.

Always when danger was close, a pulse of excitement beat in Jim's throat before the moment for action came. He could feel it hammering now. A searcher was on the other side of the two-by-fours. In a split second . . .

"Must have crawled into a hole and drug it in after him, looks like," someone drawled.

A shadowy bulk appeared beside the two-by-fours. "Come outa there, fellow, I see you," the man called, bluffing. Before the words had died away he gave a yell, "Goddlemighty, he *is* here."

The two weapons blazed at the same time. The hunter fired hurriedly, in a panic of haste. He had been taken by surprise. Jim's forty-four had been aimed deliberately, for the concealed man had known exactly where his foe must appear.

Out of the tail of his eye, as Jim dodged back of another lumber stack, he saw the man beginning to sag, the revolver dropping from his lax fingers.

The face of a second searcher showed light in the darkness. A bullet whizzed past Jim's head and buried itself in the sawn pine. The fugitive was already on the way to fresh cover.

Dodging round a corner, Delaney almost ran into the arms of an approaching man. The barrel of Jim's revolver went up and crashed down upon the other's forehead. It was a knockout blow. The fellow pitched forward at full length.

Someone was running toward Jim along the fence back of the lumber. Jim moved swiftly into the open, in order to avoid meeting him. He looked to the right and to the left.

A bulky figure closed in on him. "That you, Chuck?" a hoarse voice demanded. Almost before the question had been asked, Nagle knew the answer.

Jim's bullet tore across the flesh of the forearm and buried itself in the killer's chest. The impact of it sent Nagle's shot wild. The big man staggered and steadied himself. A second bullet ripped into his stomach. He was still firing jerkily as he went down.

Revolver in hand, Delaney walked to the gate. Even then, the furious sounds of the battle still ringing in his ears, he recalled the name of the man posted at the exit. Nagle had used it once.

"All right, Cole," Jim said as he came nearer. "We got him, Dutch and I."

"Any of the boys hurt?" asked Cole.

"Yep. Nagle is. Better see if you can help him. I'm getting a doctor."

"Hurt bad?"

Jim was close now. He saw startled alarm leap to the face of the sentinel, and he knew the man had made the discovery too late.

"Stick 'em up — quick!" he ordered curtly.

The man hesitated for no longer than the single beat of his heart. He had no chance to fight, not with that unwavering gun covering his body. Up went his hands, a weapon still in one of them.

Delaney stepped within reach and thrust the forty-four against the ribs of his prisoner. With his left hand he relieved the man of the pistol.

"Turn round," Jim commanded.

"You wouldn't —"

The question tailed away into a quaver.

"No. I ought to kill you like you meant to kill me. But I'm no murderer. Head back into the yard, with yore hands up, and don't look round."

Cole did as he was told.

Another moment, and Delaney was scudding along the street as fast as he could run. Against all probability he had come out of the ambush alive and unhurt.

At the first cross-road he swung to the right. He ran for a short distance, passed over a wooden bridge, and right-angled down a dusty deserted road. Since he knew he was not being followed, he slackened his pace to a walk. Ten minutes later he was being admitted by Colonel Corcoran to the house.

"Where in time you been?" Pike asked.

"Went to see a show at Turner Hall."

"Thought you had some sense," Corcoran reproved sharply. "Don't you know some of those scalawags might have laid for you?"

Jim laughed. The reaction from deadly danger was upon him. He was as light-hearted as a man merry with wine. "So they might," he said.

"No use joshing about it," the Colonel told him irritably. "It was a plumb fool thing to do. I'll bet Meldrum has half a dozen warriors would bump you off if they could for five pesos cash in hand."

"Half a dozen is right," Jim agreed. "You're sure a good guesser, Colonel. But you'll have to ask Meldrum what he pays for murders."

They were in the parlor by this time. Pike slewed his head round at the young man.

"What you driving at, boy?" he demanded suspiciously.

Jim sat down and lit a cigarette leisurely. He had decided to do a little grandstanding.

"There might have been seven," he said, blowing out the match. "I wouldn't be sure about that. But not less than six, counting the one that lit out when the first guns began to smoke."

"What's that?" snapped the cattleman.

"There was the one I wiped with the barrel of my forty-four," Jim counted absently. "And the two I shot. That makes four, figuring the fellow that adjourned first. Then there was the bird I took this gun off of. Cole they call him. And there were certainly one or two more maverickin' around. We'd better make it seven, don't you reckon, Colonel?"

"Did you say two you shot?" Corcoran asked, his eyes big with amazement. Then, "You're just puttin' on."[1]

"That's right. Only two." Jim brightened, and added, by way of mitigating this, "But one of 'em was Dutch Nagle."

"You shot Dutch Nagle? Or are you just running on me?" The Colonel slammed one fist into the other. "Stop joshing this minute, and tell me the story."

"Ain't I tellin' it?" Jim asked innocently. "A passle of gunmen jumped me opposite Fisher's lumber yard. We fogged awhile, and soon as I could I came home."

"Begin at the first of it," Corcoran ordered, with a spark of anger. "Tell me the whole thing — if it's not just a pack of lies."

Jim told the story, omitting only one detail, that he had gone to the theater to see Marie Corcoran. Pike listened, almost struck dumb with astonishment. He had never heard so impossible a tale in all his life, and yet he did not doubt its truth for a moment. The thing was amazing, that the boy could go through such an experience and still be alive.

"You are sure you shot two?" Corcoran said, still asking for confirmation.

"Sure they crumpled up and went down. I was in some hurry and didn't stop to get any doctor's bulletins."

"And Dutch Nagle was one of them? Boy, he has killed seven or eight men, not counting Mexicans."

---

[1] Putting on, an expression used for fooling or joking.

"I've an idea he won't kill any more." Jim added, by way of explaining his escape: "You got to remember it was dark, Colonel, and that my luck stood up fine. The best chance they had at me was while I was running across the street to the lumber yard. After that I was hoppin' around like a toad on a hot skillet. I was waiting for the first one I plugged — heard him coming round the corner of the lumber pile. The one I wiped with the barrel of my gun hadn't time to lift a hand. With Nagle it was just gilt-edged luck. He thought I was one of his own men until too late. Same way with the fellow Cole at the gate. I had him covered before he knew I was the bird they were hunting."

"Well, she has certainly busted wide open," Corcoran said. "It will be war from now on, sure."

"Yes," Jim agreed.

"The fellow they called Cole must have been Cole Glidden. He is the oldest son of Sim."

Delaney picked up the revolver he had laid on the table. "Well, he is out one ivory-handled, nickel-plated, forty-five caliber six-shooter. I've a notion to send it back to him with my compliments."

"Boy, you're in bad enough already without devilin' them any," his employer told him.

"I'm in so bad I couldn't get in worse," Jim grinned. "Might as well let 'em know I'm not scared of them. Doesn't do any harm to throw a big chest. When I was a kid I got out of more than one fight by acting like I was champing on the bit to light on the other fellow all spraddled out."

"You won't get out of this one," Pike said. "You're in it up to your hocks, you and me both."

"Sorry if I started anything," Jim said.

"You didn't start it. They brought this fuss to your door. But for heaven's sake don't go sashaying around town alone at night. This ought to be a lesson to you."

"Yes," agreed Jim mildly. "And to them, too, don't you reckon?"

"How will Meldrum explain this? Will he claim we attacked him?"

"I'm wondering about that myself," Jim replied.

"It will annoy him considerable. Nagle was his right bower, always on hand to do his dirty work."

"Likely he'll just be laid up for a spell. It would take a lot of lead to bump off as mean a wolf as Nagle."

Corcoran assented to that.

"I hope the other fellow I hit will make the grade," the young man said. "It's a terrible thing to rub a man out and give him no chance to square his sins first. I didn't think of that at the time. Nor right away after either, seeing as I was plumb tickled to have got out with my own skin whole. Do you reckon it will always give me a shiver when I think of it, Colonel?"

"No," Corcoran assured him. "I'll tell you a little story, Jim. During the war I was with General Price down in Arkansas for a while. We were lying on the edge of some woods across a ravine from the Yanks. One of their sharpshooters was right good at picking off our boys. Our colonel got annoyed. Some way he had a notion I was pretty good with a rifle. So he told me to get that fellow if I could. It took me 'most a day. The

Yank and I exchanged quite a few shots. Then I drapped him from the tree where he was hidden. He tumbled down head over heels like he might have been a squirrel. Well, sir, I was only a kid, and I worried about that considerable. I got to thinking about his home life and all that. Finally I figured it out that I hadn't killed him at all. The war had done it. After that I didn't worry any more. Same way with you, boy."

Jim tried to let that point of view comfort him.

CHAPTER SIXTEEN

Jim Hunts Cover

Jim ate his ham and eggs with divided attention. He was watching Colonel Corcoran and he was carrying on a silent conversation with the two young women. As yet he had not found opportunity to report to Rose on his expedition of the previous evening. Her father was an early riser and had been in the foreground ever since Rose and Polly had appeared.

Just now the Colonel was hidden behind the *Express*. Occasionally a hand emerged from back of the newspaper and groped for the coffee cup in front of Pike. It was one of the kind known in those days as a mustache cup. This would disappear for a few moments, then would emerge again from retirement. Jim wished the Colonel would give him a whack at the *Express* for about two minutes. There must be one piece of news in it that would interest him greatly.

Polly took advantage of the newspaper shield to frame wordless but imperative questions with her pretty lips. She did it so elaborately that lip-reading was easy.

"Did you see Marie?" she asked, spacing each silent word.

Jim nodded a "Yes." The Colonel had been still so long now that Delaney knew he must have found the significant story at last.

"Did — she — send — a — message — to — Rose?"

"Yes," Jim answered voicelessly. "See you-all soon as I can."

Pike Corcoran lowered the newspaper and looked at Jim above the top of his glasses. "Seems there was some trouble in town last night," he communicated. "Some of our worst element got into a shooting scrape. I gather from what the *Express* says that there has been a difficulty brewing for a long time between Dutch Nagle and Bill Hatch. Both are hangers-on at The Green Curtain, and both have reputations as killers. I reckon they have been jealous of each other. Anyhow, last night they fought it out and both were killed."

There was an odd dryness in Jim's throat. "Did you say — both?" he asked as soon as he was sure of his voice.

Pike's severe gaze challenged the boyish softness that was filling the young man with distress. "Yes, sir. Both. Best news I have read in a long time. All good people will be glad to know these two gunmen will no longer be a menace to decent citizens."

True enough, since the good citizens were not involved. But Jim's heart had sunk like a plummet in icy water. A chill horror drenched him. He had killed two men, rubbed them out in the twinkling of an eye. It was appalling. What right had he to take life, no matter how bad the men were? Only God could determine when a man's cup of evil was full. The Texas Rangers and the police might be His representatives, but Jim was sure he had no such claim. What he had done was wholly personal. Of course he had fired to save his own life. None the less two men lay dead in the Bat's Cave. By no wish of his own he had become a killer.

Breathlessly, her lips parted, Rose stared at Jim. Awe filled her heart. Dutch Nagle was one of the men with whom Jim had fought at The Green Curtain. She felt that the vengeance of the Lord had fallen on him. Was it not written in the Bible that he who takes the sword shall perish by the sword?

Aware of her gaze, Jim felt he must keep the talk going. Was there a suspicion in her mind that he was implicated in this killing?

"Wasn't Bill Hatch the man who shot down two Mexicans at Rancho Saco last Christmas?" he asked.

"The same scoundrel," answered the Colonel. "Shot them without any real provocation, then got false witnesses to prove self-defense. I don't know any two men who could have killed each other with more benefit to the community than Hatch and Nagle."

From the shock of the news Jim's mind swung to consideration of another angle of it. Meldrum had decided not to court investigation. His story was that the two gunmen had rubbed out each other. He was not going to ask the law for help. He and the Gliddens would attend to their own private vengeance.

Old Reuben, Aunt Becky's husband, brought in a fresh plate of hot biscuits. Polly took one, buttered it, and put it down on her plate. A thought had just come to her.

"What time was this difficulty, Uncle Pike?" she asked.

The Colonel was no blood relative, but she had called him uncle all her life.

"A little after eleven, the paper says."

Polly looked at Jim. She was thinking that he had been lucky not to meet any of the enemy faction, since he must have been coming home just about the time of the trouble. To her surprise the young man seemed nonplussed. He grew busy over his food.

After breakfast the Colonel took Jim to his office for a consultation. It was not until an hour later that young Delaney found a chance for a word with Rose.

She said, in a low voice, as she passed him in the hall: "The garden."

A few minutes later Jim sauntered into the garden. It was an old-fashioned one of roses, jonquils, hyacinths, bleeding-hearts, and others. An iron fence enclosed the property. To give more privacy rather dense shrubbery had been set out along the fence. At the far end there was a trellised seat shaded by honey-suckle.

Rose and Polly were seated in this little bower arranging a bouquet. Jim strolled down the walk to join them.

"You saw Marie?" asked Rose while he was still some feet distant.

"Yes."

"Tell me. What did she say? Was she well? Will she see me?"

"She said for me to tell you she loved you more than anything on earth," Jim said.

"Please tell me all about her."

"She is very lovely."

"Is she happy?"

"I wouldn't say exactly happy. Her smile is the sweetest one I ever saw, but I thought it was kinda wistful."

"Begin at the beginning, and don't leave anything out," Rose begged.

Jim told all he could remember except the part of the conversation that had to do with his feeling for Rose. Though greatly disappointed because her sister would not see her, Rose was rejoiced at what the young man had to say about Marie. The girl could see her messenger had been charmed by the actress, and that he brought away no impression whatever of a woman grown hard and callous. She held in her hand the gold chain with the cameo pendant, and as she looked down at it her eyes filled with tears.

"I must see her," she said, in a low voice.

"Yore sister said it was best not," Jim answered gently.

"She thinks so because she doesn't want to get me into trouble, but while she is here I am going to see her . . . somehow."

"Of course," Polly said briskly.

"You're always sure, aren't you?" Jim drawled at Miss Stuart, with a smile.

"Not always," Polly made swift reply. "F'rinstance, I might guess you had heard all about that shooting trouble last night before Uncle Pike read it in the newspaper at breakfast, but I couldn't be absotively sure."

She had caught Jim off his guard. His astonished eyes betrayed him before he slipped on the mask of impassivity. He did not deny the imputation, but slanted it off at a credible tangent.

"I heard shooting as I was coming home from the theater, but I didn't stop to ask any questions," he explained. "Someone said a man had been killed."

"You weren't sure?"

"No. How could I be sure, unless I stuck around?" He looked puzzled. "What are you driving at?"

Polly did not know, but she was convinced he knew more than he had told.

"Oh, well, I just thought —" she began vaguely.

Began, but never finished the sentence. A bullet tore a splinter from the lattice above the seat, and a revolver cracked almost simultaneously. Jim followed his instinct, which was to put as much space as possible between him and the young women. He plunged for the shelter of a live-oak tree. The gun boomed again. The young man slid back of the tree-trunk, head first, like a base-runner stealing second. He gathered his long legs and crouched low.

"Don't move," he called to the girls. "You're all right if you stay there."

Frightened, Polly lifted her voice in a cry for help. Nothing could have been better. From the street outside the garden came the sound of running feet slapping the dust of the road. Someone was getting away in a hurry.

This might be a trap to draw Jim from cover, but he did not think so. Polly was still screaming lustily. It was not likely an assassin would stay and face possible discovery while his confederate escaped. Young Delaney ran through the flower beds to the hedge, intent on finding out who had fired at him. Before he reached the fence a revolver was in his hand.

Nobody was in sight, but spurts of dust marked the runner's course. The man had cut sharply to the left into a lane which ran at right angles to the road about thirty or forty feet back of where he had been standing when he fired.

"'S all right," Jim called to the young women. "He has lit out. No harm done."

The two girls emerged from the covered seat. Both were frightened.

"Did he — hurt you?" Rose asked, white-lipped; and Polly, "Has he gone?"

He answered first Rose, then her friend. "No . . . Yes. Let's get into the house."

Pike Corcoran met them at the door. He was on his way to the garden.

"What's the matter?" he asked.

"Someone shot at us, Uncle Pike!" Polly cried, her voice shrill with excitement.

"Not at us," Rose amended. "At Mr. Delaney."

"Jumping Jupiter!" the Colonel exclaimed. "That the way of it, Jim?"

The young man nodded. "Yes, sir. From the bushes near the fence. Shot twice, then skedaddled down the road into the lane."

"See who he was?"

"No, only his dust."

Immediately Pike made up his mind on one point. "I'm going to pack you two girls back to school right now."

Polly protested. She was getting over her fright and did not want to be removed from the scene of any excitement there might be.

"Oh, Uncle Pike! Why can't we stay till tomorrow morning? We'll stay indoors and nobody will see us."

"No, missy," Pike refused. "Back you go. I'm not going to have you around where these scoundrels are shooting. Go and get ready. I'll send for Jack to take you there." His wrath exploded vociferously. "Worse than rattlesnakes. Shooting a man down in his own home with school girls present. They had ought to be strung up to a black jack, the whole caboodle of them."

"That would suit me fine," Jim agreed.

"Now you girls scat," the Colonel ordered. "I'll send Reuben to get Jack, and he'll get you to the academy."

Polly was much less afraid of Colonel Corcoran than was his own daughter.

"You'd better send Mr. Delaney to stay at the academy too," she said, with sly audacity. "He was the one they were shooting at, Uncle Pike."

The cattleman gestured her upstairs. He would not waste a word in answering her impudence.

CHAPTER SEVENTEEN

Jim Says Adios To San Antonio

"Meet Buck Burris, Jim," Colonel Corcoran said in his crisp, staccato fashion. "Buck, this is Jim Delaney. You may have heard of the young hellion."

Burris was a dapper little man with a friendly smile and gentle brown eyes. As he shook hands, Jim noted that, though his grip was firm, Buck's palm and fingers were completely buried in his own clasp. The slender body was lithe and muscular, but suggested fragility. It was carried with nonchalant grace.

"I've heard of him," Buck said. "Sundown used always to be talking about Slim Delaney, and I reckon everybody knows how he stood The Green Curtain on its head."

"Sho! It was Sundown did that," Jim explained. "All I did was help a young lady out of a window."

Pike snorted. "And I reckon Sundown killed Dutch Nagle and Bill Hatch," he scoffed.

Buck lifted an inquiring eyebrow. "I don't reckon I get that last," he said, his voice soft and low.

It occurred to Jim that Corcoran might have made a mistake. This quiet little fellow with the placatory smile and the apologetic voice did not bear the earmarks of a fighting man.

"It's more or less of a secret up to date," the cattle-man divulged. "But you might as well know, Buck. Half a dozen of Meldrum's crowd waylaid Jim Saturday night and he had to rub out Nagle and Hatch before he could make his getaway."

There was a catch to this somewhere, Burris thought. No brush-popper could casually put out of business two redoubtable killers such as Hatch and Nagle. Moreover, the *Express* had said that the gunmen had wiped out each other. None the less, Buck looked at young Delaney with increased respect. There must be something back of what the Colonel had told him.

"You can't believe what you read in the papers, can you?" Buck said lightly, with a view to getting more definite information.

"Not when Dave Meldrum gives them the story," Corcoran said. "What I just mentioned sounds like the David and Goliath yarn in the Bible, but I reckon both of them are true. A bunch of Dave's warriors caught Jim out alone. All he did was to kill Hatch and Nagle, wipe another lad with the barrel of his gun, and take Cole Glidden's six-shooter from him. You don't have to believe it right away, Buck. I didn't myself. Let it soak in gradual. Of course, it isn't possible. I get that same as you do. Only, this blamed lucky fighting fool here did just what I've been telling you." The Colonel stopped to chuckle with deep glee.

Jim was embarrassed. "Shucks, Colonel, the way of it was that I was runnin' like a scared brush rabbit and these guys kept getting in my way. I had to knock 'em over so as to get clear of them."

Still skeptical, but on the way to being convinced, Buck came to time with congratulations. "This is sure good news, Mr. Delaney. Texas ought to send you to Congress."

"It's a heap more likely to send him to jail," Pike said dryly.

Delaney cocked an eye at his chief. "Something new?" he asked.

"You have got to burn the wind out of here, boy," his employer said. "I have just had private information from a friend in the Rangers that Lieutenant Brisbane is going to have you arrested for that Pitman affair. Seems two Mexicans have come forward to testify they were present and saw you at the time of the killing."

"It's not true I was there," Jim asserted. "Like I told Brisbane, I was in town when Pitman caught up with the Mexicans driving the stock. Easy enough for me to prove that. Must be some mistake."

"No mistake," Corcoran answered grimly. "It's a doggone lie fixed up by Meldrum and Sim Glidden. But we can't stop to fight it now. I'm going to need you at the Cross Bar B. Fact is, I have just had word that my fences have been cut, a bunch of cows stolen, and two-three of my buildings burned."

"The Gliddens." Jim guessed.

"Nobody else. A knife in the back, kindness of good old Sim."

"This house is being watched," Burris said. "I bumped into a Ranger on my way here. How do you expect to get Mr. Delaney past him and out of town?"

"I don't know," Corcoran admitted, frowning. He drummed on the table with his finger-tips. "It will have to be soon, too, if at all. Brisbane won't wait all day."

"If we were up against Meldrum's outfit, we could fight our way through, but we can't do that with the Rangers," Buck contributed.

"How about a disguise?" Jim asked. His eyes bubbled to mirth. "It would be great to get into a Ranger's uniform and sashay past the fellow watching the house."

"Might as well wish for a regiment of Uncle Sam's infantry to guard you," Buck told him. "I'd say, offhand, that you are due for a short stay in the calaboose until you can get your alibi before Brisbane."

"I have a Mexican *vaquero's* costume in the house," the cattleman mentioned dubiously. "It's about your size, Jim."

"Lead me to it," the young man cried. "I can talk the lingo like a native."

"You're a blond," the Colonel objected.

"I won't be when I'm fixed up. Let's get busy."

Jim went to his room while the Colonel searched for the costume. The house had been bought by Pike two or three years before this time. For two weeks, just before Marie slipped away to join a road company, she had occupied the room that had been assigned to young Delaney. In putting away some of his belongings, he had stumbled upon a make-up box left by her. Now he brought it out and set to work. What he did not know about make-up would have filled a book. But he did the best he could with brown greasepaint and by sheer luck got just the color he wanted. Before the Colonel reached the room he had the make-up box back on the closet shelf where he had found it.

From the doorway Pike stared at him in astonishment.

"*Buenos dios, señor*," Jim greeted his boss.

"Where did you get the stuff for that?" the Colonel asked.

"Had it in my war bag," Jim said, not very convincingly. "Lemme get into those duds and see if I'll do."

In the wide sombrero, silver-trimmed velvet jacket, and faded red sash, he could pass inspection as a young *vaquero* on a holiday. Both Corcoran and Burris said he would get by if he had any luck.

Five minutes later he sauntered out of the front gate, stopped to roll a cigarette, and resumed his leisurely way downtown. The Ranger was sitting down with his back to the trunk of a live oak tree. He beckoned to the Mexican, and Jim obligingly wandered over to him from the road.

"You work for Colonel Corcoran?" the Ranger asked.

"*Si, señor*."

"Is that fellow Jim Delaney at the house?" The Ranger raised a hand warningly. "No use lying to me. I know he's there."

The Mexican looked hurriedly toward the house, as if to make sure he was not being noticed. "He was there five minutes ago, Captain," the *vaquero* said in Spanish. "I myself saw him. If you tell Colonel Corcoran I told you, he will skin me alive."

The Ranger was a private, not a captain, but it pleased him to be mistaken for one. "I never betray those who assist me with information," he said, with dignity. "Stop at the office of Lieutenant Brisbane, tell him what you have told me, and he will give you a dollar. *Vamos*."

Jim went on his way. He was tempted to do just what the trooper had ordered. It would be a great lark to drop in on Brisbane and to collect a dollar for giving news about his own whereabouts. But it would not be so much fun if Brisbane penetrated his disguise and flung him into the Bat Cave. Regretfully Jim decided he could not afford to try to play tricks on the Ranger officer.

Delaney reached Commerce Street and sauntered down it indolently. He was headed for the Travis Corral, but was in no hurry to get there. He was enjoying this improvisation of a son of *mañana* land. To get the full pleasure of it, he had to become for the time a Mexican.

In front of The Green Curtain he stopped, rolled and lit a cigarette, and leaned with his back against the wall. For ten minutes he sunned himself there, motionless, with the placid patience of one to whom time is of no import.

A man walked along the street toward him. Jim betrayed no surprise or excitement. Apparently he was still lazily indifferent. But the blood was drumming in him. For the man was Dave Meldrum.

Out of the swing doors of The Green Curtain came the gambler Wilson. He and Meldrum stopped to talk.

"Any news yet?" Wilson asked, in a low voice.

Meldrum glanced at the Mexican. "Better move on," he ordered.

"*No entiendo*," Jim said, flashing a white-toothed smile.

The owner of The Green Curtain shrugged. If the man did not understand English, it did not matter whether he stayed or went. Almost in a whisper Meldrum spoke to the pallid-faced gambler. Jim's hearing was amazingly acute, as that of one who lives in the open spaces is likely to be. To him came little snatches of the talk.

"Not yet, Frank. Brisbane . . . raid . . . Corcoran . . . arrest Delaney . . . Bat Cave alive."

Wilson's voice carried better. ". . . lives as a cat. Ought to have got him long ago."

The two men moved into The Green Curtain.

Jim continued on his way to the Travis Corral. He reconstructed in his mind, from the fragments overheard, the talk between the gamblers. It might perhaps run something like this. Brisbane did not want to raid Corcoran's house, but would arrest Delaney as soon as he appeared, in which case the prisoner would never leave the Bat Cave alive.

Jack Corcoran was busy mending a stirrup leather when a brown-faced *vaquero* strolled into the corral.

The owner of the Travis gave him one glance and continued with his work. Indolent young Mexicans dropped in frequently. When a shadow fell across him, Jack looked up again.

"Want something?" he asked.

"*Si, señor*. I come for a claybank belonging to Señor Delaney."

"That so?" The keen eyes of Corcoran swept the Mexican. "How do I know that?"

"He said for you to give me twenty-five dollars that you owe him, *señor*."

"Now I know you're lying," Jack said. He was just going on to tell the man to get out *muy pronto* when he pulled himself up short. Intently he stared at the Mexican. "You doggoned old double-action fraud," he went on. "Try to hornswoggle me, would you?"

Swiftly he rose and began to beat the *vaquero* joyously. When he emerged from the scuffle, it was to ask what the idea was.

Jim told him.

His friend nodded. "It's sure enough time for you to make yoreself scarce, Slim. The score is three to nothing now that Sundown is making the grade. They'll never rest till they have got you after what you did Saturday night, unless you light out for the brush country. Here yore enemies are thick as fiddlers in hell. It would only be a question of a few weeks, no matter how careful you are."

"About the way I figure it, only I wouldn't give myself that long here," Jim said. "That whole outfit is on the prod to get me. The Rangers would arrest me, and some night real soon these fellows would bust into the Bat Cave and shoot holes in me. So it is *adios*, Santone."

Jim saddled the claybank, waved a hand in farewell to his friend, and rode out of town. He had stayed longer than had been his intention when he arrived. It had been for pleasure that he had come, but from the first hour he had been dragged into grim tragedy. Whether it was luck or whether it was fate, he knew he could never go back and be the same boy who had wandered into The Green Curtain to see the elephant.

CHAPTER EIGHTEEN

All I'd Ask Would Be One Crack At Him

A young *vaquero* jiggled down the dusty road into Eagle Pass and swung gracefully from the saddle in front of the Palace Saloon. Three horses were already fastened to the hitch-rack. The Mexican chose a place at the end of the pole and tied his claybank with a slip knot.

He observed that two of the horses were branded on the left shoulder with a Circle G, the third on the right hip with a T Upside Down. Their owners, he guessed, were inside the Palace.

The *vaquero* eased a gun in its scabbard. He did not expect to have to use it, but in the event he had to do so, a swift draw would be essential. Indolently he sauntered into the saloon.

Three men were at the bar. Two were big rangy fellows with jutting jaws and long red mustaches. The other was very broad-shouldered and had short bandy legs. The *vaquero* knew him at once. His name was Pete Sanderson. For a short time he had been one of the King Cooper crowd. If the big rough-looking characters did not turn out to be Gliddens, the newcomer would be surprised.

The drinkers stared at the Mexican with hard-eyed insolence, and the young man returned the look with the propitiatory smile of one who recognizes a racial handicap on this side of the Rio Grande. He wished them a good morning politely.

"Where you from?" asked one of the big men brusquely.

"From Tail Holt," the *vaquero* answered.

"Know Sug Garwood?"

"I have worked on Señor Garwood's ranch," replied the Mexican, in English, but with the soft liquid tone of one used to a language of vowels.

The big man dismissed him from mind and conversation by turning an abrupt shoulder to him. He was only a Mexican.

"When do you allow Sim is coming back, Bill?" Sanderson asked.

"I wouldn't know that," the older of the two big men said. "I expect he has unfinished business in Santone." He laughed harshly, thinking of that unfinished business.

"Wish I was there helping him do it," the other rangy man cut in, with an oath. "My idea wouldn't be to pull any of this slick stuff with that scalawag Delaney, but to go make him crowbait *pronto*."

The *vaquero* ordered beer, to wash the dust of travel from his throat. He had decided that the big man who had been called Bill must be a brother of Sim Glidden. The younger one would be his son or his nephew.

There were half a dozen, more or less, of the second generation.

"Don't worry, Brad," the older Glidden advised. "Sim may be slow, but he never forgets."

"No maybe about it," Brad snapped impatiently. "He's damned slow — about settling the account with Pike Corcoran. First Uncle Bull and Rocky Parks, then Fat Clark, and now Bill Hatch. Is he waiting for Corcoran and his killers to hang all our hides on the fence before he gets busy?"

"I've felt thataway myself sometimes," Bill admitted. "Especially after Bull was killed. Hadn't been for Sim we would of gone on the warpath and wiped out a few of the gents who shot Bull and hanged Rocky Parks. Sim was right. The Rangers were on the prod those days and they were kinda anxious to get a crack at our crowd. The best break we could of got would be good-bye to Texas. Well, what happened? We lay low. Inside of five years three of the birds in that raiding party were killed in the shinnery." The teeth in Bill's prognathous jaw showed in a cruel grin. "We never lifted a hand, but they must of had enemies. It might be the same this time."

Brad slammed a heavy, hairy fist down on the bar. "The way of it is that they can kill off our boys and we dassent move a lick against them. Corcoran is the big mogul. What he says goes. We're just run-of-the-brush cowhands. If I was caporal of this outfit, I'd show him."

"Don't push on yore reins, son," Bill advised. "I reckon he will be shown one of these days."

"And this guy Slim Delaney," Brad raged on. "All I'd ask would be to get one crack at him."

The *vaquero* had his nose buried in a mug of beer. This conversation apparently held no interest for him.

"You've met this Slim Delaney," Bill Glidden said to Sanderson. "What's he like?"

Pete frowned with the effort of putting into words his point of view. Never a fluent talker, he generally confined himself to necessary essentials.

"Well, sir, he's as friendly a kid as you'd meet in a day's travel. No claim to being a bull rattler. Just a good hand to chouse longhorns."

"Big fellow — quick on the trigger — any rep as a gunman?" Bill demanded impatiently.

Sanderson rubbed his bristly chin. "Not so doggoned big. Kinda medium, you might say. I never saw him shoot. If he has got any rep as a killer, I never heard tell of it."

"What does he look like?"

"Like any brush-popper," Sanderson said, after a pause for cogitation.

"Dadgum it, does he look like Tim here?" Bill indicated the bartender. "Or like Brad — or you — or me?"

The bowlegged man looked at the bald-headed bar-tender helplessly. "No, not like Tim. Nor like any of us. I saw John L. Sullivan in Santone onct. He walks like he hadn't any weight — could step on eggs without breaking them. Same way with Slim."

"What color eyes?"

"I wouldn't remember about that."

"Hair?"

"Light, seems to me. Maybe it was red. Or brown."

"Or black," the older Glidden added irritably. "Any scars?"

Again Sanderson massaged his chin. "Might have. Couldn't say." He mentioned helpfully: "Right young and limber."

Brad laughed sarcastically. "I reckon if we want to recognize this bird, Dad, we'll have to keep the floors covered with eggs and watch him step on them."

"If I'd known you would be so particular, I would have had a tintype of this Slim taken for you-all," Pete said, a little exasperated. He was not satisfied with his own inarticulation and tried again. "Like I said, he's not fat like Tim nor sawed-off like me nor rawboned like you Gliddens. More like this *vaquero*, kinda slim and easy." He spoke to the stranger. "Stand away from the bar a minute, fellow, and let me see you."

The eyes of all shifted to the Mexican. That young man paid strict attention to his drink. The beer mug covered as much of his face as possible. He did not avail himself of the invitation to step back and be inspected. It had occurred to him that it was time to be gone. As soon as he was no longer a target for observation, he would slip quietly away.

Not being endowed with a strong sense of humor, Brad could not let his joke go without repetition.

"Can you walk on eggs without cracking them, fellow?" he asked.

"No, *señor*," the *vaquero* answered respectfully.

He was aware of a puzzled frown on the leathery forehead of Sanderson. The man was on the verge of a discovery.

"Got to be moving along," the Mexican said, putting his mug down on the bar and paying for the beer.

He was too late, had played his luck a little too far. The frown on the face of the stumpy man gave way to slow recognition.

"Jumping frogs!" he cried. "It's Slim Delaney!"

Jim had been expecting that cry. While the sound of it still echoed through the room, the forty-four leaped to the air.

"Stick 'em up!" he ordered.

The Gliddens were taken completely by surprise. They stared at him, too amazed to obey the order.

"Get 'em up before I drill you," Delaney said curtly.

Bill Glidden opened his mouth and shut it again without speaking. His son made the faintest gesture, the twitch of a hand, toward the butt of the revolver hanging in his belt.

"Don't you!" warned Jim. "Last call. Reach for the roof, or . . ."

Four brawny Glidden arms wavered into the air.

"You, too, Pete. I wouldn't want you to get ideas . . . Move out from behind that bar, Tim — with yore hands up. C'rect."

"You damned killer!" growled Bill.

"Back against the wall, boys. All four of you. And don't make any mistake — if you want to live. Now turn and face the wall. Keep 'em up."

Jim padded forward, wary as a watching panther. He stood about four feet back of the line. His eyes picked out the bartender, who was not armed.

"You can lower yore hands, Tim. Relieve these gents of their guns. Don't get between me and them. I would hate to drill you in reaching them."

"What are you fixing to do?" Brad asked angrily, and tagged the West's greatest insult to the words.

Jim did not answer him. "That's right, Tim. Now help yoreself to Mr. Bill Glidden's hogleg . . . Good. Throw them all through that back window. Never mind about the broken glass. The Gliddens pay all expenses."

There was a crash of glass as the weapons sailed through the window.

"Right-about-face, gents." Delaney's voice was soft and slurred, but it carried a threat. "You were wanting to meet up with me, Bill. Same here. I heard you were an ornery-lookin' cuss, but what I heard doesn't do you justice. You're a lot worse than that. Glad to meet you again, you and son Brad too — any place, any time. You can take that crack at me next time we meet, but right now I'll do all the cracking that's done, if any."

"If I had a gun —" began Brad savagely, and broke off into a stream of vitriolic profanity.

Jim leaned against a poker table negligently and listened with respectful attention. The barrel of the revolver pointed to the floor, but a lift of the wrist would bring it into position again.

"Such language," Jim deplored, shaking his head. "I gather you're some annoyed with me and aim to come a-smokin' next time we meet up. I'm certainly unlucky about getting in bad with you and yore friends. There was Fat Clark to begin with, then Bill Hatch and Dutch Nagle . . . No, don't you follow that impulse, Brad, unless you want to go to Kingdom Come . . . Funny how you Gliddens make me repeat. First, I had to take Cousin Cole's gun from him for fear he would hurt himself with it, then I have to do the same with you two. My advice would be for you-all to quit toting weapons. A tenderfoot is safer if he isn't armed."

Bill Glidden gave a roar of rage. He was about to fling himself at Delaney when the barrel of the forty-four tilted up and covered him.

"Not safe," Jim murmured. "You'd never get halfway, Bill." He smiled cheerfully. "Well, I'll be saying 'Adios,' gents."

Bill spat a smoking epithet at him.

"You're certainly one tough *hombre*, and I'm scared stiff," young Delaney told him. "Kinda remind me of Big Bill of Pike, you do. I'm in a hurry, but I'll stick around long enough to recite some of the poem. It runs thisaway:

At school he killed his master;
  Courtin' he killed seven more;
And the hearse was always a-waitin'
  A little ways from his door.

Big Bill was raised 'way up on the Guadalupe and wrestled with grizzly bears, I reckon, same as you. Now listen to what happened to him and take warning. This instruction isn't costing you a cent. It's free gratis."

Jim's revolver came sharply to position to quell possible action from Brad. "Don't get jealous, young fellow, because I'm giving yore dad all my attention. I'm taking folks in the order of their importance. Maybe I'll get down to you one of these days. Well, the poem gives considerable about its hero, but I'll skip to the finish.

And now Big Bill is an angel —
  Damme, it makes me cry!
Jest when he was rampin' the roughest
  The poor fellow had to die.

A thievin' and sneakin' Yankee
  Got the start of our blessed Bill,
And there's no one to do our killin',
  And nobody left to kill.

That will be all for today, boys. School is dismissed."

Jim backed to the door, flashed an amiable smile at his pupils, and vanished through the doorway.

Outside, his indolence vanished instantly. With three swift strides he was at the hitch-rack pulling at the slip knot. He vaulted to the saddle, whirled the claybank, and let out a boyish whoop of triumph.

As horse and rider dashed down the dusty street, a running man flung open the door of the Palace and pumped lead at the vanishing *vaquero*. Jim lifted his hand in a derisive gesture. Brad Glidden was a little too late. It had taken him just a second too long to reach the revolver kept by Tim behind the bar.

CHAPTER NINETEEN

Harmless As Skim Milk

King Cooper leaned against the doorjamb of the sheriff's office, located in a long low one-story adobe building. With more than casual interest his gaze rested on a *vaquero* jogging down the street toward him. The rider looked inoffensive, but Cooper had remained alive by constant unremitting vigilance. In his short span of twenty-seven years, if rumor was true, he had killed ten or a dozen Mexicans. Since the victims might have left relatives, Deputy Sheriff Cooper was taking no chances.

The rider drew up at a store, tied, and sauntered across the street, a broad smile on his face. He knew the deputy was watching him warily.

King Cooper was an eye-filling picture. He stood a little better than six foot tall and weighed a hundred and eighty pounds. Narrow-hipped and broad-shouldered, he carried himself arrow-straight, easily and lightly. He was a blond, with yellow hair and mustache, strikingly handsome. A snow-white sombrero was tilted rakishly on his head. He wore expensive boxtoed boots with fancy tops. The man crossing the road observed that he pushed back the right side of his frock coat a little. Underneath that coat tail, the *vaquero* knew, was a forty-five caliber Colt with a black gutta-percha handle and a barrel of blue bronzed steel. He had seen the gun in action, flinging bullets with swift and deadly accuracy.

A slow, answering smile broke on the face of Cooper.

"You blamed ornery scalawag. Try to fool me, would you? You've been such a hellamiler these last weeks, I didn't know whether I'd ever see you again, unless they shipped you back as freight in a box. Haven't you got any better sense than to try to hold up The Green Curtain? Come in, boy, and tell me the story. I'll say one thing. It's lucky for you Dutch Nagle and Bill Hatch rubbed each other out. That's two tough *hombres* less you'll have in your wool."

Cooper made way for the *vaquero* and put an arm around his shoulder as they walked together into the office.

"I heard another story about that Hatch-Nagle fracas," said Jim, with assumed indifference.

"All right with me, if you didn't hear that either one of 'em is still alive," Cooper said, seating himself in a chair and tilting it back against the wall. "I'm not in mourning for those birds. Once I had a run-in with Hatch and came mighty near bumping him off myself."

"Instead of leaving him for one of yore friends to collect," Jim said.

"What d'you mean, one of my friends? Nagle is no friend of mine."

"But Nagle didn't kill him."

"The *Express* said —"

"Sho, you don't want to believe everything the *Express* says, King." Jim sat on the edge of the table. His eyes bubbled with friendly malice. "The *Express* once said King Cooper was as bad as John Wesley Hardin and outside of J. W. H. had killed more men than any other bad man in Texas. It said —"

"Yeah, I know what it said." The keen gaze of Cooper drilled into the young man. "Spill your story, Slim. If Nagle didn't kill Hatch, who did?"

"I did it," Jim said mildly.

"You? But — Who killed Nagle, then?"

"Oh, I did that too," Jim mentioned.

The notorious killer stared at him. "I'm listening, Slim," he said in his soft, gentle voice.

Jim told his improbable tale, from beginning to end. When he had finished, King did not doubt a word of it.

Cooper looked at young Delaney with a new respect. He was having to revise his opinion of this harumscarum youth. It had been his judgment that Jim would do to take along, but he had not realized his destructive force, the cool and efficient deadliness that would make of him an enemy to be dreaded.

"So all you have done to date, Slim, is bump off three of these tough nuts and take the arms away from four-five more of them," Cooper said ironically. "When do you figure on starting business with them in earnest?"

"I had luck, King," the younger man explained. "It was dark in the woodyard and it worked out so I could always take the play."

"Hmp! I've noticed a fellow usually makes his own luck in a difficulty of that sort, Slim. But they were right unlucky one way — in picking on Slim Delaney as an easy pilgrim to wipe out. Sure, the darkness helped you, but they chose the time and the place, didn't they? And it wasn't dark when you walked into the Palace and collected the hardware from Bill Glidden and his son. First time I ever heard of anyone taking their guns from these wolves, luck or no luck. Watch your trail, boy. If they can pull it off, you're a goner. The Gliddens won't rest until you've turned up your toes to the daisies. I know what you're up against. I've walked for years never knowing what day will be my last. Every minute of the time I have got to be on guard, and I haven't got a pack of killers like the Glidden outfit after me either."

"I don't like it, King," said Jim ruefully. "I don't like any part of it, either killing them or being killed. I'm not made the way some fellows are. There is something soft in me."

"Don't ever let anyone know it, Slim," advised Cooper. "From now on you are marked. You'll be watched to see if you weaken. If you do — good night for you. Spend some time every day practicing with a gun. Be ready for the hour when it comes."

"I'm being driven into this," Jim said, a little desperately. "I'll be twenty-two coming grass. I'm no killer. I don't want to be one. Why should everyone look at me as if I was one of these quick-on-the-trigger warriors when I'm nothing but a waddy whose business it is to chouse mossheads? If it doesn't get out that I killed Nagle and Hatch —"

"It will get out. You can't keep anything like that quiet." Cooper laid a hand on the shoulder of his friend. "Boy, I'm telling you that you don't have to go around picking fusses now. Trouble will come to you. I know. If when it comes, you hesitate — well, you will certainly wink out sudden."

Jim felt a cold wave drench his heart. It did not matter what he was at bottom. He had been flung into a position from which he could not escape except by leaving the country. For the first time it occurred to him that perhaps King Cooper, with his long record of killings, might not be responsible for all of them.

King had been left an orphan young. He had been raised in Goliad County by a man named Burns among those of desperate character who lived on the dodge. Even before he left there, a boy of sixteen, to migrate to Maverick County, he had killed two outlaws who crowded him and gave him no choice except to fight. He had become a rustler and had driven many a bunch of stock across the Rio Grande to sell his wet stuff to Texas ranchmen. Between Mexicans and Texans there was still a bitter feeling, almost a state of war, brought down from the days of the Lone Star State's fight for freedom. The Alamo and San Jacinto were not easily forgotten. Raiders of cattle and horses swept across from both sides of the line. The life of a Mexican in Texas or of a Gringo on the other side of the river was held of little value. Once embarked on his wild career, King had shot down both Mexicans and whites.

Of late he had made an effort to reform. He was married happily and had a child. No longer did he run stolen stock. For years he had not killed anybody. He was a deputy sheriff, and a good one. The people of Uvalde liked him. King was a friendly person, kindly, generous. He was soft-spoken, never went out of his way to look for trouble, was in the way of becoming a substantial citizen.

Did King mean that the efforts he had made to change the manner of his life were of no avail? Jim blurted out a question.

"What about you, King? You have changed, haven't you?"

King Cooper's handsome face clouded. "I'll never kill another man unless it is forced on me. But there's no use fooling myself. Some day an enemy will draw on me — or some bad man who is jealous of me — or maybe just some wild hellion who wants to kill me so folks will say he is the man who killed King Cooper. As long as I'm alive I'll never be safe. That's the way it is after you have begun to kill. They don't leave you any choice."

Jim stared gloomily at a knothole in the floor. He did not want to admit that his feet were set on a path so beset with pitfalls.

"Looky here, King," he argued. "Everybody knows you. King Cooper is a name that has spread all over the Southwest just like that of Wild Bill Hickok and Billy the Kid. Different with me. I'm just a *vaquero* who got into a tight spot and had to shoot his way out. I haven't got any rep as a gunman. Nobody is going to bother me — after I get out of this jam I'm in with the Gliddens."

King Cooper laughed. "All right, Slim. Have it your own way. You're nothing but an innocent cowhand, harmless as skim milk. Let me put to you a case that happened to me when I was nineteen. I had been dragged into some shooting difficulties, and it was understood locally I wasn't a good one to run on, except by my friends when they were loading me. One day I walked into a saloon at Lockhart. A friend of mine introduced me to those present, including one mean-looking guy who started to devil me. His name was Seth Carberry. Five notches on his gun and anxious for another one. I was just a grinning kid, and I expect I looked easy. Well, it came to a showdown. He gave me my choice, to draw or to knuckle down like a yellow coyote. Understand, I had done my best to duck trouble. I had even started to walk out of the place and he had blocked the way. He wouldn't have anything but war. I left him lying on the floor with a bullet in his heart. What I mean is that he picked on me because I had done some killing and he wanted it understood he was cock of the walk. If anybody except me had walked in on Carberry, that fracas wouldn't have been forced on him."

"Then what am I to do?" Jim asked wretchedly. "I don't mean in this matter of the Gliddens. I'm in that feud with Corcoran. I 'low to stick. But after that's over, if I'm still alive?"

"I'll tell you what to do," King said seriously. "*Vamos*. Light a shuck out of here. Hit the long trail.

Move to the Panhandle, far away from here. No, that's not far enough. I'd say the ranch country of Wyoming or Montana. When you get there, reform. Never go into a saloon. Trail around entirely with the best citizens. Get converted and join the church. Settle down, get married, and have a family. That would be your best bet. If you fool around the way you've been doing, nobody is going to forget that you're the man who rubbed out Nagle and Hatch, two killers who had between them a record of more than a dozen victims. It wouldn't be so bad if you knew just who to look out for, but you never can tell. Some day you are sitting down for a little game of poker with five-six fellows you know, and one of 'em plugs you when you're not looking."

"You haven't left the country," Jim pointed out.

"I wasn't thorough enough for that," King admitted. "Too stubborn to pull my freight. And because of it, sure as I'm a foot high, someone will get me."

They ate dinner at a corner table of Hop Lee's restaurant, a table so situated that nobody could have approached any door or window without being seen by one of the two.

"You may think it's fun never to relax except when with your own family with the doors locked and the blinds down," Cooper said. "I've a different idea of it myself."

"Why don't you go away?" Jim asked impulsively.

"That's what I've been saying to you," King smiled.

Jim's rueful smile met that of his friend. "When I'm out of the jam I'm in with the Gliddens, we'll both go," he said.

King lifted his shoulders in a shrug. "Maybe."

Jim explained what he had come to get. "I stashed an outfit of clothes at yore house, in the loft of the barn. Some leathers and boots and pants. I want to get out of this Mexican costume. It's no good to me anyhow, now I've been recognized."

"Better go to the house and change, then come back to the office."

"All right," Jim assented.

At the Cooper home Jim first paid his respects to Mrs. Cooper, a pretty young brunette full of laughter and gaiety who came to meet him with a baby in her arms.

"We've been hearing about you," she told him.

"Not my fault," he assured her. "It was all wished on me."

At the barn he transformed himself from a Mexican to a Texan by the simple process of removing grease-paint and changing his clothes. He returned to the sheriff's office.

"Where do you go from here?" King asked.

"To the Cross Bar B. Corcoran will be waiting there for me. Likely he will have brought my other clothes from Santone with him . . . Well, I'll be drifting, King."

He glanced out of the door as he rose. A startled expression showed in his face. King looked out to the street. Three men were riding side by side down the road. They were Bill Glidden and his two sons Brad and Jeff.

King pursed his lips to a whistle. "I'll be dadburned," he murmured.

"Any back door?" Jim asked, and knew the answer.

"No. There's a small barred window in the other room, too small for you to pass through. We use the room sometimes to hold a fellow for an hour or two. Sashay in there, Slim. You're my prisoner. Understand?"

"In a minute, King."

Jim watched the three men draw up in front of the Crystal Mirror and dismount. If they went into the saloon, he would cross the street, get his horse, and shake the dust of Uvalde from its hoofs. The Gliddens stood for a moment in talk. They seemed to be deciding whether to go in for a drink or attend to other business first. The verdict was to postpone putting their feet on the rail. Through the dust of the street the trio of rangy hard-bitten men strode with jingling spurs. They were heading for the office of the sheriff.

Swiftly Jim moved into the back room. "Reckon I'll keep my forty-four," he mentioned. "Might need it."

King nodded and closed the door. He had no key to lock it. There was one in a drawer in the table, but he could not take time to get it.

When the Gliddens came into the office, Cooper was tilted back on the rear legs of a chair, his feet on the table, engaged in leisurely reading a newspaper.

CHAPTER TWENTY

The Gliddens Call On An Officer

King Cooper lowered the newspaper and nodded at his visitors. Not a flicker of the eyelid betrayed the fact that he was very much on his guard, that he knew these men had not ridden sixty miles for the pleasure of it. He rose and offered chairs.

"Evening, Bill — Brad — Jeff," he said, in his usual casual, friendly fashion. "Had a long ride, looks like. I reckon Mac has a bottle somewhere around here. Find seats, boys, and I'll have a look-see." King rummaged in the table drawer and produced a bottle of whiskey. He went to the water bucket and brought back the tin dipper. "Mac is out of town doing some collecting. How is everything over Eagle Pass way?"

"Rotten," Bill Glidden said bluntly. "Came to see you about that, King. Reckon you know the news. Corcoran and his warriors have started attackin' us again . . . Here's lookin' at you."

He raised the dipper and emptied it at one swallow. King renewed the supply and handed the dipper to Brad.

"You don't say. The old son-of-a-gun. Don't he know that ain't supposed to be safe?"

King retrieved the dipper from Brad, poured in a third slug of liquor, and handed the container to Jeff. He, too, said, "Here's lookin' at you, King," and poured the fiery stuff down his throat.

Cooper himself merely tasted.

"He has gathered him a bunch of warriors and aims to wipe us out," Bill explained. "We don't 'low to stand for it."

"I should say not," King said, in his most amiable voice of sympathy. "When did Pike go on the warpath? I'd heard about raiders burning his buildings, cutting his wires, and driving off his stock. But this is a new one on me."

Both men were ignoring the fact that Cooper's crowd and the Glidden gang had each been as wary of the other as strange mastiffs meeting for the first time.

"Fact is, a bunch of Corcoran's warriors surprised Nagle and Hatch and shot them down," Bill confided. "The public does not know it, but that was the way of it."

King showed the proper surprise. "Dadburn! Think of those two oldtimers getting trapped thataway. Was Corcoran present himself?"

"No, sir. Not that old fox. The ambush was fixed up by a killer called Slim Delaney."

At the mention of the name Bill Glidden stopped, his face contorted by a spasm of rage. He was remembering how that young man had relieved him of his gun.

"Slim Delaney!" exclaimed King. "Why, I know a kid called by that name. Can't be the same. He's just a brush-popper. With a grin as wide as a house. Never killed a man in his life."

"I've been told he's a friend of yours," Brad said offensively.

Cooper looked at young Glidden. "One Slim Delaney is my friend. Known him for years. Nice boy. But he never laid any trap to shoot down anyone. You're thinking of some other guy."

"There's only one," Jeff said impatiently. "What the heck! The Rangers want him for rustling. He tried to rob The Green Curtain and killed Fat Clark. He and his gang laid for Hatch and Nagle and shot them to death. I don't care whose friend he is. Delaney is a killer, and we aim to stomp him out first chance we get."

"Well, well! He's certainly been fooling me. The old slicker." Cooper chuckled. If a victim of deception, he appeared to be a cheerful one.

Bill Glidden looked at him suspiciously. "We came over here, King, because we want you to get this straight. Understand, we don't want any mix-up with you. There's no reason for one. Live and let live is our motto. But it has got to be clear that this Slim Delaney is our meat and we mean to hang his hide up on the fence to dry. He has done cut loose from yore crowd and hunted up a fuss with us. That the way you look at it?"

"I don't know what you mean by my crowd, Bill," King said, still with an amiable drawl. "I'm a peace officer of this county, and I haven't any crowd. If you satisfy me that Slim murdered two citizens of Santone, it would be my duty to arrest him when I meet up with him."

"I'm telling you he murdered Nagle and Hatch," Bill scowled.

"What were the circumstances, Bill?"

"This Slim Delaney and his gang laid for the boys at Stevens's lumber yard and downed both of them at the first volley. They never had a chance."

"Think of two old roosters like Hatch and Nagle getting caught thataway," King said. "Howcome they on the same side of the street as the lumber yard? Personally I would choose the other side to walk on at night, where ambitious guys couldn't hide behind a lumber pile and plunk me. Careless I would call it. Doesn't sound like what Bill Hatch would do."

"I'm tellin' you what he did do," the oldest of the three Gliddens said harshly. "What's the sense in chewing the rag about howcome it? I reckon it was dark. Maybe they figured they wouldn't be recognized."

"Someone must have known they were coming along there," King said helpfully.

"Sure. And fixed up a trap."

"Queer, at that," King said, still apparently puzzled. "If I had been fixing up a li'l' surprise for the boys, I would have set it around Main Plaza, or maybe outside the Longhorn Saloon. It wouldn't have occurred to me to stick around Stevens's woodyard and hope they would drift that way."

"Goddlemighty!" Bill snapped out, exasperated. "What difference does it make? They got careless, and they're dead and buried. What more do you want, King?"

"Not a thing," murmured Cooper cheerfully. "I don't aim to annoy you, gents, but — no regrets. I had a run-in with Hatch once. Never liked a hair of his head."

"He was sull," Jeff admitted. "Like a bear with a sore paw. I didn't care for him myself. But that's not the point. He was one of our crowd."

"What do you want me to do about it, boys?" King asked. "I'm only a deputy here, and —"

"We don't want you to do a thing," Bill interrupted. "All we say is for you to keep yore hands off while we run down this Slim Delaney. Just remember this is private business and you're not in it."

The steel-gray eyes of King Cooper held steadily to those of Glidden.

"Would you call that an order, Bill?" he drawled gently.

That is what the big man would have liked to call it, but men did not find it wise to give orders to that dynamic and deadly fighting machine King Cooper. Bill modified with an explanation what he had said.

"I'm just tellin' you how things are, King. We rode a long ways to talk this over friendly with you. We're going after this bird. We'll get him sure. Nothing personal in it with us far as you are concerned."

"Not at all," King replied. "Help yourself. I'm too busy minding my own business to butt into a fuss between you and Corcoran. Call me a neutral. I like

Slim. If I could help him without getting into trouble myself, I would. But that's as far as I'll go."

"What d'you mean you'd help him, King?" Brad asked, a chip on his shoulder. "What would you do for this outlaw?"

"Is he an outlaw?" Cooper asked innocently.

"You know damn well he is. If you're going to aid and abet him, we would like to know it. Nothing like having yore enemies come out in the open," Brad announced, his jutting jaw thrust forward.

"Don't push on yore reins, Brad," his father told him curtly. "You can't talk thataway to King Cooper, you dadgummed fool."

"Not for pleasure," King mentioned, with a gentleness that was a warning. "Only in the way of business."

"I wasn't aimin' to rile Mr. Cooper," Brad retracted sulkily. "We got no quarrel with him."

"Glad to hear it," the deputy said silkily. "I am a quiet citizen who wants to live at peace with his neighbors."

"Same here," Bill grunted. "Well, I reckon we'll move along." He hung on his heel to ask a question just as he was turning away. "If you hear where this fellow Delaney holes up, we would take it kindly if you drop us a hint."

"Thought you wanted me to keep out of this row," Cooper said, with a smile.

"That's right. But you could be neutral and give us a tip so we could drag in a criminal. You're a law officer."

"How far would you drag him?"

Brad laughed brutally. "If we did any dragging, it would be to the nearest black-jack tree."

"Well, I'll be frank," King said. "I like this kid. Hope you don't find him."

"If he doesn't light out of the country, we'll find him. Maybe not today — or this week — but soon."

The Gliddens strode out of the office and across the street. Brad stopped abruptly at a hitch-rack and called to the others. He was looking at a claybank horse. The three men talked for a few moments, then one of them walked into the store in front of which was the rack. Presently he emerged with a clerk, a narrow-chested little man with a freckled face and yellow hair.

The clerk shook his head. He had not noticed the rider.

"May have come into the store, but I wouldn't be sure," he said. "I don't recollect having seen a stranger. Maybe he went into the Silver Dollar here."

Jeff stayed beside the claybank. The other two Gliddens went into the Silver Dollar Saloon. After a minute or two they came out again.

"Hasn't been in there," Bill told his son.

"Betcha that double-crossing King Cooper knows where he's at," Brad cried, with an oath.

"Sure he knows," Jeff agreed. "But he'll never tell."

They could see King standing at the window of the sheriff's office looking out. Though they did not hear him say to the man in the rear room, "Three anxious gents from Eagle Pass have done discovered your horse, Slim," they suspected he was gloating over them.

"Might be right there in that back room," Brad said bitterly. "If I knew he was, I'd go dig him out of his hole, King or no King."

"Sometimes I think you haven't sense enough to pound sand in a rathole, Brad," his father remarked severely. "Can't you get it through your thick head that King Cooper is sudden death with a gun? Awhile ago you was trying to pick a fuss with him. If he ever started on you, he'd make you look like a plugged nickel."

"Three of us, aren't there?" Brad demanded.

"There would be three of us when we started to work on him," Bill replied. "Not so many when we got through. No, sir. If I wanted to be a nice quick suicide, I would walk across the street and devil King into drawing on me."

"What do we do — sneak off with our tails between our legs while he gives us the horse-laugh?" Brad wanted to know. "It's a cinch he has got that Delaney hidden somewhere, and I'll bet my boots I can tell you where. Right in the back room."

"Say he is there," Jeff argued. "That would make two to three. To begin with, as Dad says. If they had a mind to they could drop all three of us while we were crossing the road, or as we crowded into the little room. Both of them are killers. They wouldn't wait to give us the breaks. I would vote to hang around and get this Delaney when he comes out."

"All right. All right." Brad's assent was sulky, but that was only a concession to his vanity. After having considered the danger, he was no more anxious than his kinsmen to attack King in his office, whether the deputy was alone or with Delaney at his back. "Do we sit here and wait? Or what?"

"We'll go into the Silver Dollar or the Crystal Mirror and keep a lookout from there," his father decided. "It's tur'ble hot today. I'm spittin' cotton. We'll get us some cool beer to drink. The fellow can't reach his horse without us seeing him."

"If there is a back door, he will slip away," Jeff suggested.

"As I recollect it, there ain't any back door," Bill said. "They used to use the room for a kind of temporary jail till they could take a prisoner to the calaboose. But they may have changed that. Might fork yore bronc, Jeff, and ride round the block to make sure."

Jeff joined the others a few minutes later in the Silver Dollar. "No way out through the back," he reported. "If he was there when we were talking to King, he is still in his hole."

His brother Brad had drawn a chair to the front window and was seated there, a glass of beer in one hand. He was watching the front door of the sheriff's office.

"I'd bet my saddle he was in the back room all the time." Brad said angrily. "I've been in the Crystal Mirror. He's not there and hasn't been, but a guy there saw someone talking to King awhile ago. He's not right sure, but he thinks maybe the bird went into the office with King."

"I don't think it," Bill differed. "You're barking up the wrong tree, Brad. There are forty places in this town where Delaney could be. This is his old stomping ground. He knows 'most everybody."

"That's right," Jeff admitted.

"We'll watch his horse, one of us, and when he comes for it, we'll plug him. No use in being too conspicuous. We'll take turns as lookout. The others better get in a game or something, so as not to attract attention."

Jeff took the lookout seat, with orders to call the others the instant anybody made an attempt to get the claybank horse.

CHAPTER TWENTY-ONE

King Cooper And Jeff Glidden Go Shares

King Cooper locked the door of the sheriff's office and strolled across to the Silver Dollar. He stopped at the bar and asked for a glass of beer. A poker game was going. Bill and Brad Glidden had bought stacks and were sitting in. Jeff sat in a chair near the window.

"Have a beer, Jeff," proposed King.

Young Glidden did not want to decline. Gunmen had been known to grow testy when offers of a drink were refused. Moreover, he could do with another beer. But he could not very well accept without leaving his seat and moving to the bar. The excuse he gave was feeble.

"I got a crick in my leg, King. When I try to stand on it, the dadgummed thing gives way. Would you mind if I took my beer here?"

"Not a bit." King moved closer to him. A gleam of devilry lit his eyes. "Might as well be sociable . . . I see the others have got into a game. Don't you care for poker?"

All of the Gliddens were notorious gamblers, Jeff no less than his kinsmen. Given the chance, he would have played all day and every day.

"Fact is, I'm broke," he explained.

"Sho! Don't let that hold you back," King said. "I'll stake you for half the profits."

Jeff shook his head. "I'd probably lose yore money, King."

"It wouldn't be the first I have lost staking another man, but usually I'm lucky. Come on, boy. Take a whirl at it."

Glidden was embarrassed. The offer had been made so heartily he did not know how to say no gracefully.

"Wish I could, King," he blurted out at last. "But I'm watching for someone."

"Now don't you go eloping with any of our Uvalde girls, Jeff. We need them all right here for local consumption. Can't keep a reasonable supply on hand unmarried, without you Eagle Pass boys butting in."

Jeff grinned, because it seemed expected of him. "This ain't a girl, King. Point of fact, it's this bird Slim Delaney. He must be in town now. That's his claybank hitched out there."

King showed excited surprise. "The old horned toad. Do you reckon he's running a slick one on me, coming to town and not letting me know it?"

"I couldn't say about that," Jeff answered dryly. "All I know is that's the horse he lit out from Eagle Pass on yesterday."

"How do you know he was in Eagle Pass yesterday? Did you see him there?" King asked, his face a map of bland innocence.

Jeff hesitated, then told the truth. "The old man and Brad met him in the Palace. He was rigged up like a greaser. They wouldn't have known him, anyhow, but Pete Sanderson recognized him."

"Why didn't they arrest him?"

Young Glidden edited the facts. "He lit out. Brad took a crack at him, but too late. He was already burning the wind down the road."

King leaned forward and spoke in a whisper, almost into the ear of Jeff.

"There's a reward out for this guy, isn't there?"

"Y'betcha! I don't know how much. Maybe a thousand." Jeff looked alertly at the deputy. He knew that Cooper had something up his sleeve.

"How would you like to divvy that reward with me?"

"Suit me fine." Jeff was not interested in the reward, but he wanted to find out what the officer knew.

"Just you and I, fifty-fifty, nobody else in it?"

"Fine."

"I've got the bird locked up over there in my office." King was still murmuring, his head close to the other. "We'll run him over to Eagle Pass and deliver him to the Rangers. First off, we'll handcuff him. Bill and Brad can ride back with us, but they're not in on the reward."

This suited Jeff exactly. On the long ride to Eagle Pass something was likely to happen to Delaney. Moreover, he was tickled with the idea of showing up before his father and brother with this fellow shackled. Jeff was not yet twenty-one, and the family was rather inclined to regard him as a boy. After this the others would look on him with more respect.

"Good enough. We had a notion he was in yore office, King, but hadn't figured you were holding him for the reward."

"Five hundred dollars is a lot of money, boy, and I'm an officer of the law. I might as well get it as someone else, seeing that Slim is in Dutch, anyhow. Well, let's go," Cooper said coldly.

Jeff followed him out of the Silver Dollar and across the street. King closed the outer door of the office and drew a key from his pocket. Glidden made a motion toward his revolver, but the deputy shook his head.

"No need of that," King said. "I took his gun from him. If he makes a break, we'll drop him."

Cooper unlocked and threw open the door.

"Come outa there, Slim. We're takin' you —"

That was as far as King got. Jim had come out swiftly, a gun in his hand.

"Lift 'em," he ordered curtly.

King put up his hands promptly. To Jeff the officer gave advice sharply. "Put 'em up, boy. Or he'll drill us both."

Reluctantly Jeff's arms moved up.

Jim disarmed them both. "Where is my gun?" he demanded of Cooper.

King nodded to the table. "In that drawer. Where did you get that gun in your hand?"

"Found it in the back room. You're not thorough enough, King."

"By Jupiter! Mac must have left it in there and forgot it. Of all the dumb things to do!" King's face was a map of consternation.

"Tell him much obliged for me," Jim jeered.

Delaney and Cooper exchanged a swift glance. One of them was asking information, the other giving it.

Jim tossed all the guns except his own forty-four into the back room and locked the door.

"I'm saying 'Adios,'" he told them. "Tell Father Bill and Brother Brad I can't stop to say good-bye to them today. And take it easy, boys. Don't crowd me in my getaway."

He passed through the door, closed it, and dashed across to the hitch-rack. Before he was in the saddle, Jeff had reached the street and was calling to his father and brother to stop him.

King stooped, picked up the key of the inner door from the dust where Jim had dropped it, and ran back into the office to recover his weapon. When he reached the street again, Jim was vanishing in a cloud of dust. Jeff was not in sight, but his excited voice could be heard in the Silver Dollar.

Mirth gleamed in King's eyes as he ran across to the saloon, but when he pushed into the place there was none of it left on his face.

Jeff was pouring out his story to the astonished group at the poker table.

"Why didn't you have yore gun out when you opened the door on this scalawag?" Brad asked angrily.

"King claimed it wasn't necessary, since Delaney had been disarmed. Seems he found a gun in the back room Mac had left there."

"What was yore idea?" Bill asked. "Why didn't you tell us, so we could have gone along?"

"We aimed to put handcuffs on him and bring him here," Jeff explained lamely.

"Well, you sure balled it up. I don't see yet —"

"King didn't want to divvy the reward but two ways. We meant to take him to Eagle Pass to the Rangers. The idea was to have him handcuffed before you two saw him, so you couldn't cut in on the reward."

"That was the plan, was it?" Bill said, looking sourly at the deputy. "Only two of you weren't enough to hold an unarmed guy. Funny."

"It turned out he was armed," King said apologetically. "My mistake, I reckon. But how was I to know Mac had left a gun in the hoosegow?"

"I wonder if he did," Bill said harshly.

"Why, he must have. Mac or someone."

"That's right — someone," agreed Bill, a sneer on his face.

"It was mighty careless, whoever did it," King mentioned.

"I wouldn't even be sure of that," Bill demurred pointedly.

Cooper refused to take offense. "You think some friend may have passed the gun in to him through the window. Maybeso."

"I think he had a friend. He couldn't have pulled this off alone."

"I wonder who that friend was," King mused aloud, looking straight at Bill Glidden.

"Probably someone he used to run with over in this country."

Brad broke into the talk impatiently. "Are we going to sit here chewing the rag all day and let this fellow go?"

"You know damn well he's in the brush by this time," his father said sullenly. "Might as well look for a needle in a haystack."

"And to think I had him all locked up and let him go," mourned King. "Five hundred dollars easy money thrown out the window."

"Tough luck," one of the poker players sympathized, not without a puzzled bewilderment. If this had happened to anybody except King Cooper, he could have understood it.

"Sure was." King smiled ruefully. "Well, better luck next time."

He turned and walked out of the Silver Dollar.

Venomously Bill Glidden watched him go. "Mr. King Cooper got his pal away from us this time. Maybe next time it won't be so easy."

"You mean —"

Bill turned snarling on the man. "I mean what I say. Not any more or any less. Now you can go tell that to Mr. Cooper. Come on, boys."

The Gliddens strode out of the saloon, swung to their saddles, and rode out of town.

CHAPTER TWENTY-TWO

Jim Reaches The Cross Bar B

Jim traveled by short cuts, avoiding the main traveled road. He knew the country like a book, and, though he followed a devious course on account of brush and hills, he was always moving by the line of least resistance toward the Cross Bar B.

Night fell and found him still in the hills. By luck he stumbled on a cowcamp where two freckled-faced cowhands were holding a bunch of steers. One of them invited him to light and rest his saddle for the night. They were sitting cross-legged at supper. Jim swung down, hobbled his horse, and joined them.

They were riding for the W R outfit. Both of the boys were under twenty, and they were like enough to be brothers. In a day's journey one could have met twenty replicas of them. Beneath their disreputable old hats sorrel hair peeped out. From the corners of their faded blue eyes many tiny wrinkles radiated. The lips of both were swollen from sun and wind. Gangling and rawboned, they walked with the roll of dismounted horsemen. Hard, leathery hands dangled at the end of long knotted arms. They were not much to look at, but before he had met them an hour, Jim judged they would ride to hell with a friend at a pinch. This was no unusual virtue. A characteristic of the outdoor Texan was fidelity. He had to have this, just as he had to have courage, to meet the approval of his companions.

As they lounged before the campfire after supper, one of the W R men dropped a piece of information that interested Jim. He had been riding the hills looking for strays when he came on a small mountain park sunk deep in a circle of outcropping rimrock. He had heard of a Lost Park once used by rustlers to hide the stuff they had run off. Curious to examine it, he had spent a couple of hours to find a way down from the wall into the basin. At last he had struck a trail and was letting his horse pick a way down when a harsh voice brought him up short. The surprise of that challenge was almost a shock, for he had not suspected there was a human being within a dozen miles.

The barrel of a rifle peeped from above a boulder. He could see the top of a man's head and a pair of gleaming eyes, nothing more.

"Who are you, fellow?" the voice demanded. "And what you doing here?"

The throat of the W R rider went suddenly dry. He knew instantly that this was no place for him. Inadvertently he had stumbled upon men who did not want to be found. It might cost him his life. He answered as easily as he could; said he had been looking for strays and happened on this trail.

"Then happen back off'n it right damn now," he was told curtly.

Sitting before the campfire, the sorrel-topped cowhand grinned at their guest. "I done so, *pronto*. I had business anywheres but there. Boys, when I think of it goose pimples still run up and down my back. What stood out like a sore thumb was that I wasn't wanted there. If the bird back of the boulder figured I knew too much, he would sure gun me. I didn't feel safe till I was halfways back to camp."

"Where is this park?" Jim asked.

The W R rider picked up a stick and began to draw a map on the ground.

"You run into the creek west of here about a mile and follow it up till you come to a branch that joins it on the right. Take the branch for quite a ways. You'll come to a big pile of boulders. Swing to the left through brush up a kind of trough that brings you into a mighty rough country. Ahead of you is a big bald-faced rock. A fellow picks a way up a stiff rubble slide back of this and works into the rimrock. The park is right at yore feet."

"How did you get down?" Jim asked.

"I didn't," the waddy grinned. "About a half-mile to the left is the trail I started on." He stopped, for the first time suspicious that his guest's interest might not be an idle one. "You're not thinking of going there?"

"Not right away," Jim drawled, with a smile that was disarming.

"You better not, unless you want to be dry-gulched. Strangers not wanted. You're damn whistling they are not. Me, I'd wave myself around if I came closer than a half a dozen miles of the place."

"*Yo tambien*," Jim agreed lazily. He asked a question. "What was this gent who flagged yore train doing in the park?"

"I didn't ask him," the cowhand said dryly.

"Charley remembered it was his night to make supper and had to hurry home," the other W R rider chuckled. "No time for pleasant conversation."

The other boy, whose name was Charles Pierce, nodded a grinning confirmation. "That's whatever. I cut my stick. First time I ever was anxious to do the cooking. I was scared I never would get another chance."

"Didn't see any cows in the park?" Jim quizzed.

"Yes, sir. I saw quite a bunch standing on their heads.[1] From where I was, the feed looked like it might be good."

"Couldn't read the brands, of course?"

"Too far. Right then I hadn't lost any stock, anyhow."

"Likely yore friend with the gun was just an honest nester worried for fear you might lose your way back to camp," Jim said, with a sarcastic smile.

"I wouldn't have more than a guess about that," Charles replied.

They slept beneath the stars and woke up at dawn. After breakfast Jim caught, saddled, and shouted an "Adios." He rode until noon, then uncinched to rest the

[1] Cattle grazing were said to be standing on their heads.

claybank and lay down for an hour in the shade of a huisache.

Night was falling when he reached the Cross Bar B. A bowlegged, hard-faced old wrangler looked him over with suspicion until he mentioned his name.

"The old man is expecting you," the wrangler said. "Better turn yore horse into the corral and take yore war bag down to the doghouse."

Jim unsaddled and looked after the claybank, then carried his roll to the bunkhouse as directed. After he had washed up, he strolled to the big house and reported to the boss.

Colonel Corcoran caught his hand and shook it. "Where you been, boy?" he scolded. "What's this story I hear about you having a run-in with Bill Glidden at the Palace? Why didn't you ride round those fellows? Sometimes I think you haven't as much sense as a last year's bird's nest with the bottom punched out."

"Why, Colonel, I was as polite as a basket of chips to those fellows. Both times."

"What you mean both times?" Corcoran asked.

"At Eagle Pass and at Uvalde."

"You been to Uvalde?"

"Yes."

"And met the Gliddens there?" Pike snapped.

"Only one of them — Jeff. I just missed meeting Bill and Brad again."

"Any gunplay?"

"No powder burned."

"You'll wake up dead some day, Slim," Corcoran predicted. "Well, tell me about it."

Jim told the story of what had taken place since he left San Antonio. His boss grumbled at him, but with reluctant admiration.

"You got the gall of a brass monkey, son. By gravy, you act like the whole kit and bilin' of the Gliddens don't amount to a hill of beans. They will cook your goose sure if you don't look out. You keep me sweating like a nigger on election day. From now on you do as I say."

"Yes, sir," Jim said obediently.

"See you do. I'm running this cavayard. I don't want you killed too dead to skin . . . Where is your roll?"

"At the bunkhouse."

"Bring it here. You'll sleep in the northwest corner room."

Jim's wooden face betrayed no expression, but he was none the less pleased. He had been singled out from the other hands and promoted to the big house. Corcoran must feel he was on a different footing from the rest of the ranch riders. For private reasons, which he did not confess even to himself, his employer's feeling toward him had become important to Jim.

After supper the two sat on the porch and smoked. Jim rolled cigarettes, the Colonel puffed at a corncob pipe.

"How is everything at Santone?" Delaney asked after a silence. He did not specify what things he meant.

"Nothing new since you left except that Brisbane sent word to me that I had hornswoggled him about you for the last time. That business of you walking out under his nose dressed as a Mexican got under his hide. He don't enjoy being laughed at, I reckon. Even an officer of Rangers is human."

"Does Lieutenant Brisbane know where I am?"

"He will soon. The Gliddens will send word to Meldrum, who will pass it on to Brisbane. It wouldn't surprise me to see two-three Rangers here any day . . . Did King Cooper say anything about our row with the Gliddens?"

"No-o, nothing I remember. He doesn't like the Gliddens or any part of them, but he won't go out of his way to pick a fuss with the outfit. They won't like what he did for me. Probably they will grunt around about it. That will likely be all, for even the Gliddens would choose not to have King Cooper for an enemy if they can help it."

"He will be neutral, then?"

"Yes, with a strong leaning our way."

"Wish he would lean so hard he would fall off the fence on our side," Corcoran snorted. "We could use a fellow like King."

"Don't think he will. King has thrown in with law and order. He knows we're in the right, but he is so notorious as a gunman that if he took any part in a feud what he did would be misrepresented. Folks would say he had slipped back into his old ways. The only move he would make would be as an officer."

They discussed the incident told Jim by Charles Pierce.

"You could find your way to this Lost Park, Slim?" the Colonel asked.

"I'm sure I could."

"If we could tie up any of the Gliddens to this raid on my stock, it would help a lot," Corcoran said. "They have cached my stuff somewhere. Might be up at this Lost Park."

"Might be," Jim agreed.

"I have a notion to get some good men together and raid the park."

"And maybe find nothing. Why not send someone up to spy out the land?"

"Have you someone in mind who would like to commit suicide?" Pike asked bluntly, taking the pipe from his mouth and looking at the young man.

"I'm not known around there," Jim mentioned. "And it would get me out of the neighborhood while Brisbane's men were hunting for me."

"That's right," agreed the Colonel, with obvious sarcasm. "Nobody much knows you up that way except the Gliddens, and they wouldn't do any harm to you."

"We don't know this is a Glidden hangout. There are plenty of other stock thieves in the country. I'd say the odds are against it."

"What became of the Cross Bar B stuff that was stolen? Is it your notion that the thieves ate it?"

"They may have pushed the drive into Mexico, or across the Staked Plains up the Pecos. No can tell. Just because you haven't heard from this bunch of cows doesn't prove they haven't been kept moving."

Corcoran's mind harked back to the suggestion Jim had thrown out.

“I’d rather lose a bunch of cows than have anything happen to you or any of my boys,” he said irritably. “It’s a crazy idea to talk about going up to this park alone.”

That the Colonel was dallying with the thought of having someone check up on the park Jim knew. He was making objections in order to have them argued down.

“I wouldn’t have to go alone, if you feel that way about it,” Jim said. “One of yore riders could trail along with me.”

“Buck Burris will get in from Santone tomorrow,” the owner of the Cross Bar B said reflectively.

“I’d want someone who would do to ride the river with,” Jim said doubtfully. He was recalling the gentle eyes and the soft voice of Buck, his small hands and neat, trim figure.

Pike snorted. “If there is a better man than Buck Burris in West Texas I haven’t met him. You’re making the mistake of judging by appearances. He is as tough as bull hide and as game as they come. If you ever see him in action, you’ll be surprised.”

“If he wants to go, we can drift up and have a look-see,” Jim urged. “Needn’t take us long. Likely we wouldn’t have any trouble at all.”

“It will do to sleep on before we decide,” Corcoran said.

He knocked the dottle out of his pipe, rose, and stretched his arms in a yawn. It was time to go to bed.

CHAPTER TWENTY-THREE

A Family Conference

Aunt Becky by her side, Rose walked along Saint Mary's Street demurely with quick, short steps. They moved up Travis until opposite the park. A man turned the corner. He was tall and straight, and in his stride there was strength.

Rose felt a sinking within her. The man was Dave Meldrum.

He passed her without speaking.

Involuntarily Rose quickened her pace. Becky labored beside her for a few yards and stopped to voice a protest, panting for breath.

"Lawsy me, chile, we ain't runnin' no race, is we? Ise too old and too fat to go traipsin' round town like a high-steppin' colt. If you-all wants me along you shore gotta slow down."

"That man was Meldrum," Rose told her.

"You don' need to be scared of that lowdown trash. He dassent hurt you." Becky oriented herself. "This yere is the place where I saw Miss Marie go in yestidday evenin'."

After a breathing spell they climbed the stairs of the rooming-house and rang a bell. A slovenly woman in a wrapper opened a door and looked out. Her hair was in curl-papers.

"Who you lookin' for?" she asked.

"For Miss Dunlap," Rose answered. "She rooms here, doesn't she?"

"Number 15. Don't know as she is up yet." The landlady withdrew and shut the door.

Rose knocked on the door of room 15. Her heart was beating fast with excitement. She heard someone moving inside. Presently the door opened.

At sight of her sister, Rose cried "Marie," and went impulsively into her arms. The actress trembled. She was pale to the lips.

She drew Rose into the room. The sisters kissed each other. They clung to the embrace, reluctant to let each other go. Emotion throbbed through their veins.

"Why did you come?" Marie chided, in a voice shaken with feeling. "You got my message, didn't you, that you mustn't?"

Tears flooded the eyes of the younger woman. "It didn't matter what you said. I had to come, soon as I knew where you were staying," Rose cried. "Aunt Becky was out marketing when she saw you walk in here yesterday. I couldn't get here any sooner."

"You got here too soon," Marie said, with a little despairing lift of the hand. "You ought not to be here."

"No. Years too late," Rose said instantly, answering the first statement of her sister. "I'll never let you get away from me again."

"Have you forgotten — your father?"

"I don't care what he says. He isn't here, anyhow, but down at the ranch. There has been trouble there — some buildings burned and cattle run off. He thinks the Gliddens did it . . . I have wanted to see you so much."

"And I have wanted to see you." The eyes of Marie feasted on her sister. "You have grown up into a beauty, child."

"Shore am, Miss Marie," beamed Becky. "She's as purty as a painted wagon."

The eager young face of Rose was a picture of adoration as she looked at the actress. "I'll never be as lovely as you — nobody could be."

"Tha's right too," agreed Becky. She was an old family retainer and had been nurse to them both.

Mirth bubbled into Marie's face. "And I had such a sweet disposition, Aunt Becky," she derided.

"You shore was a handful, chile. But there never was anyone more lovin', when you got yore own way."

The elder sister's smile was rueful. She had learned from life the danger of always trying to get one's own way. The cost might be too high.

A knock sounded on the door. Marie opened.

Meldrum pushed into the room.

"What do you want here?" Marie blazed.

He bowed, with raffish grace. "Came for a family conference, my dear."

In dismay, Rose cried, "You followed me."

"Who wouldn't?" he asked, with another ironic bow.

The girl shrank back. He frightened her, for he had been the cause of the most violent adventure in her life, of the loss of her sister, and of the near-murder of her father. To her he was the embodiment of the Prince of the Power of Darkness.

But Marie had no fear of him. There had been a time once when she had been under the glamour of his personality. That hour was gone forever. She knew him for what he was, an evil and destructive force, one against whom she had already fought a winning battle, as a result of which she had definitely cut her life off from his. The potential violence in him was not disturbing. She could be explosive herself.

"If you have anything to say, better get it said quickly, before I call the police to throw you out," she warned.

"My loving wife, but still a little difficult," he murmured aloud.

With rhythmic grace Marie moved swiftly toward the door. He caught her wrist and swung her toward him. "Not so fast, my dear."

A passionate anger burned in the amber eyes lifted to his.

"Let me go," she ordered.

Their short life together had been filled with fiery tilts. Each had the power to stir rage in the other. Now fury leaped up and boiled out of the man.

"I'll let you go when I'm ready. You are still my wife."

"No!" she flung back vehemently, defiantly.

Rose cried out in fear. Her cry was less a scream than a wail. But it brought Meldrum back to a sense of his folly. He had not come to make a scene.

Releasing Marie, he barked a sharp command. "Stop that squalling, you little fool. I'm not hurting her."

"Suppose, now, you tell me what you want and then get out of here," Marie flamed.

"I can remember when I wasn't such poison to you," he sneered.

"You have used the right word — poison," Marie told him. "If I was a fool once, I don't always have to be one."

"You-all better git outa here, Mister," warned Becky, "or I'll ce'tainly tell Colonel Corcoran and he'll fix you-all plenty."

"I gave him a chance to fix me once at Eagle Pass," he boasted. "Maybe I'll give him another one of these days."

"Did you come here to threaten my father?" Marie demanded. She did not notice that she had claimed kinship with the man who had cast her off.

He had come because she was the only woman in the world who disturbed his peace. He had gone to see her act and had been greatly stirred by memories and desires. The glamour of the old days renewed itself in him. The conviction grew in him that he had been a fool to drive her from him. Once she had been fascinated by him. If he tried again, perhaps . . .

His mind had been dwelling on that possibility when he had seen Rose and Aunt Becky on the street, when the thought had come to him that they were going to see Marie. His intrusion had been born of overpowering impulse. But his pride and vanity would not let him admit it.

"I saw your sister come here and thought I would warn her that the old man is headed for trouble. She had better call him off if she can, though I reckon it is too late. He has pushed the Gliddens too far this time."

"What do you mean?" asked Marie. "How has he pushed them?"

"They have always hated him for killing Bull and Rocky Parks. Now that gunman of his has killed their cousins Clark and Hatch."

"What gunman?"

"Slim Delaney."

"Jim Delaney killed that man Hatch?" breathed Rose aloud.

"Killed Bill Hatch and Dutch Nagle, too. Had a little luck, just as he had the other night at The Green Curtain. But it won't last. Tell Pike Corcoran he'd better cut loose from this fellow. If he turns him over to the Gliddens and if he eats humble pie, they may call off this feud he has started with them. It is his only chance. They mean business this time."

"I don't believe it!" Rose cried, shocked into speech. "I don't believe Jim Delaney killed those men. Why should he? You are just telling lies to — to trouble us."

Meldrum looked at her curiously. "It troubles you, does it? You're interested in this outlaw and killer, eh?"

"He isn't an outlaw or a killer," Rose denied indignantly. "And whatever trouble he is in, it is because of what he did for me. If you think Father will desert him —"

"So your father knows what he did for you?"

"I'll tell him. I have been a coward too long."

Marie cut in smoothly, speaking to Meldrum. "Since you came to warn my sister, out of the goodness of your heart, and have done it, don't let us detain you from any other business you may have elsewhere."

Meldrum glared at her, then abruptly turned on his heel and walked from the room.

CHAPTER TWENTY-FOUR

In Lost Park

By unfrequented ways Jim Delaney and Buck Burris followed innumerable hill creases toward the Lost Park country. They rode warily, for by unlucky chance they might at any time jump up the enemy. Before they descended into valleys, they scanned the slopes, the ridge opposite, and the mesquite thickets below. A swirl of dust had to explain itself before they held it harmless. A coyote slipping through the brush held their alert attention.

It was not that they were expecting to meet a foe. In these solitudes such an encounter would be unlikely. But they were nearing their destination. If their suspicions were correct, some of the Glidden retainers could not be many miles from them, and the price of life for a man in the brush hunted by enemies was untiring vigilance.

The two men reached the cowcamp where Delaney had stayed with the W R riders. The place was deserted. Pierce and his companion had left.

"We hit the creek and follow it up till another branch runs into it," Jim said.

About a mile from the camp they struck the creek. The brush was thick and there was no trail, but they pushed through the mesquite, plodding up the sunbaked draw until they came to the fork. The riders took the right branch. The way grew steeper and rougher. They came to a field of boulders. Here they swung to the left and into a steep arroyo up which the horses climbed. A rough broken stretch lay in front of them.

Jim pointed to a bald-faced outcropping of rock standing out from a ridge.

"We head for that flatiron," he said.

In the shade of the big rock they unsaddled to rest their mounts.

"Not far now, I reckon," Buck guessed, lying flat on his back with arms outstretched.

"Not far," agreed Jim. "The park is back of the rimrock."

They were in no hurry. It had been decided that they would not attempt the actual descent into the park until night had fallen. There would be plenty of light under the stars for their purpose and not enough so that they could be seen at any distance. Until sunset they could lie unnoticed in the shadow of the flatiron. That would give them time enough to scale the rimrock before dark.

For supper they ate beef sandwiches and canned tomatoes, after which they caught and saddled. Through black jack they rode to the foot of a steep rock slide.

"Charley Pierce said to ride up the slide," Jim mentioned. "It makes a break in the rimrock."

The going was heavy. Loose rubble clattered down beneath the pressure of the horses' hoofs. The muscles of the wiry cow ponies stood out as they reached for footholds and clambered up the steep slope. The mounts were winded when at last they stood on the rimrock.

At the feet of the men lay Lost Park. The north end of it was wooded. That part which stretched just below them was more open. There was a good deal of brush. No sign of life met the eye.

"Filled with absentees, looks like," Jim said.

"Can't tell from here," Buck replied. "Might be a small army holed up in the timber."

"I won't kick if there's nobody at home," Jim mentioned cheerfully. "If a fellow got trapped down there, he might holler mighty loud for help without getting it."

"Have to fight our way out if we jump up trouble," Buck said casually. "We better get back in the brush till after dark, don't you reckon?"

They moved into a clump of black oaks to wait for darkness and the subsequent moon. After long silences they talked in low tones, merely to break the monotony. Like most outdoor men, they lived a good deal within themselves.

Neither of them smoked. It was not likely that anyone would come close enough to get a sniff of the smoke drift, but they did not want to take chances. Darkness descended over the land.

A big moon rose through a jagged notch in the hills. Stars spangled the sky.

"Might as well get started," Jim suggested.

They tightened the saddle girths and mounted. Along the rimrock they rode, looking for the break in the wall Charles Pierce had mentioned. Presently they found it, a wide rock platform that descended toward the valley. In the rubble, marks of hoofs showed that horses were accustomed to follow this trail. Both men scanned the prints very closely. It was important to find out whether those who had last traveled this path had come up or gone down. As to this they could not be sure.

Jim pointed out the print of a descending horse half blotted out by one pointing in the other direction.

Buck shook his head doubtfully. "Take a look at this one, Slim."

The mark superimposed over another leading from the park was heading down the trail.

"No can tell," Jim grunted. "Not in this light. I reckon we'll have to go ahead and trust to luck."

"Unless one of us went part-way on foot to see where this trail leads," Buck said. "I could sneak down and make a lot less noise than two horses. If the way is guarded, maybe I could make it unnoticed."

"And maybe you couldn't," Jim pointed out. "We'd better play this out together. If those birds have been roosting in this park for years without being discovered, they haven't been keeping a guard on the trail day and night. It's not reasonable."

"Your friend Pierce met someone on the trail."

"Going in or out, I would guess. He just happened to bump into him."

"All right. Let's be on our way."

They went down in single file, Jim in the lead. The valley was flooded with moon and star light, a bowl of silver touched to a magic vagueness, all harsh detail blotted out by the kindly night. Looking at it now for the first time, a man might well have named it Paradise Park; but both these riders knew that under the cruel sun the brush was harsh and thorny, the animal life gaunt and wolfish, and that any humans who from time to time took up their abode here were breakers of those laws which society has enacted to make our common life together possible, were foes to all the hardy pioneers who had pushed to the frontier in covered wagons to build another commonwealth for the Union.

The wide shelf dropped sharply down and ran into a shale abutment sweeping out from the lower face of the wall. From this point the road was plainly marked. It had been traveled many times and was well defined. Night riders had passed over its surface on nefarious errands, sometimes driving bunches of cattle before them.

On such errands, though not from this base, Jim Delaney had ridden more than once himself. He had been trapped as a boy by the glamour of an outlaw's free life. It had been painted for him as something heroic. Sam Bass and John Wesley Hardin and Joel Collins were figures that loomed large around the campfires in the brush. Many stories were told of them by admiring cowhands. At a critical hour Jim had fallen under the influence of King Cooper, and though King had given up his cattle-raiding habits, the reputation of other days still hovered over him. For a year Jim had swung a wide loop. He knew that he would never again ride crooked trails, but he could not know that his folly would not rise from the past to destroy his future.

The road swept around a clump of live oaks and dropped down a slope to a sizable log cabin. In the windows of the building lights showed.

Though Delaney and Burris were a hundred and fifty yards from the house, a dog began to bark.

"We better drift," Buck said. "Into the live oaks."

A man came out of the house. He bulked black against the light of the open door.

"Wha's matter, Rover?" he demanded, his voice carried by the breeze.

Rover lifted his nose toward the moon and howled.

The dismounted horsemen stood motionless. They were protected by the darkness of the live-oak clump back of them, but they could not be sure the man would not make out the shadowy bulk of horses.

Presently the man went back into the house and shut the door.

Jim and Buck retired to the live oaks.

"Not a thing we can do here, with that dog prowling around," Burris said. "I'd like to sneak up to the house and find out who these buzzards are, but the hound wouldn't let me get to first base. What say we ride down to the lower end of the valley and check up on any cattle that are here?"

"Might as well," Jim agreed.

They had come to Lost Park with two purposes in mind. The first was to find out if the stolen Cross Bar B cows were cached there; the second to discover whether the Gliddens or another band of rustlers were using this as a retreat. But Colonel Corcoran had given them explicit instructions not to get into trouble if it could be helped. Rather than run any serious risk they were to leave without getting the information they were seeking.

The two riders skirted along the wall that hemmed in one side of the valley. They kept, as much as they could, within the shadows flung out by the rocks. It was quite likely that all the inhabitants of the park were not up at the cabin. Some might be out with the stock.

Feed in the park was good, even though there was a good deal of brush. No doubt there were springs which watered the low lands. A better location for a hideout for rustlers could not have been found.

The Cross Bar B men were in no hurry. They had the night before them. In enemy territory as they were, caution was important. If they could get out of the park without their presence being discovered, it would be all to the good. They did not want to scare the rustlers from their hole.

Through heavy brush they crossed the lower end of the park looking for cattle. So far they had not seen a trace of stock.

Jim jumped up a big *ladino* which scuttled for the thicker brush like a jackrabbit. The young man swung his claybank and gave chase. The longhorn and the horse plunged through the mesquite. Delaney crowded the steer and drew closer. There was no room to swing a rope. The rider decided to tail the animal.

They crushed through the chaparral. Jim reached for the long limber tail, swung it round the horn of the saddle, and turned the claybank swiftly to the right. The longhorn crashed to the ground, turned a complete somersault, heels over head.

Instantly Jim was out of the saddle. The steer lay still, all the breath knocked from its body. By the light of the moon Jim read the brand. It was a Cross Bar B four-year-old. Swiftly he hogtied the steer.

Presently he heard the voice of Burris calling him, not too loud. He answered. Buck rode out of the darkness to him.

"Thought I heard you chousing a longhorn, Slim," he said.

"Take a look at this," Jim said.

Buck swung from the saddle, came forward, and examined both brand and earmarks.

"Belongs to the old man all right," he said. "Question before the house now is, Who are the gents that drove him here?"

"Answer is, the fellows up at the cabin. Look out, Buck, I'm turning this fellow loose. He's liable to be on the prod when he gets up."

Buck mounted. Jim made sure his cowpony was close enough to be reached on a short run before he undid the knot in the tie rope. The *ladino* struggled to its feet, shook the long horns, and charged at Burris. Buck swung his horse, as on a dime, and doubled out of reach of the lowered horns. The steer kept going. They could hear the crash of its progress through the mesquite.

"What now?" Jim asked. "Blamed if I see how we are going to find out who these rustlers are. Can't stick around till morning and ask them."

They were riding toward the lower end of the park. Buck drew up his horse sharply.

"Look, Slim."

A light gleamed through the brush. Both men stared at it.

"A campfire or a cabin," Jim said.

"Yes, sir. Some of the boys stay down at this end of the ranch, looks like. I reckon we better investigate this."

They tied to mesquite and moved forward on foot.

"Hope there is no dog this time," Jim whispered.

Apparently there was none. They drew close enough to see that the light came from the cabin. Angry voices drifted to them. Two or more men were quarreling.

"This listens good," Buck said. "Let's get closer."

They crept up to the log house, Jim in the lead. Edging along the wall, they reached a window. Jim raised his head and peered into the lighted room.

Two men sat at a table, a bottle between them. They were glowering at each other angrily. Jim moved a little to make room for his companion.

One of the men at the table thumped his fist on the top violently. "I won't have it, by Moses! When I go gallin' no shorthorn like Bert Benson can butt in. Understand?"

"Yeah, I understand," Benson jeered. He picked the bottle up, poured a half tumblerful of liquor, and tossed it down his throat. "That's what you say. Now listen, fellow. Abby Glidden ain't wearin' the Stub Ransom brand yet. Not none. What's more, she never will be. I don't scare. Savvy? You're liable to find my bronc hitched to the fence "most any time you drap around."

"Shove that bottle thisaway," Ransom snarled. He was a wiry little fellow, thin-lipped and slit-eyed. Before he said any more he too helped himself to a drink. "You're one of these bully-puss buzzards, by what I'm told. You like to run on anyone who will stand it. Well, me, I'm some bull rattler my own self. Any time you want to get on the prod, come asmokin'."

The other man looked at him venomously. "Go slow, Stub. That's fighting talk. I won't take it from any man. King Cooper couldn't talk thataway to me, let alone a squirt like you."

To those outside watching, it was clear that both of them had been drinking heavily and were in a dangerous mood. A hot fire burned in the shallow black eyes of Benson. He was a big ugly man with dark hair plastered tightly across his low forehead. A vicious man, Jim thought, but no more so than the little fellow with the cruel mouth and the lidded, sultry eyes.

Stub laughed harshly, with intent to provoke anger. "King Cooper could kick you in the pants without you liftin' a hand. If he ever started, he would make you look like a plugged dime. And, fellow, when you don't like the way I talk, you know what to do about it."

Benson spoke slowly, searching his mind for scabrous epithets with which to brand the other. He was facing the window and those outside could see the cold, fierce rage burning in his brutal face. They could see, too, that Stub never lifted his gaze from the man black-naming him. Not a muscle of his body moved, except those which controlled the fingers slipping ever so slowly toward the butt of the weapon at his side.

The big man stopped, in the middle of an insulting sentence. He had caught sight of a face at the window. Rising from his seat, he reached for his forty-four.

"Look, Stub, look — someone at the window!"

Stub thought it was a trick to distract his attention. His revolver flashed — twice — into the stomach of the big man. Benson caught at the edge of the table to steady himself from the shock. Bewilderment registered in his face, as though the surprise of this attack drove out all other thought. A curious sound, half sigh, half groan, came from his lips.

Another bullet crashed into his chest. It brought him back from his daze. He would be a dead man soon, and knew it. All the life still in him rallied for one last blow. His right hand rested on the table, still clutching the forty-four. The trigger-finger crooked. As the gun roared, he crashed down upon the table. An outflung arm knocked the lamp from the table to the floor and extinguished it.

Silence followed the booming of the guns. The men outside waited for Stub Ransom to rush from the cabin. He did not appear.

Jim spoke in a low, awed voice to his companion. "Both dead, don't you reckon?"

"Unless it's a trick. Let's not push on the reins."

The suddenness of the tragedy shocked them both. A moment ago two men had been full of lusty, furious life, now . . .

Not a sound from inside. It was not possible, Jim thought, that Stub could be waiting there in the black darkness, his victim close enough to touch, crouched to strike again if enemies appeared.

"I'm going in," he murmured.

"Keep back while I fling the door open," Buck warned. "If he's ready to get us, he'll fire soon as the door is swung."

They tiptoed to the entrance. Buck reached for the latch, raised it with a little click that sent their hearts scuttering to their throats, and flung the door wide, crouching back of the log wall.

Not the faintest alarm stirred the silence.

Jim tiptoed into the room. Clouds had scudded across the sky and shut off the light of the stars and moon. Jim waited, not in the doorway, but close to the wall. He listened, every sense keyed to taut alertness.

Something moved. Buck was edging into the cabin.

Delaney struck a match. The flame flickered up. By the light of it they saw two men lying with lax limbs stretched out, one on the floor and the other upon the table.

The match went out. Another one scratched to life. Buck stepped over the body of the man on the floor and picked up the lamp. Jim lit it.

CHAPTER TWENTY-FIVE

Lute Glidden Arrives And Departs Hurriedly

While Jim held the lamp, Buck examined the bodies.

"Dead, both of 'em," he said.

Jim put the lamp on a shelf. He discovered that he was trembling. "Never saw anything so sudden in my life," he said.

"Queer how things work out," Burris replied. "The big fellow reached for his gun because he saw us. That was the signal for the other one to kill him."

"The big one — Benson — must have been practically dead when he fired. His one shot went straight to the heart. Would you call that luck — or fate?"

"I wouldn't know," Buck replied briefly. "What stands out like a sore thumb is that if we're seen in the valley, we'll get credit for this. Time to light out."

"That's right," agreed Jim. "Soon as we've checked things up."

The cabin and its furnishings were crude. There was a stick-and-dirt chimney with a rock back. The door was made of clapboards. No puncheon covered the dirt floor. Bunks, table, chairs, and bench were all home-made. The cooking implements consisted of a skillet, a Dutch oven, and an iron pot. A broken saddle, a pair of shiny old chaps, a leather trunk, caught the eye.

They searched the cabin. In the litter of odds and ends found in the trunk was a letter from Sim Glidden to Bert Benson. It was addressed to Uvalde. The letter gave instructions to Benson to buy a list of provisions, itemized by the writer, and to take these at once to "you know where." In Stub Ransom's pocket there was another letter. The signature at the bottom of it was Abby Glidden. The girl appeared to have written it in a passion of anger. The text was short but explicit. No suitor could have missed the meaning.

> I have always dispisd you and didn't know why. Now I know. If I ever see you at the ranch again I will put a bullet in you. Go to Lost Park and hole up like the wolf you are. Go to hell for all I care. But stay away from me.

"The young lady certainly had her dander up," Jim commented. "I'd make a guess she is the kind that makes the fur fly considerable."

"Yes," agreed Buck. "I've met her only once. That was at a dance. One waddy was drunk and wanted to dance with her. She took one look and turned him down. He must have said something fresh, for she hauled off and gave him a slap on the cheek you could hear all over the room. That brush-popper sure went out with his head hanging. The way I sized up Miss Abby Glidden was that she had had her own way all her life and been spoiled. Brought up in a house full of wild men. Shoots and rides with the best of them. I've never heard a thing against her, but there are ructions in her neighborhood right often."

"Sounds like she would be interesting," Jim said. "Pretty?"

"Pretty isn't exactly the word. She has big blazing eyes and a lot of black hair. You never saw a straighter, more supple figure. Tall and dark and full of the devil. My idea is that she is born for trouble, like all the Gliddens. Her mother died when she was a kid, and she is the sort that needed a mother mighty bad."

"Rough and masculine-looking," Jim added.

"No, sir. All woman. When I said pretty isn't the word to describe her, I meant it doesn't go far enough. When she is in a room you don't see other women, if you get what I mean."

"Hmp! *You* noticed Miss Abby all right, if you did see her only once," Jim said dryly. "Well, we'll keep her letter. Maybe the boss could use it. Shows the Gliddens know all about Lost Park."

"I expect that letter was burning Spud Ransom up," Buck remarked. "He probably figured Benson had beaten his time, and hate of the big fellow was boiling up in him."

"Maybeso. I would say the lady is well rid of both of them."

The clatter of a horse's hoofs sounded and stopped abruptly outside. A voice called, "Hi yi, yippy yi!" gaily.

Someone could be heard swinging from a saddle and striding toward the house. The door opened. A tall young man, gaunt as a wolf, strode in and pulled up abruptly. To say that he was surprised is to do his amazement less than justice. His incredulous eyes stabbed here and there — at each of the dead men, at the two living ones whose guns were trained on him. He opened his mouth to speak, and closed it without uttering any words.

Jim said, in his gentle drawl, "Don't get excited."

"Who — who are you?" the newcomer gasped.

"Just a couple of pilgrims who dropped in unexpected. Have to collect yore hardware, stranger."

"I haven't a gun."

"Hope you won't feel we're doubting yore word if we make sure. You're the investigating committee, Buck."

Burris patted the long body and made certain there was neither revolver nor knife in the legs of the boots. "Harmless as Mary's little lamb," he pronounced.

Jim closed the door. "Might as well stay and rest yore saddle awhile, Mr. Glidden. We could have got along without you here, but since you've come, we might as well make the best of it."

That the man was a Glidden had been a safe guess. In spite of his gauntness he had the physical characteristics of the Gliddens, the jutting jaw, the reddish mustache, the big rangy look.

Glidden moistened his dry lips. His apprehensive glance came back from the two lax figures. "You — killed them," he said hoarsely.

"No," Buck answered. "They had a quarrel and shot each other."

He knew this man would not believe him. As an explanation this was not reasonable, not even plausible. But he gave it for what it was worth.

"How did you get here?" Glidden asked.

"Never mind about us," Jim told him. "We're here. That's enough. We'll ask the questions."

"Which Glidden are you?" Buck inquired. "Who is your father?"

"I'm Lute Glidden. Sim is my father . . . I don't know who you are, but I've never done you any harm. You' better let me go."

"We're not going to do *you* any harm if you talk straight," Buck assured him. "But we want the truth."

Glidden did not believe him. These men had killed Ransom and Benson. They would kill him, too, unless he could get away from them. But the panic of the first shock was dying down in him. He was a hard, tough man, not easily frightened. If he kept his head he might fool them yet. The odds were heavily against him, but there was a chance.

"What do you want to know?" he asked sullenly.

"How many men have you in the park?"

"There were six of us."

"Name them."

"These two." Glidden nodded at the bodies. "Myself. Uncle Mart. A fellow called Hatcher. Cousin Doug Glidden."

"No more?" Buck snapped.

"No more."

Jim reflected that what Luther Glidden said might well be true. Food had to be transported to the park at considerable trouble. There was no need of keeping many men there. Very likely at times the place was deserted.

"Were you in the party that raided the Cross Bar B pasture and ran off a bunch of cows?" Jim demanded.

"No, sir. Neither I nor any of my kin. We're not rustlers."

"We found one of Pike Corcoran's steers in the park here. Where did it come from?"

"I wouldn't know about that," the lank man made answer. "Likely it drifted in."

Jim took a shot in the dark. "Which trail into the park would it probably have used?"

"Either one." Glidden's eyes slid for an instant to the door. Was there a chance to make a break successfully that way? "Depends on whether it came from the south or the north. How can I tell which way?"

"That's right," Jim assented. "How could you — unless you happen to have driven it in? Well, Mr. Luther Glidden, we've enjoyed our short stay here and are now leaving. It may interest you to know that you're going out with us, part of the way, anyhow. If we left you here, some of yore friends might annoy us."

In Glidden's interpretation what had just been said held a sinister menace. He was to go *part of the way* with them. At the convenient moment they would put a bullet in him and leave his body as they were going to leave those of the men they had already killed. He did not doubt that they were hired gunmen of Corcoran.

The prisoner's gaze slid past the window. Wouldn't that be a better way out than the door? The chances were that he could not make an exit either way without being shot down, but he had to try one. Clark — Hatch — Nagle, and now Benson and Stub Ransom. He did not intend to be the sixth if he could help it.

Glidden played for time. "No need of taking me along, boys. I don't know who you are, either one of you. If you're scared I'll tell the other boys too soon, you can tie me up here. No hard feelings on my side. What the heck! It's all in a lifetime. I'd take a drink with you over it if that bottle of liquor hadn't been spilt."

The man got his smile working. It was intended to express good-fellowship, but the tiny beads of perspiration on his forehead betrayed his anxiety.

"No hard feelings on our side either, Glidden," Jim said, with a derisive grin. "That is, none personal. Can't say I care for yore family. I don't find Cousin Brad, for instance, what you could call sociable. Liable to run on you a little bit if you'll stand for it, wouldn't you say?"

"Brad *is* bossy," agreed Luther, with a mind divided.

His surface attention was given to Delaney, but his darting thought was for the moment on the beam which stretched from ridgepole to ridgepole just back of Burris. It would be a desperate hazard, but . . .

"Still, a fellow can't be responsible for all his kin," Jim went on pleasantly. "Since you're the white sheep of the family —"

"I don't claim to be any whiter than the rest," Luther interrupted hardily. "They suit me, fellow."

The beam was about four feet from the window, Glidden guessed. With luck . . .

"About that north trail from the park," Jim said casually. "Where would you strike it to get out of the valley?"

"Right straight back of the cabin the chaparral runs to the foot of the north wall," Luther explained. "There's a break in the rock. No trouble to find it when you are close. All you have to do is keep on going up the gulch."

Jim looked narrowly at him. Glidden had been a little too glib with his information. He had not needed any urging to give it.

"You wouldn't load us," Jim said skeptically.

"Why would I?" demanded the prisoner. "The sooner you get out of here, the better it will suit me. I'm not throwin' down on my friends any, either. They have no secrets here."

Buck smiled. "Nothing they wouldn't tell the whole world. Well, time to go. *Con su permiso, Señor Glidden, vamenos*."

Luther did not waste words in accepting the suggestion to leave. He responded by swift and acrobatic action. Arms extended, his long gaunt body shot forward and upward. Sinewy fingers closed on the beam, and a pair of booted legs swept toward the window. The fingers released their grip. The boots crashed through the glass of the window and the body followed. Glidden had got away without a shot being fired at him.

The break to escape had been a complete surprise. Neither Jim nor Buck had found time to seize the lank body as it was vanishing into the night.

Together they rushed for the doorway. Glidden came round the corner racing for his horse. Jim plunged forward to stop him, but the escaping man had the advantage by twenty feet. Luther caught at the rein and vaulted to the saddle. He drove his heels home and the animal jumped to a gallop.

Two bullets whizzed past Glidden. He crouched low in the saddle and drove his mount straight into the brush. The others could hear the sounds of the horse crashing through the mesquite. Presently these died away.

The Cross Bar B men stared at each other blankly.

Jim grinned, his smile wry. "I know a couple of lunkheads who don't know enough to pound sand in a rathole," he said.

"Goes double," Buck admitted promptly. "But I will say I never saw the beat of the way he sailed through that window. I hadn't a glimmer of a notion he was aimin' to take that way out. I give him good."

"*Yo tambien*," Jim drawled. "I don't give us much, though." He cocked an inquiring eye at his companion. "How come you didn't get him while he was doing his trapeze stuff?"

"Why ask me?" Buck asked. "You had a gun in your fist and your arm isn't crippled."

"You didn't want to drop him?" Jim charged.

"Did you?"

"Can't say I did. I'm no hired killer, to shoot down an unarmed man. As he said, he hadn't done us any harm. If I had woke up in time, I could have grabbed him."

"We're too tender-hearted to be making war on the Gliddens," Buck said grimly. "Even if he hasn't done us any harm yet, he's riding hell-for-leather to do it now. Where do we go from here? By the time we reach the trail we came in by, it will be blockaded. In the dark we can't find it easy and they can."

"What about the north trail?"

"You weren't so wooden-headed about that, Slim," admitted Burris. "He sure let out that there is another trail in here, but I'd hate to bet more than a 'dobe dollar he told us the right way to find it."

"If we don't find it, we're outa luck," Jim said. "We'd better start looking right damn now."

They trailed through the brush to the place where they had left their horses.

CHAPTER TWENTY-SIX

An Innocent Bystander

To look in the darkness for the north trail out of the park was almost a hopeless task. On account of brush, rocks, and the contour of the ground, it was not feasible to keep close to the cliff and examine it minutely for breaks which might permit of an exit. They might easily pass the gateway for which they were looking.

It had come on to rain and both moon and stars had been blotted out by clouds. They could not see twenty yards in front of them.

"Like lookin' for the needle in the haystack," grumbled Jim. "But we might as well keep going."

"Unless we want to be found here in the trap," added Buck.

"Time will be workin' for them and not us," Jim said. "It's a cinch that before an hour has passed, someone will be riding to tell the Gliddens outside that we're here. In two days a dozen of these buzzards will be lookin' for our carcases. They will comb the park thorough till they have rooted us out."

"If we're still here," Buck said by way of proviso.

"Sure. By that time we've got to be headin' for anywhere but here . . . There's one thing, Buck. If that scalawag Glidden was telling the truth, there won't be but three of them in the park for a while. If we bump into them, we'd ought to be able to stand 'em off."

"Standing 'em off won't do us any good," Buck rapped out. "We've either got to slip away unnoticed, or we've got to whop them and light out . . . Doesn't it look a little lighter over there to the left, as if there was a break in the cliff?"

"I wouldn't say so, but we might as well look. Wish it would stop raining."

"Looks as if she had started in for a soaker."

"Y'betcha! Well, we got good slickers, anyhow, and salt pork and beans enough to see us through. Might be a lot worse."

"A whole lot worse," Buck said cheerfully. "We might be lying back there in the cabin dead as the two rustlers we left there. I've been in many a worse tight than this. We'll shake the rope off sure."

"My notion too . . . No road this way, Buck."

They kept as close to the cliff as they could, following a winding, twisting path forced on them by the roughness of the terrain.

Jim murmured softly the words of an old trail song he had sung often under the stars while night-herding:

"There's hard times on old Bitter Creek
That never can be beat;
It was root hog or die
Under every wagon sheet.
We cleared up all the Indians,
Drank all the alkali,

And it's whack the cattle on, boys,
Root hog or die."

A chuckle interrupted him. "Sim Glidden and his gang sure will think you're the blamedest hell-a-miler that ever came down the trail. John Wesley Hardin and King Cooper won't amount to a notch on a stick beside you. This Lute Glidden will describe you, and they'll know right off it's Slim Delaney to bat again. Now you've bumped off two more of them —"

"You know I didn't have a thing to do with it," Jim protested.

"I do, but they don't. If we swore on a stack of Bibles we didn't do it, they wouldn't believe us. And you did it, you'll find. I just happened to be along with you."

"I have the doggondest luck!" Jim burst out. "They push me around till I'm in a jam and have to shoot my way out. Or else they lay it to me when I'm one of these innocent bystanders. But what's the use of jawing? They won't believe me. I'm a bad man from the Brazos, they claim. Pretty soon it will be so that when I'm around everybody will expect hell to break loose in Georgia."

"If you don't hunt trouble, it certainly hunts you," Buck grinned.

"I'm saying so," Jim agreed fervently. "Oh, well, what's the dif? Might as well be hanged for the sheep as the lamb."

Presently he was singing softly another stanza of his song.

"Oh, I'm going home
Bullwhacking to spurn;
I ain't got a nickel
And I don't give a dern.
'Tis when I meet a pretty girl,
You bet I will or try,
I'll make her my little wife,
Root hog or die."

"Picked that pretty girl yet, Slim?" asked Buck.

"No, sir. What would a brush-popper like I am do with a wife?"

"For an outsider you sing right fervently about her. Thought maybe you had met that pretty girl during your recent visit to Santone."

"Nothing of the sort," Jim protested. "I didn't meet any girls while I was there. Most of the time I was undercover."

"Thought I heard about a young lady you rescued from The Green Curtain. Then there were two you got a knockdown to at Pike Corcoran's house. Won't any of them fill the bill?"

"I'm not lookin' for a wife, Buck. Don't you worry. I won't offer any competition for the young lady with big burning eyes, the only one you notice in a roomful of women."

"Much obliged," Buck said. Burris was a bachelor by temperament and never looked at a woman with the speculative eye of a man interested in a home. "But not necessary, I reckon. You and I both would look like poison to Miss Glidden."

They decided it was useless to search for the hidden road out of the park in the dark. No doubt they could slosh around in the rain all night and be no farther advanced than when they started.

"Better find some shelter if we can and get some sleep," Buck advised. "What about that overhanging cliff back there? We can find a fairly dry spot, anyhow."

The two rode back to the place Buck had mentioned. The rain was from the north and a sort of cave had become eroded at the foot of the wall. The horses were unsaddled and picketed in a grassy spot, after which the riders tried to select a soft dry spot on the sloping boulder. Water dripped down upon them from above and the hard rock pushed up into their flesh. Though by no means comfortable, they snatched sleep in brief naps. Both of them were outdoor men and used to making the best of what they could get. Morning found them cold and stiff and hungry, but no more so than they had been a dozen times before.

Not daring to light a fire, they ate some leftover food from the previous day. The sun was breaking through the clouds when they brought in and saddled their mounts. Its warmth brought heat back to their chilled bodies.

"Never did get so tired of a night in my life," Jim complained cheerfully, "except onct when I was a kid and got the scarlet fever."

"I was some dissatisfied with it myself," Buck drawled. "Different with us than it was with old Sundown when he dropped into the Quarter Circle J one night and was hustled out from the bunkhouse for breakfast at four o'clock in the morning. He said a guy could stay all night quicker there than any place he had been for quite awhile."

"One thing I'm sure tickled about is that old Sundown has made the grade," Jim said. "You have to kill an oldtimer like him considerable before he'll stay dead."

They saw no sign of other human life in the park until close to noon. All morning they skirted the valley close to the cliffs, but without any success. The Cross Bar B men had agreed that if they did not find the north road by night, they would have to try to force a way out by the trail they had followed coming down. This would probably involve a battle with the rustlers, but it would not do to wait until reinforcements reached Lost Park.

By midday they had come down to the wooded end of the park. Occasionally they could see smoke drift rising from the chimney of the house they had discovered soon after their arrival. Once they caught a glimpse of two men on horseback. The sunlight flashed on the barrels of their rifles.

"Not taking any chances," Jim said. "They have heard Lute Glidden's story."

"I'll bet they are scared to death," Buck hazarded. "If they had us out in the open where they could see us, they wouldn't worry half so much. What gets a fellow's nerve is a menace hanging over him that he can't put a finger on. It is staying with them every minute that we rubbed out two of them last night and may finish the job any time. Right now they are listening for a gun to crack from behind some tree. So long as we are invisible, they think of us, not as a couple of guys trapped here, but as avengers who may strike without warning."

"If they are as goosey as all that, maybe they will let us go without putting up a fight," Jim suggested, with no confidence in his hypothesis.

Buck shook his head. "No. Soon as they see us, we'll just be two of Pike Corcoran's hired gunmen and the mystery that scares them would be blown away."

In the afternoon the situation was reversed. A bullet from an unseen rifle whistled past Jim's head and cut a leaf from a cottonwood behind him. Both men dropped at once from their saddles and took cover back of the trunks of trees. But almost at once they knew this was not necessary. They could hear a retreating rider crashing through the brush. Whoever had fired at them had taken one shot and fled while his skin was still whole.

CHAPTER TWENTY-SEVEN

Jim Says Much Obliged

The Cross Bar B men were not able during the day to find the north trail out of Lost Park. By the middle of the afternoon they gave up the attempt. It was time to be leaving. They decided they must take the only way out that they knew. The best time to make the attempt was just after darkness fell, before moon and stars came out.

About sunset they worked their way back to the upper end of the park and took cover in a clump of scrub oak about a quarter of a mile from the house and the same distance from the lower end of the road. One of them kept watch on the house, the other on the trail up the cliff.

Jim reported to his companion. "Two men leaving the house on horseback. The dog is going with them." He added, after a little: "They're heading for the trail leading up the bluff. You'll see them in a minute or two. The third fellow is standing in the doorway."

Presently Buck spoke. He was stationed at the other end of the patch of scrub. "I see 'em now. They're riding up the trail. Are they figuring on holding the road against us? Or are they riding out to meet the birds they are expecting?"

"The third guy wouldn't stay here alone and let the others leave the park," Jim shrewdly guessed. "Betcha the two on horseback will stop at the first bend of the trail and guard it."

His surmise turned out to be correct. "They are out of their saddles and parked up there," Buck announced, after a time.

"Wish we had known the way was open. Might have made a dash for it and got away."

"Too late for that now."

"Yes, unless —"

Jim stopped. A germ of an idea was being born in his brain. If the men could be drawn down from the trail by a ruse. But how?

He considered and rejected one or two wild ideas. A third stuck in his mind. He suggested it to Buck.

"Might do," Burris said doubtfully. "It's only a chance, but it's neck meat or nothing with us. Soon as it is dark, we'll try it."

They waited, apparently with stolid patience, but in reality filled with anxiety. If this did not work, if morning found them still imprisoned in Lost Park, the likelihood of ever leaving would be slight. Even now a bunch of Glidden men must be riding toward this secret rendezvous.

Darkness followed dusk. The Cross Bar B men dropped behind a little ridge back of the scrub oaks and rode down the hollow toward the house. They tied their mounts and crept forward on foot to a little tongue of land that thrust itself above the surrounding terrain.

"We're near enough, Buck," Jim said. "Let her go."

He fired two shots from his Winchester and one from the forty-four, spacing them a few moments apart. Buck did some shooting into the air after he had finished. A wild shot from the house flung defiance at them.

Swiftly they retreated to their horses and rode back up the hollow to the scrub oaks. There was no way of knowing whether the trick had succeeded in drawing the guards down the trail to the assistance of their companion in the house. Unless they happened to hear or see the men riding back, they would have to trust to luck, and in the event that they had failed, the luck was not likely to be good. In discussing the plan beforehand, Jim and Buck had agreed that such a fusillade would bring them back to the house, if they had been guarding the trail, to the aid of their friend, but it was by no means sure the rustlers of Lost Park would argue the same way. Among those they had met to date there had not been very much solidarity.

Cautiously the Cross Bar B men rode out from the scrub brush toward the ridge which ran up to meet the cliff shelf road.

Buck caught at Jim's bridle rein. "Listen," he whispered.

To them on the breeze came the beat of the feet of galloping horses. The men watching the road were hurrying to help the one at the house.

"She works," Jim murmured exultantly.

Two minutes later he and Buck were climbing the shale approach to the ledge trail.

The relief was tremendous. For more than twenty-four hours they had been under a strain of uncertainty, knowing that they must get out of the park soon or not at all; that time was working against them and for their enemies. At last they were on their way back to the world from which they had come.

The moon rode up over a hill crotch as the horses climbed the trail. With the stub of an old pencil Jim wrote a note on the back of the envelope of the letter Sim Glidden had written to Benson.

> Much obliged, boys. We did not know how to find the beginning of the trail again and you showed us. We have had a pleasant time in Lost Park and aim to come again. The hunting ought to be good here. See you again one of these days. Adios.
>
> THE AVENGERS

He weighted down the envelope with a rock in the middle of the trail.

"A fellow has to say 'Thank you' after he has been a guest," Jim said with a grin.

"Only they would like to have you say it in person," Buck replied.

"Maybe they will understand we were in some hurry and excuse us," Jim answered. "Boy, I could eat a leather mail sack, I'm that hungry. Wonder when we'll sit down to honest-to-God food again — coffee, hot bread, fried chicken. I'm so gaunt my backbone is pressing against my navel."

"When we get out of here into the hills, we'll fix us up some hot grub that will be good for that gone feeling," Buck promised.

They reached the rimrock above and put their mounts at the slide. The horses slithered down, sometimes on their hoofs and occasionally on their haunches. The escaped riders went down the creek and crossed country to the deserted camp of the W R cowhands. Here they lit a fire and prepared food. But neither of the men cared to spend the night so near Lost Park. They saddled and pushed on their way. Up and down arroyos, over countless hills, they plodded through the brush.

When they stopped on the bank of a creek and picketed their horses, Jim's watch told him it was midnight. The chance of enemies finding them here, surrounded by miles of mesquite as they were, was so slight as to be negligible. They rolled up in their blankets and fell into instant sound sleep.

A hot sun was shining down upon them when they awakened. Their weariness had gone and troubles had vanished. They were making a safe return home with their mission successfully accomplished.

Corcoran was much relieved to see them. Ever since they had left he had been blaming himself for letting them go.

"By granny, I've been worried," he confessed. "I hadn't ought to have sent you boys on no such crazy business. You might both have been bumped off there in the park."

"We 'most starved to death," Jim told him. "Outside of that everything was fine."

Pike excused himself and had a few words with the cook. In celebration of their return he was ordering a special supper.

He came back, flung himself into a chair, lit his pipe, and listened to a more detailed account of their story.

"I don't care much for this 'avengers' business," the Colonel frowned. "Sounds too much like night riders and jayhawkers."

"We might have signed the note, 'By order of Colonel Pike Corcoran.' Maybe that would have been better," Jim said, with ironic contrition. "I reckon they know who we were, anyhow."

"They don't know, but they guess," corrected Buck.

"'Course we'll be blamed for killing those two fellows," the Colonel said ruefully. "Too bad we can't prove we didn't."

"I wonder about that," Buck said. "Look at it this way, Colonel. We're off to a flying start. Score, five to nothing. Every time they have run up against us — against Slim here, mostly — they have had the worst of it. The Gliddens know the whole country is figuring them false alarms, and the warriors who have taken orders from Sim are doing a lot of guessing. It was fine while they were living at the top of the pot, but it's some different now. The scalawags who trailed along with the Gliddens have a mighty high regard for their own skins, and you can bet a lot of them are getting scared. Way they look at it there's something mysterious about this business, their crowd getting killed off so wholesale. Nary a Glidden hurt, only those who run with them. That'll make them think. I've a notion that from now on the Gliddens will pretty nearly have to play their hand alone."

The Colonel nodded. "Something to that, Buck. Probably they talk it over and explain just how they happened to get the worst of each fracas, but just the same they must have a sinking feeling, a plumb scary fear that their luck has run out at last."

"May be so, but they won't quit," Jim said.

"No, they won't quit. Fact is, they will boil over and do something that may wipe a lot of us out and ruin them too. Can't help that. What must be must. We have got to play our hand out, too." Colonel Corcoran leaned forward and patted Jim on the shoulder. "If the rest of us do as well as you have done, boy, we'll beat the Gliddens from where they laid the chunk."

Jim blushed beneath the tan, embarrassed at such praise. Fortunately the cook came out just then and beat on a triangle. Delaney jumped up at once. He departed to wash up for supper.

His shyness vanished when he found his feet beneath the table. He was sitting down to the food he had wished for twenty-four hours earlier — coffee, hot biscuits and corn bread, fried chicken, and, to top off with, peach cobbler.

CHAPTER TWENTY-EIGHT

The Weak Link In His Armor

To Sim Glidden, sitting in the office of The Green Curtain with his son Cole and his partner Dave Meldrum, came his other son Luther with tidings of disaster.

Luther blurted out his news as soon as he had closed the door behind him.

"That fellow Slim Delaney sneaked into Lost Park and killed Bert Benson and Stub Ransom."

Not a muscle of Sim's heavy body, slumped in an armchair, moved in response to the information. Only his stony, heavy-lidded eyes quickened to life.

"Did you bump off Delaney?" he asked harshly.

"No. We watched the pass, but he slipped out by a trick."

"Rode in, killed Benson and Ransom, then rode out again big as Cuffy," Sim said, with a harsh, bitter laugh. "What were the rest of you fellows doing all this time? I reckon you had other business and couldn't waste time on this buzzard. How many men he have with him?"

"We don't know for sure," Luther answered. "I got a crack at them from the brush once. Didn't see but two."

"Got a crack at them and missed?" snarled Sim. "Buck fever?"

Beneath the tan of Luther's cheeks dark angry blood ran. "Call it that if you like. They were a heap closer than I was when they missed me. Had me prisoner in the little cabin and I broke loose."

"How come they to take you prisoner?" Cole asked.

"I busted into the cabin right after they killed Bert and Stub. Hadn't any notion they were there. Had me covered before I could lift a hand. I surely thought I was a gone goose."

"How did you get away?" Meldrum asked.

"We'll come to that in a minute," interrupted Sim. "Did this Delaney find out there are Cross Bar B cows in the park?"

"He claimed he did."

"Then by this time Pike Corcoran's riders are on their way to the park. Did you leave his stuff in there?"

"No. Uncle Mart and Bud Hatcher are hustling the bunch out by the north trail."

"Where they driving for?"

"Nowhere. They aim to turn the stock loose soon as they get them outa the park."

"Good. Now about Benson and Ransom. How were they killed?"

"Don't know. Like I said, I walked into the little cabin and found them lying dead with these two fellows there. I've a notion one of the two fellows was Buck Burris. The other was Delaney."

"Tell me," ordered Sim. "Begin at the start."

Only once did the father interrupt his son. That was to slam a great fist down on the table when Luther described the trick by which he had escaped.

"That's using yore brains, son," he said heavily. "You done well that time."

Meldrum raised a question when the tale was told. "How do you know this fellow was Slim Delaney?"

"We don't know for sure, but I described him to Jeff and he said there wasn't any doubt."

"Jeff ought to know, seeing that he once arrested him," Sim said, with obvious savage sarcasm. "Yes, I reckon he was Delaney. Nobody else would have the sand in his craw to do so crazy a thing. I aim to rub that bird out, but I will say I wish I had a son that had half his guts."

Cole flushed. "Why don't you say half his luck? If you ask me, what Lute did was nervier than anything Delaney has done yet."

The opaque eyes of Sim rested on Luther. "You're right, Cole. It's not guts you boys lack, but gray matter in yore think tanks. Lute showed both once, but he couldn't keep this fellow from getting out of the park when he had him trapped."

"What would you expect me to do — stay up there on the trail while these devils were wipin' out Uncle Mart?" asked Luther angrily.

"I'd expect you to do what you did do, ride lickety-split for the house and leave the road open for

Pike Corcoran's killers to slip away," Sim told him sourly.

"You haven't answered my question," Luther retorted. "Was it more important to hold those fellows till help came or to save Uncle Mart?"

"Did he need any saving?"

"No, not the way it turned out. But how could we tell that? I'll say one thing. Uncle Mart doesn't feel the way you do about it. He thinks Hatcher and I did just right. By gravy, I think you're not fair about it. A fellow does his darnedest, and all he gets is kicks."

Meldrum defended the gaunt Glidden, principally to annoy Sim. "I don't see what else the boy could have done. Easy to sit here in a big chair and criticize him. Mart stayed at the house so as to prevent Delaney from slipping down and burning it. When it looked like he was attacked, the boys rode down to help him. Nothing else they could do."

"Nice of you to butt in and buy a stack in a private game, Dave," jeered Sim. "Lute will appreciate your sticking up for him, even if it isn't necessary. All I claim is that this Slim Delaney outgeneraled him, same as he did you, only not so much so. 'Course he didn't make a monkey of Lute when the guns were smoking the way he did of you and your crowd in town here."

Cold anger in his voice, Meldrum cut back instantly. "I wouldn't think the Gliddens have got so much to brag about. Let me see. He has bumped to date into Cole and Lute and Mart and Bill and Brad and Jeff." The gambler ticked the names off precisely on the fingers of his hand. "I don't seem to remember that any of them got so far with him."

"I claim he just has nigger luck," Cole said irritably. "When he came up to me and jabbed a gun into my belly, I thought he was one of our boys. Wasn't a thing I could do when I found out."

"We'll cut out this scrapping, boys," Sim announced abruptly. "Fact is, like Dave says, none of us have anything to crow about so far. I don't want to ride you, Lute. If you were worried about Mart, you had to look after him first off. We'll start fresh from the chunk. This Delaney has had luck. Grant you that. But he has guts and horse-sense too. Still and all, there must be a weak spot in him if we knew where it was."

"If we ever get to him with our six guns we'll find it," Cole said.

His father looked at him. "There's more than one way to skin a cat, son. When you are my age, you'll know it pays to have all the information about an enemy you can gather. Take one point, for instance. The Rangers are after him for rustling. If they pick him up, they will bring him back here. It will be up to us to collect his scalp while he is a prisoner."

"Fine, if they get him," Cole said skeptically. "I've noticed that most generally a fellow can't depend on the neighbors to round up his stock for him when he wants them."

"I can give you one tip," Meldrum said, "though I don't see what good it will do you."

"Spit it out."

"This Slim Delaney and Corcoran's younger daughter Rose are interested in each other. Anyway, she is in him. She is a mighty pretty girl, and I reckon it works both ways."

"What are you expecting us to do — attend the wedding?" asked Sim ironically.

"Not expecting a thing," the gambler answered. "You were asking for some human spot in this killer Delaney, and I have mentioned one, but by this time I know better than to look for you to do anything about it but talk."

"What could we do, Dave?" asked Cole.

Meldrum looked at him out of cold, hard eyes. "I wouldn't have any answer for that, boy. If you were smart enough you could maybe use her to trap him, but I never did believe in miracles."

"Trap him, how?" Cole persevered.

"Why, the way Dave did at the lumber yard," Sim jeered. "Only Dave wasn't there in person. He was busy that night and couldn't go. Maybe a good thing for him he was."

"Thought we were to quit this yelping at one another, Dad," Cole persisted. "There's an idea in what Dave says, seems to me, if we could work it out. Send this Slim a note from her to come and see her, say; then blast him off the map while he's on the way."

"I have a copy of the young lady's handwriting," Meldrum mentioned.

"You have?" Cole repeated. "Where did you get it?"

"She wrote to me asking me to come and see her."

"Asking *you* to come and see her? What for?" Luther wanted to know.

"On private and personal business," Meldrum replied coldly.

"Maybe the same note would do," Cole suggested.

The professional gambler rummaged around in his desk and at last produced an envelope with a letter in it. He glanced it through before he replied to Cole.

"No. My name is in the letter, and it is not the kind she would write to this young scalawag. But I'll tell you what I'll do. Fix up your plan to get him and I'll have one of my girls, Lucy Page, write a letter the way it ought to be written and imitating Rose Corcoran's hand. Lucy is clever as all get out. She will do it right."

"Sounds feasible," Sim ruminated aloud. "If it isn't boggled by someone."

They were devoting, he realized, much more time to the destruction of a cowhand than the fellow intrinsically deserved. But Delaney had become a symbol. He represented to the public a young and romantic figure who was carrying disaster to the Gliddens. It was important, first of all, that he be stamped out of the picture. His death would point the moral that nobody could defy the Gliddens with impunity.

After the Gliddens had departed, the details of their plot worked out, Meldrum sent for Lucy Page. She was a dark-eyed, handsome young woman with a better education than most girls of her profession. Her clothes she carried well, and in her gestures and manners little refinements still showed.

Meldrum laid a five-dollar gold piece on the corner of the table. “Want you to write a letter, Lucy. It is supposed to be from a girl to her sweetheart. She’s writing to him asking for his help. Make it sound natural. She’s a good girl, still in school. The letter wants to show her kind of — shy, you know. Chances are neither of them has ever spoken any love talk together. Or not a great deal, anyhow. You get the idea.”

Lucy sat down on the edge of the table and swung a foot. “I don’t know as I do, Dave. Is this a real girl? If so, who is the fellow?”

“It’s a joke some of the boys are getting up. Call the girl Mary — Jane — Kate — no, Rose. That’s what we’ll call her — Rose.”

Lucy was no fool. She knew there was something back of this. In time she would find out.

“Rose is a good name. What’ll we call him? How about Dave? That will do fine, won’t it?”

“No. He’s a cowboy. Might call him Slim, or something like that.”

“How would Bucky do?”

“That would be all right, but I kind of like Slim. It has an outdoor sound. Let’s call him Slim.”

“He has ditched her after getting her in trouble, and she’s begging him to come back to make her an honest woman. That the idea?”

“No. Nothing like that. She’s a square girl. Likely he never even kissed her. If he has, that’s as far as it went. But she is scared someone wants to do her harm — some enemy. So she begs him to come and take her down to her father’s ranch, say. Something like that.

She sets the time when she can meet him and the place."

"It's a regular play, isn't it?" the girl said, derision in her voice. "I hope you-all get a good laugh out of the joke, whatever it is. I haven't come to the joke part of it yet. Let me in on it, Dave. There's not so much to laugh about in this road-to-hell place of yours that I couldn't stand a side-splitter like this one must be."

"Not necessary for you to get funny about it," Meldrum told her sharply. "All you have to do is to write the letter — if you want the five dollars. Then you're through. If you can't use the five, I know plenty others who can."

"Oh, I can use it," Lucy said. "I was trying to combine pleasure with business. Do I write the letter here?"

"Yes. Sit at my desk. Begin by calling him 'dear Slim,' then go on to say she is frightened and worried because someone — let's see, call him You-Know-Who — is hanging around and means to do her harm. Kind of hint at kidnapping. Ask him to come and take her to her father's ranch where she will be safe. Make it read nice and smooth, like she hates to call on him, but he's the only friend she has."

"Why doesn't she write to her father? I would think that would be more natural."

"She isn't on very good terms with the old man," Meldrum explained. "Besides, the idea is to fool this young fellow into thinking she has fallen in love with him and then to give him the horse-laugh later."

Under long lashes Lucy looked at him speculatively. "Oh, that's the idea," she said dryly. "You and those in with you want to take this Bucky down a peg, so you load him with the notion that she calls on him to come and rescue her."

"That's it, except that his name is Slim and not Bucky. Fact is, this Slim is a bumptious guy who needs putting in his place."

"Then Slim is his real name?"

"Yes. Let's get busy with the letter."

"I'd better write it and then copy it later in a nice school-girl hand on some small square stationery," Lucy proposed.

Meldrum found pen, ink, and paper. Before her he laid a folded letter with two or three lines visible. What Lucy read was the end of one sentence and the beginning of another.

> unhappy because I do not know where she is. If
> you will give me her address so that I can write to
> her, perhaps God will forgive you for all the

"That's the sort of writing," he said. "Make it like that if you can. Keep the letter short. After you have finished, we'll go over it and fix it up."

"Do you mean imitate this handwriting?" Lucy asked.

"Yes."

"I see. This Slim may know her hand."

The gambler did not comment upon that. He discussed with her the phrasing of the letter and he stayed with her until she had made the final copy. That Lucy did not get a chance to see the rest of the letter the writing of which she was imitating, he took pains to see.

But after the young woman had left him, she did not dismiss the matter from her mind. She knew he had some devilry in mind. He had been in conference with the Gliddens that morning and the sending of this letter had been decided upon at that meeting. It did not take any wizard to guess that. She wondered about this Slim who was getting an urgent invitation to help a maiden in distress.

Lucy was lying on her bed smoking a cigarette. Abruptly she sat up, struck by an idea. Slim Delaney, of course, the man who had precipitated the fight in The Green Curtain and later had killed two of the Glidden men at the lumber yard. She had written a decoy letter. Unwittingly she had invited the young man to his death.

The girl was emotional, and fell into an immediate unhappy agitation. In this feud she was on the side of Corcoran and Delaney, as was every dance-girl in the house. None of them liked Meldrum or Sim Glidden. The Colonel was a good man, and they respected him. But Slim Delaney was to them the hero of this war. His youth, his audacity, his courage, and his success had taken hold of their imaginations. That she had lent herself to the plot to destroy this boy distressed Lucy greatly.

It would do no good to try to get the letter back from Meldrum. He would not give her wishes the least consideration. Nor could she go to the police. In the world to which she now belonged officers were natural enemies. Then what could she do? How could she save Delaney — and do it without delivering herself to the anger of his enemies?

She began to see a way. A young man, a cowboy, was coming to see her that evening. She had talked with him about Delaney and knew the two were friendly. It would be easy to persuade him to carry a letter to his friend Slim warning him that the other letter was a decoy.

CHAPTER TWENTY-NINE

A Ventilated Hat

Corcoran and his riders wasted no time in getting to Lost Park. They expected to find the valley untenanted, though it was possible that the reinforcements Mart Glidden had sent for might be entrenched there. This was not likely. The chances were that Mart had intercepted them before they arrived and sent them back home. So the Colonel and Slim guessed.

Their guess turned out to be correct. There were no men and no stock in the hidden valley. Pike burned both cabins to the ground after he had searched them in vain for evidence of the identity of the rustlers whose rendezvous this was.

The boss of the Cross Bar B did not linger long in the park. The Gliddens had not driven the stock out by the ledge trail. If they had done so, the evidence would have been written clear on it. Therefore, they had moved out by the north entrance. The Colonel led his men back up to the rimrock and down the slide. From here they made a wide circle, to get around to the north side of the park. It was a long ride, through rough country, for the park made a big bite into the high lands. The brush was thick. There were innumerable gullies, hills, desert stretches. They corkscrewed in and out, following the line of least resistance, but always working to the right in the end, in order to get past the barrier of rimrock and reach the other side of the hidden valley.

They made camp well to the north of it. Breakfast had been disposed of before the first sunlight flooded the hill across from the camp. Pike spread his men, though not so far apart that a rifle shot would not bring them together again in a bunch. They were on a cow hunt, but there was always the chance they might jump up men instead of Cross Bar B stock. The Gliddens might be waiting for them. This particular brush country was the habitat of the rustlers. That Corcoran would sweep across it looking for his vanished cows would be likely enough. Any one of a hundred ledges, mesquite arroyos, or clumps of chaparral would serve for an ambush.

The riders found almost no cattle during the morning. One or two mossy longhorns crashed through the brush at their approach. These were wild as deer. The only one roped and thrown was a maverick. It had never been branded.

At noon the Cross Bar B men gathered together, not for food, but to make sure none of them had been trapped by the enemy. One rider, Yorky Carpenter, reported that he had cut the tracks of a bunch of cows. They were pretty well scattered and were moving slowly, grazing as they went.

"If they are Cross Bar B stock the rustlers have turned them loose," the Colonel guessed. "Figured they daren't take a chance of being caught with them."

"We know they are the Glidden outfit, anyhow, whether we find them with the cows or not," Yorky said.

"There's a lot of difference in being sure of a thing and being able to prove it in court," the boss replied. "Nobody knows that better than the Gliddens. For years folks have known they are rustlers, but nobody has had the evidence to convict them."

Corcoran's riders followed Yorky to the place where he had cut sign. Buck Burris dismounted and examined the tracks.

"Yep," he agreed. "Moving slow and feeding as they go. When they are fed up, they will light out for the home range."

"If they are Cross Bar B cows," Jim added.

Presently they caught up with the feeding stock. There was a bunch of about fifteen of them, all carrying Corcoran's brand. The riders pushed the cows along in front of them. Later in the day they gathered in two more small groups. There were still thirty not accounted for, but the Colonel was reasonably sure these would work their way back to the ranch.

"We'd better be getting back," he said. "If we stay away too long, something is liable to break. We'll take what cows we have picked up and let the rest go for the present."

Corcoran, Jim, and Buck rode straight for the ranch, leaving the others to finish the drive. They stopped at Eagle Pass to get the ranch mail. There was a letter from San Antonio for Jim. The Colonel passed it to him, after taking a look at the good stationery.

"You haven't got a girl hidden out on us somewhere, have you, Slim?" he asked jocosely.

Jim blushed. "No, Colonel, I ain't hardly old enough yet," he said. "I'm a young thing that cannot leave its mammy."

He ripped open the envelope and glanced at the signature before reading the letter. The name written there startled him. It was Rose Corcoran. He shot a glance at the Colonel, but that gentleman was busy looking over his own letters. Abruptly he put the letter in his pocket.

Jim walked out of the post office and down the little street of false fronts to the hitching-post where they had tied their horses. Flanked by two of the animals, he drew the letter from his pocket and read the contents swiftly.

There came the crack of a gun. Jim swung one of the horses round to protect him. He drew his forty-four, eyes riveted to the front of the Palace Saloon. From one of the windows a man was vanishing.

Corcoran and Burris ran out of the post office.

"What's the matter, Slim? Who shot?" the Colonel asked.

Jim put the letter back in his pocket. He lifted the wide hat from his head and looked at it. In the roof of the sombrero were two small holes.

"I wouldn't know that, Colonel, but whoever shot had right good intentions," he drawled. "He sure ventilated my hat proper."

"Goddlemighty, don't stand there like a dummy!" the Colonel shouted. "Get a move on you before he pops you again."

"Shot came from the Palace," Jim answered. "Fired by a gent who has vamosed from the window. Anyhow, I have done swung old Baldface round between me and there."

"Some of those damned assassins," Pike cried angrily. "Son, we're going in to find out who. Spread out, boys, and close in, I go through the door first. Keep your eyes glued to that window and if you see anyone there let him have it."

The Colonel took the center with Burris on the right and Delaney on the other side. They moved forward, swiftly, revolvers drawn. Kicking the door open, Corcoran strode into the saloon. The two younger men were at his heels.

The interior of the Palace was as peaceful as old age, if one judged by surface indications, so placid that it might have been set for a scene in a play. Tim the bartender was polishing a glass with a towel. A man lay on a bench against the wall with a hat over his eyes. Apparently he was asleep. Three others were playing stud. One of them Jim recognized as Pete Sanderson, whom he had known at Uvalde a year or so ago as one of King Cooper's men.

A thin telltale drift of smoke floated near the ceiling above the bar.

"Who fired that shot?" demanded Corcoran.

The pretense of comfortable ease vanished from the manner of those inside the saloon. In the Colonel's voice was a sharp imperative, and three drawn guns backed it. Those at the stud game lost interest in their cards. The man on the bench sat bolt upright, as if he had felt an electric shock.

Tim said, the glass still in his hand, "What shot?"

"By gravy, don't chop words with me," Corcoran barked. "Who fired it? Let him stand up and take it."

From the alley back of the Palace came the clatter of a horse's hoofs. Someone was getting away hell for leather.

"He's lit out," Tim said.

Jim ran back and flung open the door. A mounted man was disappearing back of a barn. He was headed for the country. No use to follow. He would take to the brush if pressed.

"Who was he?" Pike snapped.

The face of the man in the white apron had as much expression as a wall. "Never saw him before. He came up to the bar to get a drink. First I knew he had his sixgun out and was taking a crack through the window."

"That's a lie," the Colonel roared. "You know doggone well who did it."

"Honest, Colonel, the guy was a stranger, one of these here drifters who blow in and out." Full of bland innocence, Tim offered description. "A tough, sawed-off, heavy-set fellow about forty — or maybe more. Said he came from New Mexico."

Delaney laughed, with no friendliness in his mirth.

"Speak yore little piece now, Pete. You never saw him before either, did you? Maybe he told you he came from Arizona."

Sanderson squinted up at Jim, who had stopped at the card table.

"He didn't tell me where he came from, Jim. Fact is, I didn't notice him particular."

"Didn't you notice he was a tough bird, heavy-set, forty or more?" Delaney gibed. "You want to back up Tim, don't you, if you're all playing together?"

"I was playing stud here and never looked at him," Sanderson insisted doggedly.

"And I reckon you other gents were too busy to see him," Jim said. "Never looked up as he ran to the back door after shooting. No curiosity. Doesn't mean a thing if a gunman whangs away in the same room as you."

The Cross Bar B men had put their guns back under cover. It was plain there would be no more shooting at present.

"Sure I noticed him," one of the card players said. "Well as a fellow could who was ducking under the table for fear he would get shot. He was bowlegged."

"A stranger, of course. Probably a Mexican from across the Rio Grande."

"Never saw him before, to recollect him." The man chewed tobacco as he looked at Delaney impassively.

"For a man as scared as you were you got back to yore game right quick," Jim suggested.

A boy walked into the Palace and looked around.

"Miss Abby says for me to tell her cousin Brad she has done her shoppin' and is ready to go," the youngster announced. "Where's he at?"

"He was called away sudden," Jim told the boy. "Maybe one of us had better go and explain it to Miss Abby. How about you, Buck?"

"You're a better explainer than I am, Jim," Buck said.

Delaney looked at the boss of the Cross Bar B for orders.

"All right, boy," Corcoran said. "Run along and tell her that her cousin just missed being an assassin by two inches."

Jim lingered for a parting shot at the enemy. "You certainly gave a good description of Brad, Tim. Outside of the facts that he isn't a stranger to you — nor sawed-off — nor within fifteen years of forty — and that he didn't mention he came from New Mexico — it came near being perfect. At that, you did better than the other boys. You may have seen cross-eyed, but they were all blind."

Beside the boy Jim walked out of the Palace and across the street to Barlow's St. Louis Emporium. A young woman looked up quickly as he entered. She was tall, arrow-straight, and dark. As Buck Burris had said, there was something arresting about her, a freedom that had in it some kinship to the wild things of the forest.

"Where is Brad?" she asked the boy.

"Brad went away," Jim said cheerfully.

"Away where?"

He could read the question in her dusky eyes. Who was this stranger she had never met? Why had he come with little Bobby?

"He didn't say where. Just left." Jim had taken off his hat and was looking at the crown. There were two small holes in it.

"What do you mean? Is anything the matter? Who are you?" In her voice there was a rising note of anger. This man was mocking her.

"Nothing the matter," he answered evenly. "Brad did his best, but he missed. You can't kill a guy every time you shoot at him. If he keeps on trying, maybe he'll have better luck."

"He — shot at you?" she asked, her black eyebrows meeting in a frown.

"If he wasn't shooting at me, a man as careless as he is oughtn't to be trusted with a gun," he said, smiling at her.

"I asked you who you are."

"Me? My name is Slim Delaney, if that means anything to you."

He could see the angry color pour into her face beneath the tan. "Delaney the killer!" she cried.

"No," he denied. "I never killed except in self-defense. But no need going into that. You wouldn't believe me. What I'm here for is to tell you not to expect Brad to see you home. He left, in a hurry, after he punctured my hat."

"Brad shot at you — in the street?"

"No, Miss. From the window of the Palace — when I didn't know he was there. Then lit a shuck like the heel flies were after him."

"I don't believe it." Her black eyes blazed into his. "He isn't afraid of a murderer like you. Get out of my way, or — or —"

She swept past him out of the store, gathering her skirts so that they would not touch him.

CHAPTER THIRTY

Buster Eaton Delivers A Letter

Jim followed Abby Glidden out of the store. As he watched her moving across the street, he thought he had never seen a woman to whom anger was more becoming. The passion in her seemed to set fire to the long, supple grace of her body. He could imagine that Queen Elizabeth in her brittle youth might have carried herself with the imperious rage of this girl. Queenly was the word Jim had in mind. She walked as though she spurned the common earth.

At the hitch-rack she stopped, then turned abruptly. Jim was in front of the store. Out of the Palace Colonel Corcoran and Buck Burris were just coming.

The young woman spoke to Corcoran, her voice trembling, a long arm outflung toward Delaney. "This man — this killer — said my cousin has gone. His horse is here with mine, Brad's horse. He can't have gone. Don't lie to me. Did that murderer kill Brad? Is that what he means?"

Corcoran took off his hat. "No, Miss Glidden. Slim told you the truth. Your cousin fired at him without warning and lit out before we could settle with him. I reckon he took the first horse handy."

"Three of you to one," she cried scornfully. "That's how you Corcorans fight."

She freed one of the horses at the hitch-rack. The bay gelding with the side saddle she held by the reins, her furious eyes searching for a mounting block. "Steady, Black Hawk," she ordered.

Jim stepped across the street. "Let me help you, Miss Glidden," he said.

Abby hated his young debonair grace and his mocking smile. Her dark eyes flamed anger. The quirt in her hand swept up — and down across the young man's derisive face.

He tore the whip from her and flung it away, bleak gaze fixed on her.

"If you're ready, Miss Hellcat," he drawled, at last.

Surprisingly, as their eyes locked in battle, the fury of hers died away. The blow that had brought the crimson streak to his cheek had exhausted the explosive force in her. An inner emotion had swept her, one wholly unexpected, wholly new. It paralyzed her will, left her strangely shaken. She drew back, as if in fear of him, the color dying from her face. Her breasts rose and fell faster than usual, as with one who has been running.

He had offered to help her, and the quirt in her strong hand had lashed his face. Some stubborn instinct in him held Jim to his ironic tender of service. He would not let her angry scorn defeat him.

"Always tromped on men, haven't you?" he said, almost in a murmur. "What you need is a boss, someone to beat hell out of you."

"You brute," she told him, but without the usual lusty conviction of her epithets.

"Give me yore foot," he said curtly.

To her surprise she lifted it obediently and put it in his hand. He gave the lift and she found herself in the saddle. Automatically she arranged her skirts, then looked down at him, an odd shyness in her big dark eyes. She opened her lips to speak and closed them without saying anything. From her throat there came instead a strangled sob. She gave her gelding the spur and lifted it to a gallop.

Jim dabbed his bleeding face with a bandanna. "Nice gentle little catamount," he said to his friends, with a laugh.

Corcoran shrugged. "She's one of the wild Gliddens, but I wouldn't say you weren't to blame some, Slim. She knew you were mocking her, and she cut loose the only way she could. What beats me is why she let you help her up finally."

"Must be his winning ways," Buck jeered amiably.

Jim made no comment, but he, too, wondered exactly what the meaning was of that wordless drama which had leaped to life between them. One moment she had been all furious scorn; the next a girl troubled by misgivings. During that long meeting of the eyes drums of excitement had beat in her heart and the sound of them had echoed in his.

He put that speculation from him, to set his mind on a more practical problem. Rose had written and asked him to come to her at once and take her to the ranch. She had suggested she was in danger, or at least was afraid, and she had asked him not to tell her father. Since she did not want to worry him, it would be soon enough for him to know when she reached the Cross Bar B.

Jim would have to go to San Antonio. He realized that. Yet there was something about this he did not like. It was for Pike Corcoran to decide whether he wanted his daughter brought to the ranch during these troublous days. Delaney was drawing his pay as an employee. There seemed to him a species of disloyalty in moving without his authority, something almost underhanded.

Reluctantly he asked the Colonel for leave of absence.

"Got to go to Santone for a couple of days if you can let me off," he explained.

Corcoran smiled. "He gets a letter from his girl, Buck. And right away he wants to get off. But he hasn't got any girl, he claims. What do you make of that, Buck?"

"You tell me, Colonel," Buck drawled. "Claims he's got no use for girls. Claims they are poison to him. Claims —"

"Go ahead, Buck," Jim interrupted. "You sound like you're wound up like an eight-day clock. Have yoreself a good time."

In spite of his apparent insouciance, Jim was uneasy. The random guess of the Colonel had hit too near the mark. Rose was not his girl, of course. He was just a waddy hired by her father and she was the daughter of one of the richest men in Texas. But when he arrived at the ranch with her, it would be hard to explain to Corcoran that he was only a good Samaritan. The chances were that the boss would give him his time and tell him he could go down the road.

Jim rode with the others to the ranch to get a fresh horse. He was still mulling the thing over in his mind. It seemed to him strange that Rose had not appealed to her cousin Jack Corcoran. He was on the ground, could help her more promptly, and was in the family. If it had been Polly Stuart now, with her flair for dramatics! But Rose, shy and a little proper and quite unsure of herself — it did not seem in character.

Jim saddled a fresh horse and went into the house to eat dinner. After he had finished, he walked out to the porch and untied his mount.

"Look out for yourself, Slim," the Colonel told him anxiously. "Don't forget you have enemies in Santone. I hate like Sam Hill to see you go."

A man on horseback came down the road at a jogtrot. At sight of Jim he threw up a hand of greeting.

"'Lo, you old son-of-a-gun, I been lookin' for you all over West Texas. Got a message for you. Where you been keepin' yoreself at?"

"'Lo, Buster," Jim called back. "Someone was tellin' me you got hanged or shot or drowned, or something. I see the guy was premature a li'l' bit. What you mean message? Who from?"

Buster rode up and swung from the saddle. "Say, am I in time for grub? I ain't seen food since last time."

Colonel Corcoran had stepped to the porch. Jim introduced the cowhand to him.

"Colonel, this is Buster Eaton. Buster, meet Colonel Corcoran. Who is the message from?"

"From a lady."

Buck Burris had followed the others outside.

"Another one, or the same girl, I wonder," he murmured aloud.

The Colonel laughed. Jim turned a brick-red.

From Eaton he took the letter handed him. It was on the same kind of stationery as the other letter in his pocket. He tore open the envelope, looked at the signature, and frowned.

"I don't know any Lucy Page," he said.

Buster coughed, a trifle embarrassed. He glanced at Corcoran. "She's a — a friend of mine. A dance-girl at The Green Curtain."

Jim's eyes raced back and forth over the written lines. He read the letter twice. The second time he was making up his mind on a certain point.

"Like to see you, Colonel," he said.

Corcoran led the way to the little room that served him as an office.

"What's on your mind, Slim?" He added, with a smile, "Breach of promise or divorce?"

Jim did not know how to begin. He had to be careful to say nothing that would lead up to the adventure he had had with Rose in The Green Curtain.

"I've had a letter, Colonel," he blurted out, and then stopped, an embarrassed young man.

"Two of them, Slim," corrected the owner of the Cross Bar B.

"That's right. I don't want you to get me wrong, Colonel. Fact is, the first letter is signed by Miss Rose."

Corcoran stiffened. "By my daughter?"

"Yes, sir. It didn't look just right to me. She would get Jack to help her. Or she would write you."

"Help her! What do you mean? Give me that letter, Slim."

Jim handed over to his employer the first letter he had received. Corcoran read it, frowning.

"I reckon it's a forgery," Jim explained.

"Why would my daughter ask you to bring her here? Why wouldn't she write to me?" The Colonel fixed harsh, steady eyes on Delaney. "Is there something going on between you and her I don't know about? If so, what?"

"No, sir. I was surprised to get the letter and I didn't know what to do."

"You ought to have known what to do — turn it right over to me. I'm surprised at you, Slim."

"Couldn't throw a young lady down, could I? Anyhow, that's not the point. I think it's a fake. Would you say that was her writing, Colonel?"

Corcoran could not immediately disengage his mind from resentment.

"Not your business to wait on her. If there are any orders in my family, I'll give them. I'm the one to say where she is to stay."

"Yes, sir," Jim agreed. "It was dumb of me to think Miss Rose could have written that letter."

The Colonel examined the handwriting. "Looks like her fist," he said, and added suspiciously, "What makes you so sure it isn't?"

"Like you say, she would not have written to me, but to you. Besides, I got another letter."

"Not from Rose?" the older man snapped irritably.

"No." Jim opened the second letter. "She signs it Lucy Page. Says she works at The Green Curtain and Meldrum got her to write the first letter. Says she didn't get on to what was doing until she had turned it over to Meldrum, then she figured out it was a trap to get me to Santone where they could kill me. So she is getting Buster to bring this warning to me. Begs me for God's sake not to pay any attention to the first letter and not to tell anybody she has written me. Here's the letter."

Pike read it. "Same person wrote both, I judge," he said, comparing the two. "The capital D is alike in both, and notice how the E is made."

"No doubt about it. Look at this M and this one." Jim pointed them out, standing beside the Colonel.

"You don't know this Page girl, Slim. That's what you said, didn't you? Why is she taking so much trouble to protect you?"

"Don't know. Buster might tell us something about her."

"Might." Corcoran stepped outside and called Eaton into the room. He flung an abrupt question at the cowboy. "Young man, how well do you know this Page woman?"

Buster flew flags of embarrassment. "Why, Colonel — I — I —"

The owner of the Cross Bar B brushed aside the young man's stammering explanations.

"I don't care anything about your personal life. What I want to know is how reliable this girl is. What is she like?"

"She's right reliable, Colonel. As nice a girl as you'd ever meet in a dance-hall. Good-hearted and — and square."

"You know what was in that letter you brought Slim?"

"I didn't read it, but I know what was in her mind. She was plumb worried. I had to promise I'd get her letter into Slim's hands soon as I could."

"If she works for Meldrum, why is she so anxious to save Slim?"

"She doesn't like Dave. None of his girls do. When she figured out he had used her to help trap Slim, she felt awful bad. If you knew Lucy like I do, you'd understand. She's a good girl. Maybe that sounds funny to you, but it's so. She'll do to ride the river with, Lucy will."

"Unless she has you fooled," Corcoran said.

"She hasn't got me fooled," Buster denied stoutly. "She's all right."

Though Pike Corcoran was now a wealthy citizen full of responsibilities, and also a member of the church in good standing, there had been a time not so many years before when he had been a wild young buckaroo. Experience had taught him that character and respectability are not synonymous. A woman from a dancehall might have in her reservoirs of goodness and decency, and one riding in her carriage might be empty of everything but selfishness and vanity.

"Why did she write the other letter?" he asked.

"Dave told her it was a joke, that they were loadin' a young squirt who needed taking down," Eaton explained. "Afterward, when she thought it over, that didn't look good to her. She worked it out that Dave was fixing to rub out Slim."

"One thing is sure," Jim said. "The same person wrote both letters."

"Lucy finished writing the one I brought while I was in the room," Eaton said.

"Since that is so, there wouldn't be any sense to it unless it means just what it says," Jim pointed out.

Eaton was only a brush-popper and Pike Corcoran was one of the big men of the State, but Buster resented this suspicion and said so.

"I've ridden a heap of miles to bring you a message from a girl who risked a lot to send it. If this letter had fallen into the wrong hands, she would have been in trouble up to her neck. I'll tell you one thing, Slim. Sure as God made little apples Lucy sent me to save yore life. Far as I'm concerned, you can do as you damn please, except for one thing. You'll padlock yore tongues about having been warned by her."

Jim grinned his friendly smile at Eaton. "We'll sure do that, Buster. I'm satisfied it's the way you say, and when I get a chance I'll sure thank the lady for what she did. Don't get on yore ear, son. We've got to check up on any funny stuff Meldrum pulls off. We're where we daren't make any mistakes. This is war."

"That's all right with me," Eaton said. "All I'm saying is you can bank on Lucy all the way — just as far as you can on me."

"I'm satisfied, too," Corcoran said, patting Eaton's shoulder. "We're obliged to you, boy, and to your lady friend. Tell her if I can ever do anything for her, she can count on me." He drummed with his finger-tips on the table. "But there's one thing worries me some. Meldrum would go a long way to do me a meanness. This first letter is a threat against my daughter. Of course he wouldn't dare do her any harm, but he might annoy her."

Pike stopped, his jaw square and set. He was remembering that this villain had taken one of his daughters and ruined her life. Was there any possible way he could touch the other?

"Dave hates you like poison, but he couldn't do a thing against Miss Rose, not unless he has gone plumb crazy. This country wouldn't stand for it a minute." Buster spoke with blunt finality. Texans held women high.

True enough, Jim admitted to himself. But Meldrum must have sent the letter because he suspected Jim was in love with Rose. Since this was so, since Meldrum and the Gliddens felt they could strike at both their enemies through Rose, was it so impossible they might try to use her as bait to trap them, even though they had failed this time? It was ridiculous to suppose she was in actual danger, yet they might frighten her. Would it not be better to get her out of San Antonio to a place out of their reach?

After Eaton had gone he suggested as much to her father.

Pike was of that opinion himself. But he did not want to bring her to the Cross Bar B, where at any time there might be serious trouble. "I'll have Jack take her down to Tom Stuart's ranch near Laredo," he decided. "He will look after her till this flare-up has settled down."

So it was settled.

CHAPTER THIRTY-ONE

Jack Corcoran Gets Out Of A Buggy

From the wheels of the buggy rose a cloud of yellow dust. On both sides of the road mesquite stretched to the edge of the horizon. In places branches brushed against the side of the rig.

Rose grumbled a little to her cousin. She did not want to be shipped away where news would reach her only after a long delay.

"I don't see why I couldn't go to the Cross Bar B," she complained. "It's nice of Uncle Tom to ask me down there, but I'd rather be at home."

Jack Corcoran flicked the buggy whip close to the left ear of the right horse. "Uncle Pike figured you would be safer at the Stuart ranch," he said.

"Safer? Good gracious! Wasn't I safe enough at school? Who would bother me? I'm just a girl."

"You're Pike Corcoran's daughter," Jack mentioned. "Already Dave Meldrum has tried to use you to trap Slim. No knowing what he would do next. 'Course they wouldn't hurt you. We know that. But they might use you to get an advantage somehow. Anyhow, Uncle Pike didn't want you so near Dave."

"How do you mean he used me to trap Slim?" she asked.

Jack told her about the letter. Down the back of the girl a chill traveled.

"I worry all the time," she explained, in a low voice. "I keep getting afraid they will hurt Father — or someone — and do something terrible. Last night I woke up and couldn't sleep. I had dreamed the Gliddens had captured Jim Delaney and meant to torture him. It's horrible. Why don't the Rangers stop it?"

"Maybe they will soon," Jack said. "Lieutenant Brisbane told me yesterday they are waiting for something to break. He knows the Gliddens are rustlers and a bad outfit generally, but he hasn't got enough on them yet. They haven't had any luck lately. Though they started the fighting, they have always got the worst of it so far. The Rangers can't very well arrest them for getting their own men killed."

"First thing you know these men will kill Father — or Jim — or some of our friends," Rose said, a worried frown on her young face. "Isn't there any law? Do we have to wait until — until —"

Her sentence tailed out despairingly.

By way of comfort Jack assured her that both her father and Jim Delaney were pretty well able to look after themselves.

Out of the brush three men rode. They surrounded the buggy. Jack looked from their drawn revolvers into the masked faces with a heart that seemed to have been plunged into a lake of icy water.

"Get out of that buggy," one of the men ordered.

Jack hesitated, and played for time. "What do you want?" he asked. "I haven't got but about ten dollars with me."

He knew they did not want his money. Subconsciously he was telling himself that it would do no good to reach for a weapon. They would drill him through before his hand could travel six inches from the rein.

"Reach for the sky — and get out *pronto*," the spokesman commanded.

"No use us getting out," Jack argued. "I take it you are road agents, gentlemen. I'll give you every cent we have and you can let us go on."

The blue barrel of a forty-five was pushed nearer to Jack's head.

"Did you hear me? *Get out!* Or I'll let you have it and feed yore carcass to the buzzards."

Rose spoke, in a small, frightened voice. "Please get out, Jack. Maybe if I explain to these — these gentlemen —"

A strong arm reached in and plucked her from the buggy seat. She was lifted to the saddle in front of the rider. Another of the men disarmed young Corcoran.

Jack said quietly, driving down the panic in his breast: "You're piling up trouble for yourselves if you interfere with this young lady. Leave her out of it and do business with me."

One of the men ripped out a sudden furious oath.

"I've a mind to do business with you, fellow. You're a Corcoran. That's enough for me." The barrel of his revolver jerked toward Jack.

"Don't be a fool, Cole," another man cried urgently. "He's not in this."

Jack noticed that all three of the men were lanky, rawboned fellows, the last speaker thinner and gaunter than the others. That would be Lute Glidden.

"The whole tribe is in it," snarled the one called Cole. "What's the idea of us settin' back and lettin' them kill our boys while we do nothing about it?"

"Let me down!" cried Rose, struggling to free herself.

The horse carrying the double load danced nervously. Jack caught sight of a Circle G branded on the left shoulder. The long-legged rider steadied his mount.

"Be still, you little fool," he snapped at Rose.

To Jack crisply Luther gave an order. "Last call. Get out."

Young Corcoran got out, as if he had been released from a spring. From the step of the buggy he dived at the gaunt Glidden's throat. One arm went round the neck, the other closed on the protuberant Adam's apple. Both men went down into the dusty road, Luther head first. They struggled, Jack trying to get the gun. In the mix-up Luther Glidden's mask came off.

Jagged lightning flamed before Jack's eyes. He sank into unconsciousness.

"That'll hold him," Cole said with savage satisfaction. He had wiped Corcoran with the long barrel of his forty-five and he felt better.

"We'll light out before he comes to," Luther said.

They rode into the brush.

"Where are you taking me?" Rose wailed, in terror.

"Don't be scared," Luther told her. "We won't hurt you any. You'll be back with your friends inside of forty-eight hours."

He led the way, winding to and fro in the mesquite.

CHAPTER THIRTY-TWO

Colonel Corcoran Gives Orders

One of Corcoran's line riders dropped into the ranch house and reported to the boss. When he had finished telling about the fences and the stock, he added, almost casually, a bit of information.

"Funny thing, Colonel. I was camped on Hog Creek last night. The hound woke me with his barking. Three men and a woman were riding along the hillside about fifty yards from me."

"What time of night?"

"I'd guess around eleven o'clock."

"Sure it was a woman?"

"Yes, sir. The light wasn't any too good, and I wouldn't know any of them. But one sure was a woman."

"Did they stop and talk?"

"No, sir. Rode straight on, like they were ghosts. When I hollered they didn't answer."

"Queer," admitted Corcoran. "Where would a woman be going with three men at that time of night?"

"Search me."

Pike said, with a smile, “Sure you weren’t dreaming?”

“Dead certain,” the waddy said positively.

“Which way were they headed?”

“Northwest.”

“Oh, well! None of our business. I reckon even outlaws have wives . . . If you are going to comb the brakes below Hog Creek for those strays, better get Homer and Shorty to go with you.”

Two hours later Jack Corcoran rode in on a horse covered with lather. His face was drawn and his eyes haggard with anxiety. He flung himself from the saddle and ran into the house calling for his uncle.

Pike was down at the corral with Delaney examining a lame horse. At sight of his nephew’s face, he straightened abruptly.

“Rose! They’ve got her,” the young man blurted.

“Who?” asked her father, alarm in his rasping voice.

“The Gliddens. They held us up a little way out of town and took her with them.”

“And you let them take her?”

“They knocked me cold. When I came to they had gone.”

Pike Corcoran looked like a man with a mortal fear in his heart. He put a hand against the flank of the horse to steady himself.

Jim Delaney carried on with the questions. “How many of them?”

“Three. One was Cole Glidden. Another was Lute, I reckon.”

“How do you know?”

Jack told his story.

The Colonel broke in with a little cry. "Yorky saw them last night. On Hog Creek. They passed close to his camp."

Delaney crushed down the dread in his heart. He spoke with a crisp confidence he did not feel.

"They won't hurt her. They know better. This time they have passed the border line. We'll rouse the country and hunt them down. They'll be stomped out like rattlesnakes."

"They were going northwest," Pike said. "Heading for the home ranch. Get busy, boys. We'll tear them from their hole. Get horses — guns. Call in our riders."

The Cross Bar B woke to furious energy. Men caught, saddled, rode away to call in those who were out on duty with the stock or riding the line. One went to Eagle Pass to notify the sheriff, another to Uvalde with a letter from Jim Delaney to King Cooper. A third carried the news to a body of Rangers camped on Wolf Creek. Within a few hours the whole countryside would be seething. A sheep-herder reported that he had seen four riders at daybreak. They had been riding through the brush at a distance. He could not tell whether one of them was a woman.

Jim was of opinion that they would draw a blank at the Circle G. The Gliddens had made a bad mistake, one that might very well break them, but Sim was not fool enough to have taken their prisoner to the ranch. He would put up the bluff that this abduction was none of his doing or of any of his friends.

Beside the Colonel rode his nephew Jack and Jim Delaney. A man cantered down a draw waving a bandanna.

"What is it, Nelson?" shouted Pike as soon as the man was within hailing distance.

Word had reached Nelson of what had taken place and he came with news. He was a nester on Big Creek. Four riders had crossed the valley below his house not three hours ago. He was sure one of them was a woman.

Jim was surprised, and told his companions so. There was something queer about this affair. Three times the kidnappers had let themselves be seen since they had taken Rose. In a country such as this, with vast stretches of uninhabited brush, they ought to have been able to reach their destination unseen.

"The answer is they didn't," Pike said impatiently. He was not interested in theories. The one thing that obsessed his thoughts was the need to get Rose back safely.

Yet Jim persisted. "I'm wondering if there isn't a better answer," he replied. "These Glidden boys know this country. They didn't have to come within miles of Nelson's place. Why did they risk being seen — unless their idea was that they wanted someone to see them?"

"Why would they want anyone to see them?" the Colonel asked, the rasp of anxiety in his voice.

"That's what I'd like to know," Jim said. "What's in their minds? They're trying to fool us somehow. One thing is sure. They won't hurt Miss Rose. They daren't, and they wouldn't, anyhow. Why did they take her? For a ransom? I wouldn't think so. They are not that crazy. Why, then?"

"Does it matter why, since we know they did?" Jack asked.

"Sure it matters. They are not covering their tracks either. Do they want us to catch them? That doesn't make sense."

Jim could not work out the problem, but his mind continued to dwell on it.

By the time Corcoran's forces were ready to close in on the Circle G, the posse had swelled to more than thirty men. Sheriff Moore had cut across from Eagle Pass to join them.

If the Gliddens were not completely surprised by the avalanche of riders who swept down upon them, they gave a very good imitation of it. Sim, Mart, and Bill were sitting on the porch smoking. They vanished into the house and closed the door.

Pike flung himself from his horse and ran up the porch steps. He hammered on the door.

"Come out of there, you rats, and bring my daughter with you!" he shouted.

Sim had caught sight of the sheriff. "What's all this about, Moore?" he called from inside.

"You know what it's about, you dirty wolf!" roared Pike. "Come out of there, or we'll shoot you down like coyotes."

Sheriff Moore stepped forward. "First off, we want Miss Rose Corcoran, Sim," he said.

"What in Mexico you talking about?" Sim asked.

"We know she's here, and we mean to get her," Corcoran broke in angrily.

Sim flung open the door. "What crazy idea is this? She's not here. I don't know where she is. Far as I know I never set eyes on her. Is she lost?"

His brothers stood back of him. Both of them held revolvers in their hands. Sim apparently was unarmed.

"You'll tell me where she is, or I'll hang the whole caboodle of you," Corcoran threatened.

Jim was standing just back of his chief. He watched the three Gliddens, one after another. He was convinced they knew nothing about the disappearance of Rose. That looked reasonable to him. Hot-headed youth had been responsible for this crazy attempt at reprisal.

"You talk like a fool, Pike," Sim said. "Do you reckon we've gone plumb crazy just because you have? Even though your killers have been shooting down our friends, we Gliddens don't fight women. If the young lady has got herself lost, we'll help hunt for her."

Sim's voice was suave and conciliatory. He was talking really to the sheriff and the non-partisans, trying to make out a case for the Gliddens as injured parties. None the less, Jim thought he read in the man's heavy face a bewildered doubt. Young Delaney's guess was a shrewd one. This was the first that Sim had heard of the disappearance of Rose, but a wave of dread was drenching him. He remembered the conference in Meldrum's office at The Green Curtain. Cole had been very keen to trap Slim. It was possible that when the first plot failed, he might have done this fool thing. Sim knew his son well enough to be sure that he would not under any consideration injure Rose Corcoran. But if he had mixed himself up in an abduction, Texas would not ask what his intentions were. It would move to swift vengeance.

"Step out of there and give up those guns," Pike said harshly. "I'm searching the house, and I don't care whether I do it with you dead or alive."

The sheriff said hastily, to prevent bloodshed: "Don't push on the reins, Pike. I'm in charge here. We'll search the place, but there isn't going to be any shooting. You all had better surrender to me, Sim. I'll see you get protection."

"All right," Sim said quietly. "I'm not armed. Boys, give your guns to the sheriff. You can search the house and the whole ranch. The young lady isn't here and never has been. I don't know why you come to the Circle G looking for her."

"I'll tell you why, you damned wolf," Corcoran answered. "Because you're in this outrage up to your neck. You set your worthless sons on to kidnap my daughter, and now you're in trouble you stand there bleating innocence like a sheep. You've gone too far this time."

The stony, heavy-lidded eyes of Sim were expressionless . He asked a question. "Who says my boys kidnaped your daughter?"

Jack Corcoran answered him. "I say so. Your sons Cole and Lute and one other man. They were masked and held us up on the Laredo road."

“If they were masked, how do you know who they were?” Sim snapped.

“I had a rough-and-tumble with Lute and his mask came off. Before this one of them called Cole by his name.”

“Don’t believe a word of it,” Sim replied. “It’s a trick. First off, I don’t think the young lady is lost. If she is, my boys hadn’t a thing to do with it. Since your men began murdering us, Corcoran, you’ve got so you won’t stick at anything.”

Bill spoke up savagely. “You’ve got that killer Delaney with you now. That’s a dead giveaway.”

“We’ve nothing to hide,” Sim told the sheriff. “We’ll surrender to you if you’ll give us fair play.”

“You’ll get it,” Moore said.

He collected the guns from Bill and Mart Glidden.

The house was searched and no sign of Rose discovered.

Colonel Corcoran returned to the three brothers. His heart was filled with fear, his frozen face grim as the Day of Judgment.

“We’ll comb this place. I don’t expect to find her here. If we don’t, you’re going back to the ranch with me as my prisoner, Sim, and if any harm has come to her, I’ll shoot you down like a coyote.”

“I object to that,” Sim cried, appealing to the sheriff. “I’m your prisoner, not his. It’s a trap to rub me out, that’s what it is. I’ll not stand for it.”

“You’ll go back with me alive, or you’ll stay here dead,” Corcoran said, and stressed his words with an oath.

"You going to let him murder me, Moore?" Sim asked.

"No, nothing like that," the sheriff said stoutly.

But he was troubled. Corcoran's men outnumbered his three to one. He knew the Colonel would not let Sim Glidden out of his hands until Rose was found. The best he could get was a compromise.

"We want this thing cleared up," Moore went on. "I don't think Sim or his brothers had a thing to do with this. But we'll hold them prisoners until we know where we're at. I'll go along with them back to your ranch, Pike. They're *my* prisoners. Understand that."

Jim asked the Gliddens where the young men were. "I reckon they're all away at a camp meeting somewhere getting religion," he added.

"That's right, Sim," Moore said, "Where are the boys? This would be a fine time to give them an alibi if you can."

"How do I know where they are?" Sim replied, with irritation born of anxiety. "I don't ride herd on them. They might be at Eagle Pass, Uvalde, or anywhere else. You know how young fellows hell around, Moore."

Delaney drew Jack Corcoran and Buck Burris aside.

"Sim doesn't know any more about this than we do, looks to me," he said. "They pulled this off without consulting him, I'd say. If that's the case, they won't bring Miss Rose here."

Buck nodded. "My idea, too. I'm guessing Lost Park."

"Reasonable," agreed Jim. "They would have a safe line of retreat there, for if we came down the ledge road in force they could get away by the north entrance."

"Let's try the park," Jack proposed.

"Just the three of us," Buck said. "We'll travel faster that way."

They consulted with Corcoran. After a moment of consideration the Colonel approved.

"All right, boys. But be careful. Don't let these wolves get you."

"We won't," Jim promised. He added, "I'm expecting to bring Miss Rose back with us."

"I hope to God you do," her father said fervently.

The three young men rode to Eagle Pass, bought provisions, and took the trail.

CHAPTER THIRTY-THREE

A Hostage

Excitement filled the little town of Eagle Pass. Difficulties were common enough. The place was not unusually wild, but occasionally men passed out to the sound of roaring guns. Texas had not yet emerged from its turbulent early days to a state of law and order. But a good woman was as safe as she would have been in New England. The abduction of Rose Corcoran profoundly stirred the citizens. The storekeeper from whom Delaney and his friends bought supplies expressed the general feeling. "Those Gliddens have done torn it this time, sure enough," he said.

Jameson, of the Long Trail Corral, was equipping another posse. It was certain that very shortly the Rangers would get into action. No doubt King Cooper would set out with a posse from Uvalde.

The three young men rode out of town knee to knee.

From her doorway a woman called with vehement bitterness, "Get those wolves, Jack, and bring back Rose with you."

"Used to be my cousin's nurse," Jack explained to the others. "The Gliddens are certainly in trouble up to their hocks."

"They made a bad mistake when they left you to carry the news," Buck said. "After Lute's mask came off, there was nothing to do but put you out of the way."

"None of them knew I had seen him before," Jack answered. "The idea must have been to play like they were just a bunch of scalawags on the dodge. Probably they had an alibi fixed up to prove it couldn't have been them, don't you reckon?"

"Must have been drinking hard," Buck guessed. "Otherwise, they would not have been so crazy."

"I don't get it," Jim said, frowning down at his horse's ears. "There's no sense to the doggone thing. What did they take her for? They can't mean to hurt her — nor to hold her for a ransom. There's something else back of it. This business of letting themselves be seen three times. They're not plumb idiots. Must have done that on purpose. Why?"

"You tell us," Jack said. "It's like Buck says, crazy as a hoot owl. If they had been figuring a way to stop the clock of the Glidden outfit in this country, they couldn't have picked a better one than this. Say they were drunk and that they didn't expect to be recognized. Even so, it was dumb to take a chance when it couldn't get them a thing."

"They must have thought it would buy them something," Jim insisted. "If we only knew what."

They rode hard but carefully, resting their mounts whenever they thought it necessary.

It was after dark, by their campfire, that a possible answer to Jim's speculative search for a cause jumped to his mind.

"Could it be a trap they're springing on us, boys?" he asked suddenly.

"What kind of a trap?" Jack wanted to know.

"Say they fixed up a plot to seize Rose and hold her just long enough to stir us up. The plan might be to turn her loose then. Of course, she wasn't to know who they were. Maybe they balled that up by getting drunk. Anyhow, they want to toll us along, the way folks do hogs with an ear of corn, until they've got us where they want us. Then they expect to crack down on us and bump off a few Corcoran men. That would explain why they have been seen two-three times. They want to give us a line on where they are going."

"So half of Texas can follow them," Buck murmured ironically.

"They knew a few of us would get there first, on the jump. They could wipe us out and light out."

"Rose still being with them," Jack commented. "After they had massacred us they would still be up Salt Creek themselves."

Jim nodded. "That's the weak spot of my argument. They still have her with them, and by this time they would have had to turn her loose to play it safe."

"You must have been reading Deadwood Dick stories, Slim," Buck derided. "Still, part of what you say may be right at that. I would hate to wake up and find I was caught in a bear trap. The Gliddens are tricky. They've got something up their sleeves. Well, we'll see what we'll see."

They slept a quarter of a mile from the spot where their campfire had been. There was a chance someone might have been watching them, and they objected to being shot down while asleep.

As soon as the first faint streaks of light were in the sky, they were afoot. Breakfast finished, they took the trail for Lost Park again. Late in the afternoon, they looked down from the rimrock into the valley. Without waiting for night, they rode down the rock trail.

It would not have surprised them if they had been attacked before reaching the bottom. Riding down was a goosey business, since a challenge might boom out at them any moment. They rode well apart, scanning every boulder and shrub as they went.

Unmolested, without having seen a sign of any other human being, they dropped down into the park.

"Looks like we're barking up the wrong tree," Buck said in his gentle drawl. "I'd hate to travel this far to meet a lady and not find her."

They rode into the live oaks near the foot of the trail and drew up to consult.

"Look," cried Jack Corcoran, and his finger shot out to point at a rider.

A woman was coming up the little ridge toward them at a canter. Apparently she had caught sight of them and had turned aside to investigate.

Over Jim there swept a chill blast, the premonition of disaster. For this woman, tall and straight and dark, was not Rose Corcoran, but Abby Glidden.

She pulled her horse to a halt in front of them.

"What are you doing here?" she demanded sharply.

"We came to find Miss Corcoran," Buck said.

"Who?"

The amazement in her voice was unmistakable.

"Rose Corcoran," explained Jack curtly. "No use playing innocent. She was brought here by some of your family. We want her."

"Have you gone crazy?" she asked. "Why would they bring her here — or anywhere else?"

"How long have you been in the park?" Jim asked. His voice did not betray the growing conviction in him that they had been trapped to destruction.

"We came in last night, if that is any business of yours," Abby told him haughtily.

"How many of you?"

She answered angrily. "Four of us."

"You and three men?"

"Yes. What is this fool talk about the Corcoran girl?"

Jim turned to his friends. "Tricked us nice. This is the woman Nelson and the others saw."

"But where is Rose?" Jack asked.

"She is probably home by this time," Jim said. "All they needed her for was as bait to lure us here."

"I don't know what you're talking about," the girl said stormily. "You've got no right to be here. You had better ride out hell for leather. If my brothers find you here, you'll be sorry, I can tell you that."

"Some of them are liable to be sorry, too," Buck said, stroking his little mustache. "You can tell *them* that."

Corcoran swept a hand toward the trail down which they had ridden. "They're not losing any time, boys. Got it blocked already."

Three horsemen could be seen moving toward the foot of the trail.

"Watched us come in and lay doggo," Jim said. "Didn't want to attack us too soon for fear they might drive us back. Now they have us in a bottle with the cork jammed in the neck."

The girl's eyes flashed. "You'll get what's coming to you now for all the killing you've done," she cried.

Delaney needed information. He set out to get it. Indifferently he said, "I reckon we can hold up our end against the four or five men in the park."

"Four or five," she flung back, picking up his words swiftly. "We've got eight — nine — no, ten men here. You'd better throw down your guns and give up."

"You'd guarantee they would treat us well," Jim said ironically.

"As well as you deserve."

"Doesn't sound any too good for us," Buck mentioned. "No telling what we deserve. Who is in charge of your friends, Miss Glidden, if we decide to surrender?"

"I don't know. Brad or Cole, I reckon."

"So you didn't know you were brought along to lead us into a trap," Jim said, studying the girl.

"That's not true," she flared.

"We thought you were Miss Corcoran, and we came here to rescue her. Whoever fixed this up fooled us thorough."

"That's a lie. I wouldn't believe a word you said."

"When you see us laid out cold, you'll be glad to think you had a hand in it," Jim went on evenly.

"Lies — all lies!" she cried, eyes hot with anger.

"You'll get a good laugh out of it. I'll bet when you saw us riding down the ledge road, you chuckled plenty."

She tried to stare down Delaney's hard gaze and failed. As once before, she felt strange drums of excitement pounding in her blood. A weakness that she hated ran through her.

"I didn't see you coming," she broke out. "I wasn't expecting you. When you say anything different, you're not telling the truth."

Jim smiled grimly. "Then you'll be glad to help us out of the hole we're in." He ranged his horse up beside her mount. "I reckon you'll want to stay with us as a guest for a while till we're sitting high and handsome."

"I'll not stay with you a minute!" she cried. "I hate the whole mess of you."

"When you know us better, you'll get over that," Jim explained to her.

"I'm not going to know you better — ever," Abby retorted glaring at him.

She started to swing her horse away, but Jim caught the bridle. "I reckon you don't quite understand," he said. "They used you to get us in here. We'll use you to get out. Fair enough, isn't it?"

"How do you mean — use me?"

"You've heard of a hostage of war, I expect."

The angry color dyed her face. She cut at her horse with the quirt and it began to plunge. Jim clung to the rein. Furiously, she lashed at him.

"Get that quirt, Jack," Jim said; and to the horse, "Quit yore crow-hoppin'."

Corcoran tore the whip from the young woman and moved up on the opposite side of the animal. Between them the two men quieted the horse.

"Let me go!" ordered Abby, her face a map of rage.

"Not yet," Delaney snapped, and his eyes were hard as jade. "This isn't a courtesy game. You're going to stay with us to save half a dozen lives."

"Hiding behind a woman's skirt!" she flung out scornfully.

"Y'betcha! Just that. And glad to get one to hide behind." Jack Corcoran grinned amiably at her.

"That's the way the Corcorans fight," she charged contemptuously.

Jack's smile asked her to forgive. He had inherited the Southern attitude toward women. They were to be treated with chivalrous gentleness. He wanted her to know that, though he was backing the play of Delaney, it was only because her kinsmen had forced their hands.

"We won't do you a mite of harm," he promised. "Don't you be scared."

"I'm not afraid, but you are," the girl told him proudly.

"You wouldn't want yore brothers hurt, and long as you stay with us they won't be. We're playing the hand that's been dealt us. It's neck meat or nothing with us, you might say."

Jim laughed, without mirth. "They won't be hurt if they lay off us," he corrected coolly. "But we don't aim to be slaughtered, and if there's any killing done, we'll do our share."

Abby turned her hot, defiant eyes on his insolent, sardonic face. Some spark from him lit churning emotions she could not control — fear, hatred, anger, and a strange, passionate excitement. He seemed to her cold and implacable as fate, yet he set fires burning in her blood.

"All the killing so far has been done by you!" she cried tempestuously. "My father says you're the worst villain ever came into this country. You shoot down poor Mexicans trying to get back their stolen cattle. You rob and steal — and kill in cold blood. Billy the Kid was no worse than you. Now — when your devil-hatched chickens are coming home to roost — you whine about being trapped by the men you have injured. If my brothers . . . rub you out . . . it will be a good thing for this country. Good men will sleep in peace."

"Now you've got that off yore chest, we'll be moving," Jim said coldly. "I reckon we'll head for the other end of the park where the brush is thicker."

He turned the heads of his horse and hers. The others followed.

CHAPTER THIRTY-FOUR

On The Horns Of A Dilemma

Through San Antonio the rumor that Pike Corcoran's daughter had been abducted ran like a prairie fire driven by the wind. It came to Marie early. She went straight to police headquarters and asked if it was true. The officer in uniform hesitated.

"I'm the sister of Rose Corcoran," she told the sergeant at the desk imperatively.

At once he took her in to see his chief, a full-bodied, red-headed man whom he introduced as Wesley Harper.

The chief of police told her all he knew. Jack Corcoran had been taking Rose to the Stuart Ranch near Laredo and had been held up by three men who had forced Rose to ride away with them. The men were masked, but during the struggle one of the masks had fallen off and Jack had recognized the man as a Glidden. The Rangers had set out at once in pursuit. The chief thought there was no reason to be unduly alarmed. Even the Gliddens would not dare injure her.

Harper's assurance did not allay Marie's alarm. She went at once to the Travis Corral and learned that Jack had set out for the Cross Bar B to notify her father. The man in charge of the corral gave her Jack's home address.

Marie found Milly Corcoran at home. "I'm Marie," she told her cousin's wife. "I want to know about Rose."

"I've wanted to meet you," Milly said. "Please come in and sit down."

The actress followed Milly into the house, but did not sit down. She was anxious, and therefore as restless as a caged panther.

A brown-faced young cowboy who was in the parlor rose to meet her. Milly mentioned his name, Buster Eaton, by way of introduction.

"He is a friend of ours, and he came to tell Jack something he knows," Milly added. "He didn't know Jack had left for the ranch."

Marie lifted her tawny eyes to Buster.

"About the kidnapping of Rose?" she asked.

"Yes, ma'am. In a way." He turned his big dusty hat awkwardly in his hands. "I reckon I better start at the beginning."

He told her of Meldrum's trap to catch Jim Delaney and of how Lucy Page had frustrated the plot.

Swiftly Marie's mind moved. "Dave Meldrum is in this, too. I'll see him and make him bring Rose back."

"What about Lucy?" asked Buster. "If Meldrum finds out what she did, he'll sure make her pay for it."

Marie took a turn up and down the room, her lithe, graceful body more than ever suggestive of a panther's rippling muscles. She thought furiously.

"Yes, we've got to take care of her — get her out of town where he can't find her. Better bring her here if you can, Mr. Eaton. Tell her it's very important."

Buster nodded. "I'll do that."

"As quickly as you can, please. I'm worried. I want to move fast."

"Y'betcha, ma'am."

Within half an hour Eaton and Lucy Page rolled up in a hack. Buster was beaming, the young woman shy and not at all sure of her reception.

Marie thanked her warmly for what she had done and started to explain why she thought it necessary for her to leave town. She suggested Denver or St. Louis as a destination.

A little slyly, Lucy smiled. She looked at Eaton. The cowboy flushed beneath the tan. He began to roll his hat in his hands.

"Colorado, ma'am, but not Denver. It's this here way. I'm going up the trail on a drive for Shanghai Pierce to Trinidad. I got an uncle runs stock near there, and he's been pesterin' me to go in with him. I'm gonna take him up on that. Lucy starts for Trinidad on the train soon as I can get her to the depot. We fixed it up to get married soon as I reach there."

"The depot?" Milly asked.

"Trinidad." Buster looked at her reproachfully. "You know doggone well I didn't mean the depot."

"How long have you had this idea in your mind?" Milly asked, her eyes bright with interest.

"I've been milling it over considerable for quite a spell," Buster admitted. "But Lucy kinda hung back till she got this jolt today."

"I hope you make a good husband. If you do, you'll be happy yourself and make her happy," Milly told him.

"I don't aim to beat up on Lucy much," he laughed happily. "It wouldn't surprise me if I turned out one of these henpecked husbands."

Lucy smiled, but said nothing. Her heart sang with joy. The dead days would come to life. She expected their marriage to be a success. If it was not, the fault would not be hers.

After the proper felicitations, Marie asked a pertinent question.

"Have you money enough for the journey and to take care of yourself until Mr. Eaton gets to Trinidad?"

"Yes. I'll get a job in some restaurant when I get there," Lucy said.

Half an hour later, Milly, Marie, and Buster stood on the station platform waving handkerchiefs at a departing train.

Marie lost no time. She sent a message to Meldrum that she wanted to see him at once. The negro boy who had carried the note returned to report that Meldrum had said he was too busy to come.

Ten minutes later, the boy was on his way with a second note. It said, bluntly:

If you don't come immediately, I shall raise the town against you. I can prove you are back of the kidnapping of Rose. I give you twenty minutes to get here.

Inside of the twenty minutes Meldrum was knocking on the door of the Jack Corcoran house. Milly admitted him.

The gambler bowed to Milly and again with ironical deference to the woman who had been his wife. Eaton he ignored.

"I must have misunderstood you, sweetheart," he jeered. "Last time we met you mentioned that you never wanted to see me again."

Marie looked steadily at him. "Where is Rose?"

"Alas, I don't keep up with my in-laws as well as I should," he said. "There's a story that she is flying around the country with some wild young bloods. I hope it isn't true."

"You had better know where she is," Marie told him rigidly. "Or I'll see that you are lynched before night."

The mockery left his face as the light does a snuffed candle. "What do you mean? Have you gone crazy?" he asked harshly.

"I mean that you had a letter written about Rose that will hang you to a live oak before dark if you don't bring her back to me."

He frowned, trying to make out what she could possibly mean. Then he remembered, with a heart drenched cold, the letter Lucy had prepared at his dictation. Yet they could not know his part in it, not unless someone had betrayed him. He tried a bluff.

"I don't know what you are talking about."

"I am talking about the letter you had Lucy Page write to Slim Delaney," Marie said, her eyes never leaving his face.

He shook his head. "I always thought you were daft."

At a nod from Marie, Buster Eaton took the floor.

"No use puttin' on, Mr. Meldrum. Lucy figured it all out and sent a letter by me warning Slim not to come. We've got both letters."

"You can't prove I had a thing to do with it," Meldrum blustered.

"You forget Lucy. I'll have to warn you that Lucy has left The Green Curtain. We have her hidden where we can produce her when we want her."

Meldrum looked him over insolently. "So you're in this plot, too, you lunkhead."

Buster knotted his big fists to keep them away from the butt of his gun. He owed this scoundrel something on Lucy's account and he would have liked to pay it.

"I'm in it, all the way," he said, with slurred voice. "Any remarks?"

Meldrum turned his attention back to Marie. "You've taken to blackmail, have you? Well, I won't stand for it a minute. I don't know where your sister is. Probably it's a slick trick Corcoran and that side-kick of his Delaney are trying to pull on me. I see you've gone back into the fold. It will make lovely slush, all about the black sheep welcomed home again."

"Never mind about what I've done or am going to do," Marie said quietly. "This is your funeral, unless you do as I say."

"Why is it?" he demanded. "Say I had Lucy write that letter to trap the killer who has become a menace to this country. That doesn't prove I meant to do your sister any harm. I'm not a plumb fool. I've got more sense than that."

Marie's smile had in it neither warmth nor friendliness. "No, it doesn't prove it, but you know as well as I do that the good people of San Antonio won't ask for complete proof. The letter shows you had it in mind to do her harm — that you were thinking about it."

"Go ahead, then," he retorted. "We'll see about that. Maybe you can destroy an innocent man and maybe you can't."

He turned to leave the room.

Marie stopped him with a lift of the hand. "Just a moment. If you go out of that door now, you'll be a dead man before night. We'll cry our story all up and down Commerce Street and on the plazas."

The gambler stopped. What she said was quite true. If Lucy betrayed him publicly, that cursed letter would be enough to damn him. No mob bent on lynching, with the lust of blood in their nostrils, would take his word against hers. He had not even threatened the Corcoran girl, but the mind of the man in the street would jump that hurdle easily to a conviction that he had organized this kidnapping. It would not be true, but he would be just as dead as if it were.

"What do you want me to do?" he asked sullenly.

"I want you to guide Mr. Eaton and others chosen by him to the place where Rose has been taken."

"I don't know where she has been taken. I hadn't a thing to do with this. Not a thing. I'm as innocent as you are."

Marie lifted scornful eyebrows. "With your friends the Gliddens in it?"

"You don't know they are in it."

"I do know it. My cousin Jack knocked the mask off one of them."

"That's probably another lie fixed up by him and Pike to ruin me."

"It's no lie, but it will ruin you all right," Eaton said, with manifest satisfaction.

"If some of the Gliddens did this fool thing, it doesn't follow that I was in it with them," Meldrum said uneasily. "They don't ask me what to do."

"You've always been hand in glove with them," Marie told him sharply. "If you don't know where she is, you can find out."

"How can I find out?" he asked irritably.

"I don't know. I don't care. But you can. I'm not asking you a favor. I'm telling you what to do."

"You're backing me into a corner with a gun," he said, anger and resentment in his voice. "That's what you're doing. Why drag me into this? I've told you a dozen times I don't know anything about it."

"And I've told you that you had better find out — soon." In her eyes was the feminine ferocity one sometimes sees in a wild beast at bay with her young.

"You always were a little devil," he said bitterly.

Meldrum was in a hole, one from which he could find no safe escape. He knew nothing about this kidnapping. He doubted very much if Sim Glidden had planned it. More likely young Cole, his brothers, and his cousins had pulled it off. There was a crazy recklessness about it that suggested impetuous youth. From the location of the holdup he could guess where Rose Corcoran had been taken. A rendezvous existed near Horse Crossing where the Gliddens had been wont to cache wet stock. The place was hard to get at and was known to few. The chance was better than a fifty-fifty one that the girl might be found there.

But Dave Meldrum knew that if he led a posse to this cache, it would probably mean a complete break with the Gliddens. They would regard it as a betrayal and no explanations would clear him. Without their support he could hardly carry on in San Antonio, and instead of allies they would be active enemies.

He was on the horns of a dilemma. A choice had to be made. In her passionate attachment to her younger sister, Marie would not hesitate a moment to throw him to the lions. That was the more immediate danger. Perhaps he could talk himself out of the other; or perhaps something might occur to avert it.

"I'll do what I can," he said sullenly. "I can't promise to find her because I don't know where she is. But I'll do my best." The gambler turned angrily on Eaton. "Get together your posse, fellow, and don't lose any time. I'll meet you in forty minutes at the Travis Corral."

He swung away abruptly and strode out of the house.

CHAPTER THIRTY-FIVE

Cole Glidden Keeps A Promise

From back of a rise a voice came to the riders.

"Hello, Abby!"

Instantly Abby called an answer. "'Lo, Cole!"

The three men closed about her horse. They drew up and waited, rifles in hand. A rider cantered over the brow of the hill and came toward them.

"That's far enough," Buck ordered.

Cole Glidden pulled up his horse abruptly.

"The Corcorans have got me!" Abby shouted to him.

"Tit for tat," explained Delaney cheerfully. "We're doing a little kidnapping on our own account."

"You turn my sister loose right now, or —"

Cole did not finish his threat. He could not think of any conclusion dire enough.

"Don't think it for a moment," Jim said, raising his voice just enough to carry across the intervening forty yards. "We're keeping the lady with us till we get out of the park. You brought her here to trick us. Go back and tell yore friends if they want to bring a woman into this, two can play at that game."

Cole sat his horse, silent, motionless. The urge was in him to challenge the Corcoran riders to battle instantly. But he was checkmated. He could not lift a hand while they held Abby prisoner in their midst.

"Come out of there, you Delaney," he finally cried. "Don't hide behind a woman, you yellow coyote. Ride to one side and fight it out with me."

"No!" the girl cried swiftly.

Jim paid no attention to her sharp protest. "What would that buy us?" he asked. "I'm not interested in killing you. I had my chance to do that once and didn't take it. We came to the park to get the girl you kidnapped. Where is she?"

"Don't know a thing about that. I'm telling you to let my sister go."

"We'll make a deal," Jim told him. "Take us to the north gateway of the park, and soon as we're on that trail we'll turn the lady over to you."

After a moment Cole said, "That's a trade."

He rode cautiously toward them, watching to make sure that none of them made a move to lift their weapons. The five riders started down a draw. Jim and Buck kept pace with Abby, one on each side of her.

"What's this lie they're telling about you boys kidnapping the Corcoran girl?" Abby flung out at her brother.

"Brad heard something about that from a nester over Uvalde way," Cole said glibly. "We figure the Corcorans have hidden her somewhere to put the blame on us. That's the kind of a trick they would do."

Jack Corcoran looked at him, with rising anger. "You wanted to kill me, and yore brother wouldn't let you do it. He called you Cole."

"Sure," young Glidden said, with an uneasy laugh. "That's an old trick, using false names in a holdup."

The black eyes of Abby flashed over her brother. She wished she felt more sure the charge was false.

"Of course," she cried impatiently. "They would never have used his name if it had been Cole."

"I wrastled with Lute Glidden, dragged him from his horse, and knocked off his mask," Jack said to the girl. "I had seen him once at Eagle Pass, but I don't reckon he had ever noticed me."

"You made a mistake, Cole, in not bumping off the witness," Buck said in his gentle, mocking voice. "Not your fault. Blame Brother Lute for that. Likely that error will hang all of you."

"Where did you take Rose Corcoran?" Jim snapped at the dark, sullen young man who had joined them. "Who is with her now?"

"I didn't take her anywhere," Cole answered sulkily. "You Corcorans fixed up this story to get us in bad. I'll bet she's right in Santone with her friends this very minute, or else hidden out where you want her to be."

"You wouldn't stop at any trick to do us a meanness," Abby broke out explosively, her dark gaze on Jim.

The insolent eyes of Delaney met the stormy ones of the girl. "I've a notion, boys, that the young lady isn't in this skullduggery," he drawled. "She's either an innocent bystander or a doggoned good actor. I wouldn't be sure which, but I'm giving her the benefit of the doubt."

Abby flung away restraint and poured on him a flood of invective.

Her brother ordered her to shut up. "We can do any cussin' of this scalawag that's necessary without the women of the family bustin' loose," he reproved. "That's no way for a lady to talk, and you know it."

They moved into the brush and worked toward the upper end of the park. Cole guided the party. He led them past the ruins of the burnt cabin where Benson and Ransom had been killed.

"Take a good look at the place," Cole suggested vindictively. "That's where two of you ambushed Bert and Stub — shot them down while they weren't looking."

Buck looked at Jim. "Think I'll tell him how that was, Slim."

"Might as well," Jim agreed. "Not that he'll believe it."

Leaving Abby's name out of the story, Buck told the tale of how the two men in the cabin had shot each other to death.

Harshly Cole laughed. "You're right, Delaney. I don't believe a word of it."

"Nor I," echoed Abby. "What would they quarrel about?"

Jim turned his ironic smile on her. "I wonder," he said, almost in a murmur.

They came to a rock face built in the shape of a flatiron. Cole swung around it and pushed through a tangle of mesquite. From this a trail ran up a kind of trough filled with rubble.

"There you are," Cole said. "I've done what I promised."

Jim caught in his eye a flicker of triumph and did not understand it. This was the trail. There could be no doubt of that.

"I reckon maybe you'd better speed the parting guests on their way," Jim said derisively. "Ride up with us to the top to make sure one of our horses doesn't fall and bust a leg."

"No, sir. I told you I would show you the trail. You said you would turn my sister loose if I did."

"That's right, Slim," corroborated Jack.

"I'd like to make sure we're on the right trail," Jim said. He turned to the girl. "You wouldn't mind riding a little way farther a nice day like this, would you?"

His mockery always infuriated her. "I won't go another foot!" she cried.

She whirled her horse and plunged into the mesquite.

"Hold this fellow!" Jim cried. "I'll get her."

He dashed into the brush after Abby. She was twenty yards ahead of him when they rounded the rock wall, and she was going like the wind. To him there came the sound of shots.

Jim pulled up abruptly. He had no time to run down her horse even if his mount had the speed. Back on the trail he might be needed. Someone crashed through the mesquite fifty yards to his right. Cole Glidden making his getaway probably.

When Jim caught sight of his friends, the day went suddenly chill for him. Jack's horse was down, shot through the head. Buck Burris was clutching at his shoulder.

"Hit bad?" Jim asked.

"Might be worse," Buck answered. "That fellow showed us up. He did all the damage before we got a crack at him. I see you didn't get the girl. Just as well."

"We'll look at that wound and fix you up so you can travel," Jim said. "Those fellows will be on our tail soon as word reaches them. Have to take turn about riding double. We sure made a bad job of this. Right at the last I saw that bird had something on his mind."

While Jim was dressing Buck's wound, Jack shot his horse to put the animal out of its misery.

"In the shoulder and not into the lung," Jim said to Buck. "That's good. Expect it will hurt like sixty after a while. Wish we didn't have to jolt you over sixty miles of rough country."

Buck shrugged. "I have to take what's been handed me. It's only a clean flesh wound. The bullet went right through. Don't you worry about me. I can travel all right."

"Travel where?" Jack asked.

He was looking up the trail at the cliffs above them. Two men were standing on a rock gazing down. Jim lifted his eyes to the place where Jack was pointing a finger.

The reason for that gleam of triumph in Cole Glidden's eyes was apparent now. He had led them to the foot of the trail, but he had known all the time that it was blocked.

The spiteful whine of a bullet whistled past their ears.

"We'd better get out of here into the brush," Buck said.

They lost no time in hunting cover. Plunging into the mesquite thicket, they pushed through it to the park.

"Where do we go from here?" Buck asked, grinning ruefully.

"About half a mile below here there's a boulder field close to the wall," Jim said. "There's a spring there, Buck. Don't you remember? Better hole up there, I reckon."

"Good as any place, I dare say," Buck agreed. "We're going to have a whole passle of bees stinging us pretty soon anywhere we go."

That was true enough. Ten minutes ago they had been riding pretty, or so at least they thought. The road out of the park was open for them. Once more they had scored off the Gliddens. Now the situation was completely reversed. They were caught like rats in a trap.

CHAPTER THIRTY-SIX

In The Firing Zone

All day the firing of the guns had echoed from the rock wall across the park. The sound of it had shaken Abby's nerves. There was nothing she could do about it. She had begged from Cole and Luther and Brad in turn for these men's lives, and they had waved her petitions aside as of no moment. They had their foes cornered and meant to make an end of them. Young Jeff would like to arrange some compromise, she felt sure, but he was only a boy, and his wish had little weight against the implacability of the others.

Time and again Abby had ridden to the farther end of the park in the hope that the booming of the rifles would not reach her. Distance only increased her anxiety. She found herself listening with strained attention. There would be silence for many minutes, then perhaps a single shot, or half a dozen in quick succession, like the popping of a bunch of firecrackers.

The stillness tortured her. The explosions set her heart fluttering with fear. Each time she wondered if that was the end. Unable longer to bear the uncertainty, at last she would gallop back to the spot where three men were fighting for their lives against a dozen.

For more than twenty hours the battle had continued. After the defenders had taken their stand among the big rocks, their enemies had formed a half-circle around them so as to make escape impossible. Just before dark there had been one wild rush to storm the rocks. The Gliddens had been driven back with two men wounded.

At break of day the sniping had started. Gradually the ring of attackers had worked closer, taking advantage of all the cover that offered. But they had paid for their gains. Brad was wearing his arm in a sling, a red bandanna supporting it. He had stopped a bullet from Jack Corcoran's Winchester just after dawn. His uncle Mart had been shot in the foot and had done a good deal of swearing about it, though he returned to his place in the firing line after Abby had bound up the wound. Whether any of the trapped men had been hit since Cole had struck Burris's shoulder, the girl did not know.

But the end was inevitable. In imagination she saw the hour when the victors would move in to look down on the three lifeless bodies, and the thought of it was a knife in her heart. Always she had known the men of her family were hard and ruthless. She was fierce and wild herself. The Glidden lawlessness had brought them to this, a day of grim vengeance she would never be able to forget.

It was horrible to think of the lithe, graceful figure of Slim Delaney, so captivating in its debonair ease, lying lax and stricken in the dust, the sardonic face staring with unseeing orbs into the blue sky above. It was terrible to know that the insolent, mocking eyes which stirred in her strange fires might soon be no longer quick with life. That she was in love with this man she hated, she could not disguise from herself.

Inside, she was a river of woe. Unwittingly she had drawn Delaney and his companions here. She had always wanted to come to Lost Park and when her brother Cole had offered to bring her, she had been delighted. Not until she had met the doomed men yesterday did she know why she had been brought.

She rode back to the battlefield, dismounted, and dropped the reins of Black Hawk. Through the brush she crept forward to a little hollow where her brother Cole had been lying two hours earlier. The place was empty. The empty shells showed where he had been. Abby guessed he had slipped closer to the rock fortress at the foot of the park wall.

In the sand she picked up his tracks. He had slipped into the brush to the left, creeping on hands and knees. Abby followed, her heart thumping fast. This was the deepest she had been in the firing zone. Through the mesquite she caught a glimpse of the rockpile which concealed the defenders. From it came a puff of smoke and the crack of a rifle.

She could see Cole now. He had dug in back of a black jack. So silently did she come on him that he jumped round with an oath.

Angrily he demanded what she was doing here.

"I can't stay away," she told him piteously. "Don't go on with it, Cole. Don't kill these men."

"Doggone it, haven't you got a lick of sense?" he exploded. "First thing you know you're liable to get shot here. Why for do you come bustin' in when it's none of yore business? Someone ought to wear out a hickory on you."

"It's got to stop," she said, and her face was wan with distress. "This is murder. That's what it is."

"You're crazy," he told her. "This Delaney is the gunman who has been killing our friends. Burris was with him when he bumped off Bert Benson and Stub Ransom. They're a bad bunch, but we've got them right at last, and we aim to finish the job we've started . . . You get outa here and stay in the other end of the park. Hear me?"

A bullet whistled past them and cut a leaf from the black jack. Cole dragged his sister down into the hole.

"You crazy little fool! See what you've done. One of 'em saw you. Like enough you'll get hit before you get away."

"I don't care if I do!" she cried wildly, and suddenly gave way to collapse into violent sobs.

"If you're so scared, why did you come?" Cole asked, much exasperated. "Stop that yowling and scrouch down here. I'll get you out of it, you doggone little fool."

"Why don't you stop it, Cole?" she begged. "Some of you will get killed — you or Lute or Uncle Mart or someone."

"I can tell you who'll get killed," he said callously. "That bull rattle up there in the rocks — him and his friends too . . . We'll wait awhile before we work back in the brush outa here."

"All right. If you won't, you won't."

The sobs of Abby subsided. An idea had come to her. It was a wild and crazy one, maybe, but there was a chance it might succeed. At any rate, it would postpone the hour of the defenders' last stand.

CHAPTER THIRTY-SEVEN

In The Rocks

The big boulders had broken off from the cliff above more than a million years ago. They had crashed down pell-mell upon one another, so that the position was ideal for defense.

Jim and his friends were not huddled together, but were stationed about twenty yards apart, Buck in the center and the others on his right and left. Communication was easy by a passage back of the boulders.

Buck's shoulder pained a good deal and he was running a fever. He made no complaint, but his grin was a little tighter than usual. He was close to the spring. Frequently he bathed his neck and face with cold water.

All three of the men at bay knew that unless help came from outside they were doomed, but they intended to make the best possible fight of it. Occasionally they called back and forth remarks more or less cheerful and jocose. They had scored four hits to date, or perhaps five, and each one was the cause of public jubilation. In their conversation all of them assumed that they were going to get out of this alive.

A bullet had creased Jack's forehead. Another had ricocheted from a rock and struck Jim in the arm, but with so little force as scarcely to break the skin. So far they had been lucky.

An hour would pass without a shot being fired, then for a time there would be almost a fusillade. Even during the lulls they exposed themselves as little as possible.

It was during one of the periods when the sniping was the liveliest that Jack let out an exclamation of warning.

"Look out, boys! Someone coming licketty split," he yelled. A moment later he added: "Good God! It's a woman."

She came out of the brush, her skirts gathered, running fast. When she reached the rocks she began clambering over them, moving straight toward the three beleaguered men.

The firing died.

Someone from the brush cried out, "Come back, you crazy fool!"

Cole Glidden left cover and cut across the open to intercept her. He was too late. For a moment he hesitated, as if about to follow her into the boulder field, but a bullet from Jim's rifle struck within a yard of his feet. To advance farther would be suicide. He shook his fist in their direction, cried out an oath, and scudded back to shelter. None of those among the rocks fired at him as he retreated.

Abby dodged in and out among the boulders. She was carrying a bucket. For a little they lost sight of her.

When she reappeared, it was just below the pile where the Cross Bar B men were hidden.

She lifted her face toward them and asked a question.

"How do I get up from here?"

"Swing round that big rock to the left," Jack told her.

Abby did as directed. Using some broken boulders as stepping-stones, she crossed a natural stile and came down into the runway connecting the posts of the three men.

She looked at Corcoran, at Burris, and then at Delaney.

"I've brought you some food," she said. "I thought maybe you might be hungry."

They stared at her in astonishment. She had run a gauntlet of fire to bring food to those for whom she held a lusty hate.

Buck said gently: "That was right foolish, Miss Glidden. You might have been shot before we noticed you were a woman."

Ironically Jim smiled. "If you'd only beat the triangle, we would have come out for dinner and saved you the trouble of bringing it," he said.

His sarcasm passed Abby unnoticed. Fear and anxiety had been so present with her for many hours that her mind had no room for anything else.

"You aren't hurt?" she asked, her eyes still on Delaney.

"Hurt? Why, no! What made you think we might be hurt? We're just picnicking in the rocks." Jim drawled it out with bitter derision. "Jack is playing pirate. That's why he is wearing that bandanna round his head. Buck is in the game, too."

"You'd better move one way or the other, Miss," Jack said. "Where you stand yore head can be seen by some of them. They might make a mistake."

Abby moved toward Jim. "They have sent men up by the north trail to the cliffs above to shoot down at you," she said. "I came to warn you."

"We've been wondering when they would think of that," Buck mentioned. "How long ago did they send them?"

"About half an hour."

"That ought to give us an hour yet," Jack guessed. "After that we'll have to lie mighty low." He looked at Jim, for information. "What about Miss Glidden?"

"I'm going to stay here," she announced definitely. "They won't shoot at you while I'm in the rocks."

"Do you figure on spending the rest of yore life here?" Jim asked. "Or is it yore idea to go out and forage food for us once in a while?"

"I don't know. I couldn't stand it any longer." Abby's big eyes were fastened on Jim. They betrayed shamelessly her secret.

Young Delaney felt his pulses hammering. His cynicism was a fraud. The thing she had done set excitement strumming in his blood. He knew she had come to save him if she could.

"Got to get back to my post," he said abruptly. "Yore friends may be getting busy."

He moved to his place. Abby followed him. An out-jutting mass of quartz shut them off from sight of the other men.

Through a loophole he swept the mesquite valley just below.

"Do you see any of them?" Abby asked.

"No. They keep out of sight."

"Let me look."

"You stay down there," he told her roughly.

"Yes," she said obediently.

It was strange, this change that had come over her. Through the countryside she was known for her heady willfulness. She had followed her own lawless impulse. No man had ever restrained her, except her father on rare occasions. Now she was taking orders meekly from a man who still at times stirred in her passionate resentment. The anxious hours had taken their toll of her pride. She was just now chastened and subdued.

The space between the rocks was narrow. There was room for the two of them and no more. Jim paid as little attention to her as possible, but he was acutely aware of her presence. She could not move without brushing against him. If he turned, his eyes looked into hers and he found gifts in them that set fires blazing in him. She was elemental and knew none of the arts of concealment.

"We're crowded here," he said bluntly. "There's more room farther over."

Immediately she left him. That he had hurt her feelings he guessed. He wanted to call her back and show that he was friendly, but he did not do so. To have her so near him was disturbing. She had the vital beauty and grace of a wild young forest creature. Jim Delaney was no ascetic. The hot youth in him responded imperiously to the call she made on him.

CHAPTER THIRTY-EIGHT

You Doggoned Old Trouble-Hunter

A man waving a piece of white cotton cloth emerged from the brush. Abby offered her handkerchief to Jack. He stood on a rock and held it up. The man below moved forward into the boulder field.

"It's my brother Lute," Abby announced.

Jim let the envoy come to within easy talking distance before he stopped him.

"You can talk from there right comfortably," he said.

"I want to talk to my sister first," Luther said.

"Go ahead. Nobody is preventing you."

"Come out where I can see you, Abby," her brother ordered.

Abby climbed on a rock and stood beside Jim.

"I'm ashamed of you, girl," Luther reproved. "No right-thinking young woman acts the way you're doing. It ain't modest for a girl to go throwing in with a bunch of strangers. You'll get a bad name through the country if you don't look out. You got no right to throw your own family down for these Corcorans. Folks will sure talk."

"What will they say — that I'm the sister of a lot of killers who used me to trap the men they couldn't get the best of any other way?" she asked waspishly.

"You know doggone well what they'll say — that there must be something between you and this scalawag Delaney or you wouldn't be so anxious to protect him from what he has earned. A girl must look after her good name, Abby. Now you come along back with me and we won't say any more about it."

"And what about these three men, Lute?"

"That's our business, girl, and we'll 'tend to it without any help from you," he told her brusquely.

"Then I'll stay here."

Luther lost his patience. "Goddlemighty, girl, you can't stay with an outfit of strange men. Haven't you got any decency? We're your kinfolks, and we'll look after you."

"You looked after me fine when you brought me here as a decoy for the men you wanted to kill," she flung at him bitterly. "I'm not going with you. I'll stay here till I know these men are safe."

"But it's not right," argued Luther. "It's scandalous. That's what it is. Dad will wear you to a frazzle for this."

That was possible, since Sim had the Glidden unruly temper. But it was more likely she would be punished some other way.

"That will be his business and mine," Abby retorted.

Luther appealed to Delaney. "Fellow, I don't like you any better than I do a sidewinder. But if you have a lick of sense, you know you're only making it worse by letting her stay with you. We've got you dead to rights, and we'll clean up on you sure."

Jim grinned maliciously. "I'm only a strange man. I wouldn't have more influence with her than a loving brother."

"If you're white men you don't want a girl mixed up in this," the lank Glidden urged. "You're game enough to take what's coming to you, ain't you?"

"We didn't mix any young lady up in it," Jim countered. "You did that. You mixed two in it. As to yore sister, it's not our fault she has been brought up so badly she won't stand for cold-blooded killing."

Dark anger boiled up into Luther's face. "You're a nice guy to talk about cold-blooded killing after what you did to Benson and Ransom."

"If you're quite through —"

Once more Luther tried to persuade his sister. "Be reasonable, Abby. There's no sense in acting thisaway. It's not the proper way to do, dadgum it."

"The proper thing would be for me to leave here and let you murder these men," she cried scornfully. "Well, I won't do it. No use talking any more."

"What's that?" Jack cried, and pointed to a cloud of dust in the chaparral. "It's a bunch of horsemen heading this way."

All of them turned to look. He was right. A compact body of riders could be seen moving through the brush.

Luther ambled back on a long-legged lope to his friends. It was time to be getting out in a hurry. Those holding the rocks dropped back to cover. From their points of observation they saw the newcomers open out and sweep through the mesquite.

The crack of guns sounded. Men shouted hoarsely one to another. Riders scudded in and out of the brush, dodging out of the net spread for them.

"The Gliddens are heading for the north trail!" Jack cried excitedly. "One of 'em is down. He's up again and has grabbed his horse."

The firing continued intermittently. It would die away, and then another shot would sound. Jim drew a bead on a galloping rider. Before he could fire, his rifle was pushed violently aside.

Abby had flung herself at the barrel. She was white to the lips.

Jim nodded. "That's right," he said gently. "They are yore kin."

"We'd better be moving down from here," Jack suggested. "The fracas is about over."

A man on horseback rode out of the brush to the edge of the boulder field and waved at them.

"It's King Cooper," Jim said, and he let out a glad shout.

Five minutes later Cooper shook hands with him. "You doggoned old trouble-hunter," he drawled.

"How did you find yore way into the park?" Jim asked.

"Charley Pierce guided us. He's on my posse. Half a dozen Rangers are with us."

"Anybody hurt?"

"One Ranger killed, another wounded. We've captured two or three of the Glidden gang and killed one. A fellow called Hatcher. I reckon this business will spell good night for the Gliddens." He turned a quizzical eye on Jim, nodding toward the rocks above. "Who is your lady friend, Slim?"

"Abby Glidden. She ran up here an hour ago to stop them from firing at us."

King showed surprise. "That was right clever of her," he said.

"Has anything been heard of Rose Corcoran?" Jim asked.

"Yes, she came home." Cooper added dryly, "You'd never guess who found her."

"Then there wouldn't be any use trying."

"Your friend Dave Meldrum."

Jim stared. "Meldrum?"

"That's the name of the gent. Haven't heard particulars yet. Maybe he was scared. He'd better be if he was in this skullduggery."

The captured Gliddens were Brad, Cole, and Luther. They sat together, guarded, sullen, and silent. When Abby walked over and tried to talk with them, they turned upon her in bitter anger.

It was decided by King Cooper and the Ranger sergeant that the party should be divided for the home trip. Part of them would push on down to Eagle Pass with the prisoners, the rest would follow more slowly, bringing the wounded with them. Abby Glidden and Jim Delaney went with the advance guard.

Abby rode with her relatives, though they treated her as if she were responsible for the disaster that had befallen them. All day she was very low in spirits. Her father would probably blame her for the stand she had taken. Moreover, she knew that her infatuation for Jim Delaney could bring her no happiness. From what her brother had told her, she guessed he was in love with Rose Corcoran.

After supper Jim fixed blankets for her a little way from the others. She watched him silently.

"Anything more?" he asked, after he had finished.

"Nothing," she said, in a small voice bleak with despair.

Jim felt immensely sorry for her and greatly drawn to her. He straightened the blankets a little so as not to look at her.

"You're getting a bad break," he said gently.

"Does it matter?" she broke out. "I'm only a Glidden, and besides — I'm a fool."

"It's the kind of foolishness a man could . . . think a heap of you for," he murmured.

"If he wasn't too busy thinking a heap of another girl," she said bitterly.

There was nothing he could say to that — nothing that would comfort her. But he had to say something. He rose and took her hands in his.

"Some day you're going to love a man who will think all the world of you," he told her.

"Am I?" she flung at him. "It's nice of you to say so."

"It's true. And this won't amount to a hill of beans then."

She made a prophecy. "I'm never going to see you any more, unless it's after you have married that other girl. You're going away from me. Do you think I don't know it?"

"Maybe. I don't know about that. But you may be right. I wouldn't be welcomed by yore father and brothers, would I? But I'll say this. If I live to be a hundred, I'll never forget you — never. There is nobody else in the world like you."

"But you like that Corcoran girl better," she said drearily.

Then, with passionate ferocity, she threw her arms round his neck, held him savagely tight, and kissed him again and again.

Her hands fell away from him. She dropped her head and turned it aside. "Please go away," she begged in a voice ready to break.

Jim walked out to the *remuda*, as if to take care of his horse. He did not want the other men to see his face yet.

CHAPTER THIRTY-NINE

Lock, Stock, And Barrel

Lieutenant Brisbane of the Rangers was talking to an audience that listened intently to every word. Those present included six Gliddens, Pike Corcoran and his two daughters, Jack Corcoran, King Cooper, Jim Delaney, Buck Burris, and three Rangers.

"We've been waiting for years to call the turn on you, Sim," Brisbane said. "Of course, we've been satisfied your outfit is responsible for a lot of this rustling that has been going on around these parts. I have in my hands evidence that three of you were implicated in that holdup of the Austin stage."

Brad Glidden cut in harshly. "If you can prove that, why don't you send us over the road?"

"Did I mention your name, Brad?" the lieutenant asked suavely.

"You looked at me."

"All right. I'll look at you again and answer your question. My evidence isn't quite strong enough to convict. At least, it wasn't a week or two ago. Now you're in so bad a jury might think it was sufficient. Want me to find out?"

Brad glared at him angrily, but did not answer.

Brisbane went on, addressing Sim. "You had folks afraid of your crowd. Scared to tell what they knew. But since all this trouble flared up again and they saw your side getting the worst of it, their tongues have unloosened a lot. For instance, you hired those two *vaqueros* to testify Slim Delaney was present with Charley Pitman when the two Mexicans were killed. I sweated it out of them."

"That's a lie," Sim said. He sat heavy and inert in a chair, his big body overflowing from it. No expression registered in his opaque eyes to show that he knew the Gliddens had come to the end of their trail in Texas.

"Two of your sons and one of their cousins kidnapped Miss Corcoran," the officer went on evenly. "At least two of their kin were in cahoots with them before the crime and several others were accessories after the fact. The job was done to trap Delaney and Burris into Lost Park. After your outfit succeeded in that, they did their best to kill them. If it hadn't been for Miss Abby, they would probably have done it."

"We deny the kidnapping," Sim said, in a voice that lacked any life. "Only Corcoran evidence as to that. My boys had a right to go with their sister to the park. This Delaney and his confederates followed them there to drygulch them. After all the killing of our men he has done, would you expect my boys to let the wolf go?"

"We've gone into that," Brisbane said. "No use taking it up again. Delaney has never been the aggressor in any of these difficulties. We have confessions to prove that."

"He never gave Ransom and Benson a chance."

"He didn't kill Ransom and Benson. At least, there is no evidence to show he did. We've already covered that, Sim . . . Your gang killed one Ranger and wounded another when my men went into Lost Park to arrest them."

"They didn't know they were Rangers. Thought they were a bunch of Pike Corcoran's killers come in to wipe 'em out."

"Too thin, Sim. Sergeant Haines yelled to your crowd two or three times that they were Rangers. They deliberately resisted arrest."

"What's the use of all this talk, Brisbane?" demanded Sim heavily. "Why don't you say right out that Corcoran has got control of the Rangers to frame us Gliddens?"

"Because it wouldn't be true," the lieutenant told him quietly. "Fact is, that at last your chickens have come home to roost. You thought the law wouldn't ever reach you. Well, it has. One of two things. You can take your choice. Either we'll press every charge to the limit — and we have at least nine against different members of your family and friends — or your whole outfit will move out of Texas, lock, stock, and barrel. You can gather your stock and drive it out when you go."

"Can we drive our ranches with us?" Sim asked.

"You can turn them over to agents to sell for you. I'm stretching the law in your favor. You know that. This has all been talked out by those in authority. We know that if we hang one or two of you and land one or two in the pen, we'll make outlaws of the rest. It's better to get you out of the country. In another state you can make a fresh start."

"How long do we have to gather our stock?" Sim asked.

"How long will it take you?"

Sim consulted with his brothers and named a time. Brisbane accepted the date as fair.

"There's to be no trouble in the meantime," the officer added. "If you start anything, the deal is off. We'll go through with the charges against you."

Brad stopped Delaney on the way out of the room.

"Fellow, you're lucky," he said, with restrained anger. "I'd give all I've got in the world for one crack at you."

Jim smiled grimly, and passed him without speaking.

Colonel Corcoran walked down the street with Jim, his nephew and Buck Burris behind them.

"Yes, Brad is right," Pike said. "You're lucky. I reckon the Glidden girl saved all three of you. I'm lucky too. I have my daughters back — both of them. I've been a damned stiff-necked fool, Slim." His voice broke a trifle. "I always wanted to make up with Marie and was too stubborn. If I hadn't been so bull-headed, she would never have married Meldrum. Thank God, it's all past now."

"Miss Marie is a fine woman," Slim said. "I knew that soon as I met her."

"About Abby Glidden," Pike said abruptly. "Nothing between you and her?"

"No," Jim said, and added no details.

The Colonel laid a hand affectionately on Delaney's shoulder. "Glad of that, son. It wouldn't work out, not with the Gliddens hating you the way they do."

A warm glow passed through Jim. He felt that Corcoran meant more than he said. It had passed through his mind more than once of late that he would be acceptable to his employer as a son-in-law.

Jim tried his luck with Rose that afternoon.

Left alone with him, Rose was seized with a sudden shyness. She knew what was in her mind and suspected what was in his.

"I'm glad it's all over," she murmured. "I've been so dreadfully worried — for Father."

"We've been some worried for you," he said. "Till we heard you were safe home."

"They didn't hurt me. They kept telling me not to be afraid."

"Yes, but they didn't tell us not to be afraid," he answered, smiling. "They kind of forgot that. I didn't think they would hurt you, but I couldn't be sure after they were crazy enough to take you away."

"Anyhow, everything is all right now," she said.

"Or will be soon."

Rose looked at him quickly, then looked away. She felt the color flushing her cheeks. He was going to speak now. She wanted to run away.

"If you feel the way I do," he added.

Her gaze came back to his reluctantly, as if drawn by a magnet.

"Soon the Gliddens will be gone," she mentioned, dodging into a side path.

He waved that aside. "They've gone already far as we are concerned. I'm not talking about them, but about us." He took her little hand in his big brown one and glanced down at it. His fingers closed on hers. "How about — for always, Rose?"

She nodded, ever so little, then buried her face in his shoulder.

CHAPTER FORTY

He Had It Coming

For the last time Dave Meldrum was walking down Houston Street. Men looked at him askance. If they could avoid meeting him, they did so. If not, they nodded curtly. For Meldrum was leaving town in disgrace, driven out by the force of public opinion.

The Green Curtain had been closed and an ultimatum given him to get out of San Antonio at once. It would be impossible for him to realize anything on his investment in the gambling-house and dance-hall. Nobody wanted to buy the lease, furniture, and good will of a house in such ill repute as his.

He laid this disaster to the hands of one man, and black anger surged in his heart. Slim Delaney was responsible for it. From that first hour when they had met at The Green Curtain there had been nothing but trouble. Dave thought of the man now with savage fury. The fellow had been invulnerable. The battle at the lumber yard was still an impossible mystery. The escape from the gambling-house was another. Time and again he had been within reach of the Gliddens and they had failed to make an end of him. His success had been so astonishing that many accepted it as fatalism.

That was nonsense, of course. The fellow had been lucky. Meldrum would have liked a chance to prove it. Not now, for he would not dare kill Delaney at this time in San Antonio. But somewhere else, if by chance they ever met.

At that moment Jim Delaney swung round the corner and came straight up the street to meet him. Gone was the gambler's caution, gone his judgment. A wave of black hatred swept all other considerations aside.

He ripped out a furious oath. His revolver jumped from the scabbard.

"Come a-shooting!" he cried, and blazed away.

Three times his weapon sounded before that of the younger man got into action. That Meldrum missed can be accounted for only because of the fact that his consuming hate would not let him wait until the other was close.

Both men emptied their revolvers.

Someone, amazed, cried down from a window, "By jinks, not a single hit."

He spoke too soon. Meldrum stood for a moment after the roar of the guns ceased, straight and rigid, malice still frozen on his face. A quiver ran through his body. A slack arm fell to his side and from nerveless fingers the revolver dropped. He swayed on his feet, plunged forward to the ground. Once his shoulder twitched. After that not a muscle moved.

Slowly Jim moved forward. He looked down at the inert, sprawling body.

"I call you all to witness he fired first," he said.

From the doors of stores men began to trickle. They came out slower than they had gone in. Half a dozen of them confirmed Delaney's claim.

"He had it coming," an old cattleman said. "Ever since that day he shot down Pike Corcoran at Eagle Pass."

"Y'betcha."

"Sure had."

"Been askin' this boy for it."

Jim turned and walked slowly away. It came to him clearly that this hour had been preparing ever since that day, half a lifetime ago if one measured time by its fullness, when he had sauntered into The Green Curtain to see the elephant.

THE END

ISIS publish a wide range of books in large print, from fiction to biography. Any suggestions for books you would like to see in large print or audio are always welcome. Please send to the Editorial Department at:

ISIS Publishing Limited
7 Centremead
Osney Mead
Oxford OX2 0ES

A full list of titles is available free of charge from:

Ulverscroft Large Print Books Limited

(UK)
The Green
Bradgate Road, Anstey
Leicester LE7 7FU
Tel: (0116) 236 4325

(Australia)
P.O. Box 314
St Leonards
NSW 1590
Tel: (02) 9436 2622

(USA)
P.O. Box 1230
West Seneca
N.Y. 14224-1230
Tel: (716) 674 4270

(Canada)
P.O. Box 80038
Burlington
Ontario L7L 6B1
Tel: (905) 637 8734

(New Zealand)
P.O. Box 456
Feilding
Tel: (06) 323 6828

Details of **ISIS** complete and unabridged audio books are also available from these offices. Alternatively, contact your local library for details of their collection of **ISIS** large print and unabridged audio books.